TEN LORDS A-LEAPING

Ida 'Jack' Troutbeck, rumbustious Mistress of St Martha's College, Cambridge, has been elevated to the peerage. Although she finds the dafter aspects of the House of Lords hilarious, from the first day she becomes enthusiastically involved in its work. Disinclined to watch her language or moderate her manners, she appals conventional peers, but plots vigorously with others – including a mischievous duke – to scupper an anti-hunting bill of which she violently disapproves.

To assist her, Baroness Troutbeck conscripts her friend Robert Amiss, whose initial liberal dithering about the rights and wrongs of fox-hunting quickly gives way to a determination to defeat the puritans and fanatics who abound among the abolitionists. Though hampered by the eccentrics and bores on his side, he and the baroness are feeling confident of winning this contentious battle, when animal activists begin a campaign of intimidation. An attempt is made on the life of one of the baroness's allies, and shortly afterwards the peers suffer horrifying carnage.

Amiss and the baroness – with some assistance from the cat Plutarch – throw themselves into helping the police with their enquiries.

TEN LORDS A-LEAPING

Ruth Dudley Edwards

ST. MARTIN'S PRESS
NEW YORK

CIP DATA TK

First Edition
10 9 8 7 6 5 4 3 2 1

To John, my muse, and Jill, my versifier

and with special thanks for advice and help
to Pippa Allen, Gordon and Ken Lee, Carol Scott,
the Lords Denham, Dubs and Morris,
and Messrs Ede & Ravenscroft.

While I have tried to remain true to the spirit of the House of Lords, in the interests of the plot I have taken some small liberties with details of geography, customs and procedures.

Oh! glory of youth! consolation of age!
Sublimest of ecstasies under the sun;
Though the veteran may linger too long on the stage,
Yet he'll drink a last toast to a fox-hunting run.
And oh! young descendants of ancient top-sawyers!
By your lives to the world their example enforce;
Whether landlords, or parsons, or statesmen, or lawyers,
Ride straight as they rode it from Ranksboro' Gorse.

From 'The Dream of the Old Meltonian'
W. Bromley Davenport

PROLOGUE

'A baroness? What lunatic would make you a baroness?'

'I'll have no aspersions cast on Her Majesty the Queen, my boy,' said Jack Troutbeck, 'especially now I'm about to become a pillar of the Establishment.' The cackle that followed was so loud that even at a distance of 4,000 miles Amiss had to move the receiver away from his ear.

'You know perfectly well what I mean. Which of your multifarious admirers decided that what the House of Lords really needed to liven it up was you?'

'Mainly Bertie.'

'Bertie?'

'My God, you've got so slow since you've been in India, Robert. Been on the hippy trail, have you? Been losing your marbles at the feet of some guru while in quest of your inner being?'

'It's not just that you're out of date, Jack, it's that you revel in it. Hippies went out when I was in kindergarten. Rachel and I've been around half of India on the cultural – not the mystical – trail, since before Christmas. Which is, of course, why we missed this bizarre announcement in the New Year's Honours List. Now, who's Bertie?'

'The Duke of Stormerod, of course, you idiot.'

'You mean the Tory Party's *éminence grise*?'

'The very one.'

'What's he got to do with you?'

'Gab, gab, gab. The purpose of this phone call is to tell you to come home and help me, not to give you my life story.'

'Listen, you old villain, if you want to get me back to

participate in some foul plan or other of yours, your only chance is to coax me. Railroading is out. So is being so fucking elliptical that you leave me in more of a fog than I was when this conversation started.'

'Oh, very well then.' Her sigh came through the ether like a March gale. 'When Bertie was but Lord Bertie Whittingham-Sholto, heir to the dukedom, and was in the House of Commons, he was Minister for Central Planning. Do you follow that?'

'I even remember that, Jack.'

'I afforded him light relief.'

'You were his moll?'

'More his hitwoman. My job was to duff up those of my colleagues who were putting bureaucratic spikes in his radical wheels.'

'It's a pretty poor metaphor, if you don't mind my saying so.'

She ignored him. 'So now he's in the Lords he wants me to do down the forces of evil.'

'Which ones?'

'Wets, trendies, enemies of England. You know – the usual lot.'

'In the House of Lords?'

'More there than you'd think, I'm sorry to say. That's why I need you. They're mustering for a dastardly attack on our heritage.'

'Which bit?'

'I'll tell you when you get here.'

'Why should I?' Even to his own ears Amiss sounded petulant.

'Because you'll have fun.'

'Fun? Last time we collaborated . . .'

'Yes?'

'. . . it involved death, disaster, trauma, temptation, capitulation, emotional upheaval and general mayhem – all ending up in the triumph of Jack Troutbeck.'

'Exactly,' she trumpeted complacently. 'It was fun.'

Amiss shrugged. 'Well, while I'm job-hunting, I suppose I might be persuaded to help you out a bit. As long,' he added hastily, 'as what you're at doesn't offend my moral susceptibilities.'

'Bugger your moral susceptibilities. When are you due back?'

'In about two weeks.'

'Ah, good timing. I'll have done the palace by then and you'll be just in time for my introduction to my peers. You can help me carry my ermine. Twelve o'clock sharp, Tuesday fortnight, lobby of the House of Lords, best bib and tucker. We'll have lunch first, and then you can watch me turn into a noblewoman. Further celebration that evening.'

'It's the day I get back, Jack, after an all-night, twelve-hour flight.'

The familiar words, 'Don't be such a wimp,' were followed by, 'Must fly. Enemies to swat. See you then.'

Slightly dazed but, despite himself, feeling a rush of adrenaline, Amiss rang Rachel's office.

1

Rachel threw a pile of newspapers on the sofa. 'I can't say these reports add much to the sum of human knowledge.'

Amiss picked up the three-week-old *Independent*, from the front page of which Jack Troutbeck's photograph stared out defiantly. 'Among the predictable rewards to the party-faithful and the generous captains of industry,' said the report sniffily, 'was the surprise announcement of a peerage for the Mistress of St Martha's College, Cambridge. Miss Ida "Jack" Troutbeck, CB, (61), was a Deputy Secretary in the Department of Central Planning when she retired three years ago to become Bursar of St Martha's, where last year she succeeded as Mistress in tragic circumstances. In only a short time she has acquired a reputation in educational circles as an outspoken critic of what she terms "fatuous liberal poppycock."'

The *Telegraph* noted approvingly that in her sparse *Who's Who* entry, under hobbies, Miss Troutbeck had put 'enjoying myself'. The *Guardian* registered concern that in a recent speech to the Annual Conference of Heads of Colleges, she had poured scorn on 'namby-pamby ill-thought-out educational fads'. Although she would not be taking the whip, she was a Conservative Party nominee, so it was probable, observed the commentator darkly, that the Tory Party was playing its usual trick of promoting the disadvantaged only when they were extreme right-wingers. Amiss wondered how the *Guardian* would react if they knew that under Jack's mistress-ship a black bisexual had been appointed to the bursarship of St Martha's; then, reflecting on Dr Mary Lou

13

Denslow's opinions, he realized that it would scarcely undermine their argument.

The tabloids, of course, had got hold of what the broadsheets had been too tasteful to discuss. Although Jack Troutbeck had been relegated to page two of the *Sun*, with the front pages being reserved for minor decorations for a long-serving soap star ('our Lenny'), a popular comedian ('"No, I never" Dwayne') and a lollipop lady ('Toddlers' Angel'), the new baroness had two short paragraphs describing her as having been at the centre of a 'Highbrow Double-Murder Saga', which led to her getting the 'Top Job' in a 'Snob College'. It had also got hold of a photograph of Jack looking murderous – if not highbrow – in gown and rakishly tilted Tudor cap on the occasion of her being conferred with an honorary doctorate.

Amiss finished the last of the papers and chucked it in the bin. 'Drink?'

Rachel nodded.

'Gin?'

Eyes closed, she nodded again.

As he reached for a couple of glasses from the kitchen cupboard, a familiar voice said, 'Oh, no, sahib. It is inappropriate that you should demean yourself by entering the servants' quarters. What is it that you want?'

A few days had been enough for Amiss's spirit to have been broken by Ravi's contemptuous subservience, arising from his view of Amiss as a guest, and therefore privileged, while being also an immoral parasite who shared the bed of the mistress of the house without having the common decency to make an honest woman of her.

'Two gins and tonics, Ravi, and could you put in a lot of extra ice, please? Rachel is feeling the heat.' Ravi assumed the expression of fastidious pain suitable to a servant hearing an employer spoken of informally. Amiss affected not to notice. If Ravi got his fun out of behaving like a stereotype from the last days of the Raj, that was Ravi's problem.

'Sahib.'

Amiss turned back. 'Yes?'

'There is no ice.'

'Why not?'

'There has been a calamity. Laxmi, that miscreant, has left the door of the refrigerator open and it has all melted.'

'I don't suppose you could get some anywhere?'

'Oh no, sahib, there will be none by now, because, you see, it will all have gone.'

Amiss already knew Ravi's almost infinite capacity for ensuring that what he didn't want to do couldn't be done. He strode over to the refrigerator, extracted two lukewarm cans of beer and marched out of the kitchen, his ears ringing with imprecations about the impropriety of memsahib drinking out of anything but a glass.

'How can I leave you to the mercies of that old fraud?'

Rachel sat up wearily and took a swig out of the open can. 'No choice.'

'It's just so unfair that you're lumbered with him.'

'There's no point in going on about it, Robert.' Rachel sounded rather testy. 'He comes with the apartment, he's got thirty-eight dependants, he's worked for the High Commission for twenty years and I'm stuck here until Personnel release me.'

'In June,' said Amiss hopefully.

'Maybe. Now, would you explain to me what a middle-of-the-road, well-meaning liberal like you is doing taking up arms against the future with someone who makes Margaret Thatcher seem rather left wing.'

'It'll fill in the time while I'm looking for a job.'

'Don't give me that, Robert. You could fill in the time looking for a job by looking properly for a job.'

'Anyway, she's really a libertarian rather than a right-winger.' Amiss realized he sounded defensive. 'And, for as long as I've known her, I've always found that her enemies deserve to be enemies.'

'You just can't resist her.'

'Who could?'

'Lots of people, from all I've heard. All I can say is, "God help the House of Lords".'

'And all who sail in her,' said Amiss gravely.

15

Rachel raised her beer can. 'Let's drink to a smooth voyage.'

'There's no point in wishing for the impossible. With Jack as skipper, I aspire only to disembark alive.'

2

'My God, you look magnificent.' Stunned, Amiss gazed at the vision in scarlet with trimmings of gold lace and white fur that plunged into the lobby to greet him. 'You should dress like that all the time.'

'Costs too much to rent.'

'You'd think a grateful government would throw the uniform in free.'

'Well, I'll be sending it back to Ede and Ravenscroft tomorrow, so you'd better make the most of it now.' She pirouetted girlishly and at such speed that she tripped on the hem of the robe and, without Amiss's rescuing arm, would have sprawled on the great marble floor. As it was, she dropped her black hat and her parchment, which rolled swiftly across the floor. 'After it!' she cried. 'That's my Writ of Summons. If I don't have that they'll chuck me out before I'm in.'

Amiss retrieved the document, put it in her hand, brushed down her cocked hat and placed it tenderly under her arm.

'Now you see why I needed you.' She smote him on the back affectionately, but painfully.

'I'm to be your dresser?'

'And much, much else.'

'Why aren't you wearing a coronet?'

'Disappointing, isn't it? But that's only for coronations. If I wasn't such an admirer of the Queen I'd be looking forward to the chance to sport it. But you like, I trust, my lace and miniver.'

'What's miniver?'

'Some kind of stoat, I think. Now, enough of this sartorial

17

chitchat. Pity you missed lunch. I had something I wanted to tell you. Where were you, anyway?'

'My plane sat on the tarmac for five hours. I've come straight from the airport.'

He knew her too well to expect any sympathy. 'Well, you'd better head off to the gallery in a minute. You'll find Mary Lou and Myles there. He'll explain what's going on, nobs being in his line.'

'You've brought both your lovers? Is that etiquette?'

'Correction. I've brought two of my lovers. What's wrong with that? You're so suburban. Now stop making objections and go and join the plebs. I've got to go off with my nob escort – sorry, sponsors – in a minute. I want you back here, seven-thirty tonight for dinner in the Counsels' Dining Room. Black tie.'

'Why?'

'Have to do these things properly. We baronesses have a reputation to keep up.'

The weariness of someone who has endured seventeen hours in a plane along with dozens of fractious children began to engulf Amiss. 'Must I?'

'Of course you must. The sooner you get to know people the better. We've a lot to do here.'

'Do I gather you're going to throw yourself into the spirit of this potty establishment?'

'You betcha,' said the baroness.

At this moment, two elderly, scarlet-clad men materialized and stood beside her.

'M'Lords Bedmorth and Deptford, otherwise Joe and Sid,' she explained. 'Mr Amiss, otherwise Robert – one of my sidekicks.'

The three shook hands.

'Jack,' said Deptford. 'It's time to go in.'

'What happens now?' asked Amiss.

Deptford called across the hall. ''Ere, Mr Hudson, this young geezer, take him up to Miss Troutbeck's mates, will you?'

Deptford turned back to Jack Troutbeck and began to rearrange her robes to best effect and straighten up her Peter-Pan fur collar. A gigantic man in a black tailcoat and knee breeches advanced purposefully and bowed to Amiss. 'Perhaps you'd like to follow me, sir.'

Amiss looked over his shoulder at the disappearing backs of the three robed chums and then pursued Hudson upstairs. A few moments later he was in the gallery, hugging Mary Lou enthusiastically. Catching Hudson's eye, they sat down. 'Do you know Myles Cavendish?'

'Only by reputation.'

Cavendish grinned as they shook hands. Amiss tried to imagine a physical encounter between this dapper little man and Jack Troutbeck, and pushed the thought out of his mind. As Jack had once observed to a puritanical policeman, 'Who can tell where Eros will strike?'

'Here they come.'

Amiss gazed around the cathedral-like chamber, a vision of carved mahogany, red-buttoned seats, blue carpet and lashings of gold leaf, and saw to his right a stately procession hoving into view, preceded by a haughty-looking chap in a black brocaded tailcoat, white stock, black knee breeches and a gold chain with dangling bits.

'Black Rod,' whispered Cavendish.

Amiss nodded, delighted to see in person the dignitary who annually banged on the door of the Commons to summon its inmates to join the Queen and the peers for the state opening of Parliament. He was a bit on the elderly side to have to parade with a heavy baton, and on the wizened side for his leggings, but he had presence. He bowed to the Lord Chancellor, who was smartly turned out in a black-and-gold gown which contrasted strikingly with the bright red of the woolsack on which he perched and then walked slowly forward.

'Now comes Garter King at Arms.'

'The chap who decides what coat of arms you can have.'

'That's right.'

Amiss looked respectfully at a stately figure in black leggings and an extraordinary multicoloured tabard dominated by heraldic emblems. Any man who could turn out dressed like a playing card and still look dignified had, he felt, enviable chutzpah. His bow was a model of solemnity.

19

'What's he carrying?' he whispered.

'The Peers' Patent.'

Amiss was left no wiser.

Next came Deptford, whose features Amiss had been finding teasingly familiar and whom he now suddenly identified as Sid Peerless, who as a transport union leader had been the terror of commuters in the 1970s. Jack Troutbeck processed several feet behind him, apparently concentrating hard on not tripping over or dropping anything. As she passed them, she took her eye off Deptford's back, looked up and gave her friends an enormous wink. Bringing up the rear was Bedmorth, whose relaxed demeanour betrayed a man born to the purple and well used to negotiating his way round the place gravely and in full regalia.

With a pause for another bow, the leaders proceeded until Jack was deposited beside the woolsack. She knelt, was handed her patent by Garter and presented both documents to the Lord Chancellor, who passed them to a hovering chap in lawyer's wig and gown. She got up successfully, though inelegantly enough to elicit a stifled giggle from Mary Lou, walked to the table in the middle of the chamber and stared fixedly ahead as the chap with the parchments read out their contents sonorously, with splendid anachronistic phrases like 'realms and territories . . . Oh ye, that we of our especial grace, certain knowledge and mere motion . . .' reverberating around the chamber. When he got to 'by these presents advance, create and prefer our trusted and well-beloved Ida Troutbeck to the state, degree, style, dignity, title and honour of Baroness Troutbeck of Troutbeck', she beamed, then recollected herself and stood expressionless throughout the rest, even at the improbable moment when instructed solemnly that it was her duty at all costs to attend 'our Parliament for arduous and urgent affairs concerning us, the state and defence of our United Kingdom and the Church'. He then took her – phrase by phrase – through the affirmation of allegiance to the Queen, which she performed faultlessly, and indicated where she should sign her name on an ancient-looking document.

As she picked up her cocked hat, Black Rod and Garter

suddenly took over with a bit of processing and bowing, the sponsors took up position with Jack Troutbeck between them, Black Rod peeled off and the trio were shepherded by Garter to the back row of the benches on Amiss's left, which he recognized as the cross benches, reserved for independent peers.

Mary Lou began to giggle again – with Amiss finding it impossible to keep his face entirely straight – as the trio sat down in the back row and gazed intently at the Garter King at Arms, who stood in the row beneath, gazing at them fixedly. At some prompt imperceptible to onlookers, they rose and doffed their hats with a courtly bow in the direction of the Lord Chancellor, who raised in acknowledgement the tricorn hat which perched on his full-bottomed wig. They repeated their manoeuvre; he responded. After the third exchange, the procession regrouped and the new girl was led down the right-hand side of the chamber, the three peers bowing once or twice as they went. When Jack drew level with the Lord Chancellor, she hesitated for a moment and then bowed again, shook his proffered hand and then, flanked by her startlingly dressed old men, she was led from the chamber to cries of, 'Hear, hear!' from the packed benches of the House. 'Hear, hear!' shouted Mary Lou, until Cavendish warned her she'd be kicked out. 'It'd take a lifetime to learn the rules in this place,' she grumbled.

'That's what's so much fun about it,' said Cavendish.

'Is that it?' asked Amiss.

'That's it. The peers have indicated she's acceptable, so she's now one of them. She'll be off disrobing.'

'What a shame. That gear really suited her.'

'Yes, but she'd be liable to break her neck if she tried to carry on in her usual way wearing floor-length clothes. Now, are you joining us in the bar for champagne?'

'No, she told me to be back at seven-thirty tonight.'

'Ah, yes. Presumably she thinks you need a rest. Wants you to sparkle tonight, I gather.'

'Sparkle! I feel on the point of death. Mind you, it's uncharacteristically thoughtful of her to think I might need a few hours' kip. Will I see you two tonight?'

21

'No. Tonight's business, I gather. Where the House of Lords is concerned, we're strictly pleasure.' And Cavendish and Mary Lou laughed merrily.

3

Amiss awoke from an exhausted sleep at 6.45, hurled himself into the shower, flung on his clothes, hailed a cab just outside his front door and reached the Lords on the dot of 7.30 to find the entrance blocked by a struggling mass of police and screaming demonstrators. It was too dark to read the banners and the only words he could make out from the shouts and chants were 'murderers' and 'sadists'. He watched idly for a few minutes as the police finally got the upper hand. A van drove up and a dozen or so noisy protestors were bundled inside, banners and all. The entrance was still blocked by the more peaceable but still obstinate protestors, so Amiss decided to cut his losses and enter via the House of Commons entrance.

'I have an appointment with Lady Troutbeck,' he explained to the policeman on the door, 'but I couldn't get through to the Lords entrance. What's going on?'

'H'animal h'activists,' said the policeman heavily. 'Bunch of no-good riffraff if you ask me.'

'What are they complaining about? Export of calves to France?'

'Fox-'unting, of course. 'Aven't you been reading the papers?'

'I've been away.'

'Well, it's coming up in the Lords soon. The Commons voted for abolition, their lordships look like throwing it out, so there's merry hell.'

'Thank you, officer.' Amiss proceeded through security checks to the Commons lobby and turned right down the corridor, meditating rather enviously about people who had such certainties about issues where he was ambiguous.

'Thank heaven,' he said to himself, expelling hunting from his mind, 'that I'm not going to have to take sides on this one.'

And so, wrote Amiss to Rachel, of course the first thing she announced as I came into the Counsels' Dining Room was that here was the back-room boy who would provide some intellectual clout to preserve the glorious chase. And naturally because of my misplaced notions of propriety, I didn't think this was the moment to get into an explanation of my liberal dilemma on the matter. Not when I was being gazed at by Joe, Sid and what turned out to be ten other members of the nobility, all of whom were welcoming me enthusiastically as one of their own. 'Why didn't you warn me?' I hissed at Jack when I got the opportunity. 'Stop being such a fusspot,' she replied helpfully.

Piecing it together with a little help from Bertie, the excellent Duke of Stormerod, I learned that they're the inner circle or hard core dedicated to defending hunting – particularly of foxes – against the House of Commons, the animal activists and all comers. And needless to say, Jack has thrown herself enthusiastically into the cause for, as you might guess, the Troutbecks have ever been tremendous enthusiasts and participants in this noble sport. And because it was necessary to get cracking with the conspiracy, her celebratory dinner was limited to this group, for, as you will remember, when Jack throws herself into something she doesn't hang about.

Well, I don't know how productive animal activists' planning meetings are, but I can't say I was overimpressed with this one; I think in her exuberance Jack overdid the hospitality. Before we got through even the first two courses – quails' eggs, wild salmon and plenty of champagne and Chablis – and were proceeding to get stuck into our noble roast, several of the gathering seemed decidedly squiffy. And although Jack has a head like a rock, she had had enough herself to be treating the evening as a rave-up rather than a sort-out.

By now I was already even more ambivalent than I had started out. For while Bertie, on my left, was so charming and so very persuasive on the subject of the traditions of our way of life that need to be preserved in the interests of society, m'Lord Poulteney, on my right, had turned out to be a nightmare.

I am, as you know, a connoisseur of bores and until last night I thought no experience could be worse than that man who trapped me on the plane the last time I went to Delhi and turned out to be a kind of talking motorway atlas, but Poulteney is a talking hunting diary. You know the sort of thing the Victorians wrote up: 'Good start, early scent, ran him into small cover. Lamed gee and had to call a halt.' Riveting.

As insensitive as he is thick, old Poulteney required of me little more than attention and although he suffered a slight shock when he learned that I kept neither hounds nor horses, it never even crossed his mind that I didn't hunt. So he bored on with his interminable and incomprehensible reminiscences of 'View Halloa and into Braggs Wood'. Fortunately Bertie – one of those aristocrats who justifies the hereditary principle – recognized that I had fallen into a catatonic state and rescued me. It turned out that one of his ancestors had been a Viceroy of India and he loves it well and we had a very jolly chat about all of that with lots of chummy anecdotes along the way. He was also full of amusing sidelights on the Lords, on the dotty customs of which he expounds affectionately and very amusingly. The reason he had not been one of Jack's sponsors, it turned out, was that he outranked her. 'Oh, no,' he explained gravely. 'You see I'm a hell of a feller, with four miniver bars to her two and a gold coronet with strawberry leaves for best, while Jack – poor old thing – 'll have to settle for something plebeian in silver gilt with a few silver balls. And rules say you can only be sponsored by two from your own grade. Pity. I'd have been proud.'

Jack, meanwhile, was the life and soul of her side of the table, smacking her lips over the food, demanding that the glasses to the left of her and right of her and indeed in front of her be refilled, and generally celebrating her elevation like

25

a good 'un. 'I like being a baroness,' I heard her announce when someone asked her how she was feeling.

At about 9.30 or so, when we hit the port, a feeling of camaraderie was universal. Jack leapt to her feet with such energy she knocked over her chair as she called us all to order. 'Friends!' she shouted. 'Before we get down to the serious business of the evening, I want you to drink a toast.' Everyone staggered to his feet. 'Her Majesty the Queen!' she cried, somewhat conventionally, and then as an after-thought, 'and confound her enemies . . . and ours.'

As she sat down, Bertie got up and made a speech about our noble hostess. He reminisced fondly about their days together in the department, where apparently she endeared herself to him on the very first day they met by denouncing a colleague for talking a lot of bollocks.

'Jack,' he explained towards the end, 'though perhaps short on diplomatic skills' – (she looked surprised at this; it's impossible to get it through to her that she is anything other than suave) – 'is a trooper. Some amongst us have never quite adjusted to the arrival in this House of peeresses. First they feared women were not intellectually up to the position. And though this view has altered, there are now those who feel our lady members are worryingly puritanical.

'I am pleased that is a criticism no one has ever made of our noble friend, Baroness Troutbeck, who thinks Round-heads exist to be target practice for Cavaliers. We now have an important challenge facing us as the forces of puritanism attempt to encircle us. We have lost the first hunting battle: it behoves us to ensure we don't lose the second.

'I am delighted to welcome, as part of our counterattack, such a doughty companion in arms. We require much of her. Sid's beloved Surtees declared that among the qualities possessed by the ideal Master of Foxhounds should be' – he peered at his card – "the boldness of a lion, the cunning of a fox, the shrewdness of an exciseman, the calculation of a general, the decision of a judge and the liberality of a sailor". My dear old friend Jack has all these and more qualities in abundance. She is a great addition to our struggle and we can rely on her.

'My friends, let us drink a toast.' There was another scraping of chairs. 'To Baroness Troutbeck.' 'Baroness Troutbeck!' shouted us all. 'Hoicktogether!' shouted Poulteney, 'Huick-holler!' or something similar shouted someone else, and a cheerful-looking cove beside Jack launched into 'For She's a Jolly Good Fellow', thus inspiring the more jovial elements of the gathering to embark on a sing-song in which, for most purposes, I was unable to participate, owing to being a bit short of experience on the hunting-song front. I could make a shot at:

> D'you ken John Peel, with his coat so grey
> D'you ken John Peel at the break of day

but that was about it. Still, as the port went down, I quite enjoyed listening to ever louder and jollier verses like

> Hark forward, my boys, tally-ho is the cry,
> Tantara! Tantara! resounds the blithe horn

I was vividly reminded of Wodehouse's *The Mating Seasons*. Do you remember when Bertie Wooster got sloshed with Esmond Haddock and they ended up singing Bertie's version of Esmond's aunt's hunting song:

> Halloa, halloa, halloa, halloa!
> A hunting we will go, my lads,
> A hunting we will go,
> Pull up our socks and chase the fox
> And lay the blighter low

while Bertie stood on his chair waving the decanter like a baton and Esmond on the table using a banana as a hunting crop. We didn't quite get to that pitch of excitement, probably because some rather serious-looking waiters shimmered in from time to time, but we came close. We roistered away, Jack to the fore, until midnight, when we were persuaded to leave.

When we stood outside waiting for a taxi, I expected to

be the last to be allowed to get one, being both the most junior and the only commoner, but to my surprise, Jack had one of those flashes of consideration that saves one from throttling her and shooed me into the first taxi ahead of all my elders, somewhat spoiling the effect by saying, 'Breakfast, Park Lane Hotel, seven-thirty, and be on time.' Before I could deliver a protest she had slammed the passenger door and was waving me off.

Not wishing to get involved in an altercation in front of a group of her fans, and not knowing where she was staying, I had little choice but to obey orders. And yes, I know you are thinking, 'How can you let this old bag push you around like this?' The answer is, of course, that I am congenitally inclined to take the line of least resistance, except when I take a stand on principle. And do bear in mind that it was principle that got me where I am now, i.e., out of work . . .

4

'Mmmmmmm. I was afraid they wouldn't have any.' The baroness heaped on to her already well-filled plate a pile of black pudding and looked at Amiss solicitously, spoon poised.

He shuddered. 'No thanks.'

'Why not? What's wrong with you? You need building up.'

'Sorry, Jack, but at this time in the morning, wimp that I am, I can't face eating dried blood.'

The baroness rolled her eyes heavenwards and shook her head incredulously. 'I like black pudding.'

'Good, good. I'm happy for you.'

Together they carried their trays to the booth where they had left their coats and settled in, Amiss to breakfast modestly on bacon, egg and Cumberland sausage, the baroness to weigh into kidneys, bacon, tomato, mushroom and black and white puddings, while punctuating her eating with grunts of satisfaction.

'Enjoying it?' she enquired anxiously.

'Very nice, thank you. And you?'

'Kidneys a bit of a disappointment. I like them bloody.'

'You would,' said Amiss grumpily. 'Now, why am I here?'

'Plan of campaign, obviously. We didn't get very far last night. I don't know what you were thinking of.'

'Me?'

'Well, you're supposed to be coordinating all this.' She took a mighty swig of coffee and chomped happily on some crispy bacon. 'That's what I've hired you for.'

'First, you haven't hired me and second, you omitted to tell me what I was supposed to be doing.'

'Well, I've sort of hired you. I'll foot any bills you incur and give you a couple of hundred quid a week. After all, I make a bit on expenses.'

'Even with the price of London hotels?'

'I don't stay in hotels.' She grinned happily. 'Myles is based in London, I should remind you.'

'So you're still two-timing Mary Lou with him?'

'Or vice versa.' She laughed. 'Not that two-timing is an appropriate accusation. We're not all such prigs as you. Neither Myles nor Mary Lou is exactly sitting wistfully by the fireside waiting on my return. Anyway, stop being so nosey. What you're supposed to be finding out about is how to sort out the killjoys.'

'Dammit . . .' Amiss put his cup down with such force that it slopped coffee into his saucer and on to the tablecloth. He swore and mopped it up.

'Tsk, tsk. Can't think what's got into you. You're becoming awfully ratty.'

'I don't suppose you'd regard jet-lag, lack of sleep and a hangover as mitigating circumstances? Not to speak of having to get up at six-thirty in order to come in to watch you scoffing a fat breakfast.'

She wasn't listening. 'Right, now for your instructions. What with having to fly up and down to Cambridge to do my mistressly duties, I can't run things at the Lords. You're going to have to help this crowd function. Marshal the arguments, the facts, and help them with the speeches. For although right is on our side, I have to say we've got some pretty weak vessels to make its case.'

'Jack, I don't even know whether I'm for or against fox-hunting. That is' – he raised his voice as she opened her mouth – 'I don't like it and I don't want to do it so I can hardly be said to be for it, but I'm not clear if I'm against it. Instinctively I hate an activity that involves chasing a small animal over hill and dale. Yet I do dimly grasp the arguments about tradition, esprit de corps and all the rest of it.'

She shook her head so vigorously that several hairpins were dislodged from her bun. 'You disappoint me. I can see that I'm going to have to spell everything out. Right. Let's start with cruelty.'

'Yes, I know. Foxes are vermin that have to be kept down and gassing, trapping and even shooting are far more cruel than hunting.'

'Right. Now conservation.'

'I suppose you're going to tell me that hunts are interested in preserving the traditional countryside.'

'Yep, including planting woods to make coverts for foxes and keeping a varied landscape to increase the enjoyment of the huntsmen. You don't get farmers who hunt clearing hedgerows and turning their farms into prairies. With me so far?'

'More or less. Pass the coffee.'

'Now, economics. What with hunt-staff and farriers, feed merchants and vets, saddlers and bootmakers and all the rest of them, you're talking of more than thirty thousand jobs. Then there are the horses and hounds. I can tell you there would be a pretty sharp drop in the horse population if you abolished hunting, and most of them would be slaughtered to be fed to dogs. Although there would be a lot fewer dogs since the hounds would have to be put down too, so they'd have to flog the horse carcasses to the Frogs.'

'Oh, I suppose it's aesthetics.' Amiss felt driven into a corner. 'It seems faintly distasteful to have all this going on for the benefit of a few thousand nobs and City types prancing around in scarlet coats.'

'Where'd you get that figure? What with those who follow by car and on foot, it's closer to a quarter of a million, few of them nobs and the majority of them women. Mind you' – she paused to pull her pipe out of her pocket and ram into it a vast quantity of tobacco – 'you can see what we're up against if, even you, the confidante of a baroness, are demonstrating class prejudice.'

'I wouldn't call it that.'

'Well, I would. You know bloody well that that is one of the two motivating forces for the anti-hunt lobby. Why do you think the Great British Public regularly declares itself in favour of abolishing hunting while being perfectly happy with fishing? I'll tell you why. It's because there are four million anglers in this country, and most of them are plebs.'

'You're not saying that the huge majority against hunting consists of people actively participating in the class war?'

'Not necessarily. But I am saying that they don't know what they're talking about. If you know sod-all about an issue like this, it's very easy to get all sentimental about a fox. It's good old sloppy thinking. That's what happened over deer-hunting. The populace had a vision of brutal toffs pursuing Bambi and his mother over hill and dale with blood-curdling whoops. And bingo, in the blink of an eye and without giving the matter any serious thought, a collection of ignorant parliamentarians – opposed only by some ineffectual wimps – put an end to the Exmoor and all the other historic hunts of the West Country. That mustn't happen this time.' She took a mighty pull and enveloped the table in smoke, which she sniffed appreciatively. 'Now, let's turn from the ignorant to the nutters.'

'Usually a pretty wide classification in your book, old girl.'

'Well, on this occasion it's pretty specific. I'm talking about fruitcakes like half those who were carrying on last night outside the House. Their object is to change human nature by legislation. When they've got rid of fox-hunting, they'll move on to shooting and when they've had that abolished it'll be angling. Then, before we know where we are, we'll all be vegans, forbidden from eating or wearing any animal products. Result?'

'Gradual extinction of farmyard animals, I suppose.'

'Got it. Now, are you satisfied? Ready to fight the good fight?'

'I just can't warm to it, Jack. Look at Poulteney, for God's sake.'

'There's more to hunting than Poulteney. Why not take me rather than him as a hunting role model?'

'Do you hunt?'

'Well, I haven't had time for some years, but, if I may say so, I cut a pretty dashing figure with the Cottesmore until I was in my forties.'

'Did you wear pink?'

'Sometimes I wore pink, sometimes black.'

'And jodhpurs and high boots?'

'But with a skirt and side-saddle, of course. Only way to ride.'

'For reasons of decorum, no doubt.'

'No, though I admit to an element of vanity. Don't look my best in trousers. But it was more that riding side-saddle allows you to control a horse much more powerful than your size or weight would normally allow.'

'Where would one find a horse bigger than your size and weight would allow?'

The baroness chuckled; she always took insults as an obscure form of flattery. She looked at her watch – 'Zounds!' – and energetically signalled a waiter for the bill. 'I've got to be off. Train to catch. College council meeting at ten. If I don't see you later I'll ring you tonight. In the meantime, get to work.'

'What sort of work?'

'Immerse yourself in the literature. Read up on the facts. Drop by the Lords and get to know your fellow conspirators. See how you can help. Start thinking propaganda. Surely I don't need to tell you. You're a bloody ex-civil servant.' She threw some money on the bill.

'I can't just march into the House of Lords and start flinging my weight about.'

She jumped up. 'Of course you can. You're working for me. I've arranged for you to have a research assistant's pass. Get off to the Lords and sort out the details with Black Rod's office. Now, come on, I'm late.' She pulled on her coat and headed for the door. Amiss chased after her.

'Who's my best point of contact?'

She hailed a taxi. 'King's Cross!' she shouted to the driver. 'And go like the clappers.' She jumped in. 'Bertie's the smartest, but Sid's got more time. Tally-ho!' she cried, as she slammed the door behind her.

Amiss stood irresolute on the pavement. After a couple of minutes he set off towards the London Library.

5

'Morning, Violet,' said Deptford. 'And how are we today? OK on the taxi front last night, I hope?'

'Indeed yes, my lord. Debate kept going until ten-thirty-two, I'm pleased to say. What can I get you, my lord?'

'My guest would like a gin and tonic, please.' Deptford saw Amiss's baffled expression. 'Staff get taxis paid for after ten-thirty. If it's a matter of a few minutes we try to spin the debate out long enough.'

'Commendably humane.'

'Yeah. But don't tell the Public Accounts Committee. Some of them buggers would probably denounce it as a wicked waste of taxpayers' money. Inflexible bastards.' He took a substantial sip of his whisky and soda. 'Oh, that's better. I tell you, I didn't 'alf feel in a right old state this morning. A fellow of my age shouldn't be led astray like we were last night. Dangerous woman, Jack. Always was.' He sniggered in a reminiscent sort of way.

'You've known each other a long time?'

Lord Deptford grinned. 'Twenty years or so. No more than that. But there was a time when we knew each other very, very well.'

Amiss preferred to ignore the implication. 'I see. But as I was saying, I'm a bit baffled by some of what happened yesterday.'

'Like what?'

'For a start, I'm a great admirer of Jack's, but how did she get such a turnout of peers yesterday. Someone told me the audience for her introduction was about three times the usual.'

'Bertie Stormerod, of course. He's always had a soft spot for our Jack, so he leaned on his mates to put on the best show possible. Throw in us pro-hunting lot and you've got a lot of people wanting to make a fuss of her. You see, if she's going to play a major part in defeating this bill, even while she's still wet behind the ears in Lords terms, she needs to be given all the backing she can. Adds to 'er stature, you might say. She's going to be making her maiden speech about eleven months earlier than usual, so she 'as to be seen to be special so as to square the fuddy-duddies. Next?'

'OK. I could understand the connection between, say, Lord Poulteney and Stormerod and hunting. But you?'

Deptford emitted a throaty chuckle. 'Can't see what a jumped-up member of the working classes is doing defending a gentleman's pursuit, eh? That what you're getting at?'

'I suppose it is.'

'It's quite simple. Wanted to be a jockey as a kid. Did three years as a stable boy after I left school at fourteen and fell in love with the local 'unt. You can't imagine what that was like for a city boy. Glamour, excitement, danger. For a time I was like that description of Mr Jorrocks.'

Amiss raised an eyebrow. Deptford sighed. 'I suppose no one reads them now – R. S. Surtees's stories about a Victorian cockney tea merchant who became a Master of Foxhounds. I love 'em: try this.' He declaimed emotionally: '"I am a sportsman all over, and to the backbone – 'unting is all that's worth living for – all time is lost what is not spent in 'unting – it is like the hair we breathe – if we have it not we die – it's the sport of kings, the image of war without its guilt, and only five and twenty per cent of its danger." Ah, it's wonderful stuff. Would you like to borrow some?'

'I have one already. I spent an hour this morning collecting hunting books from the library – including *Handley Cross*.'

'Well done, mate. You'll enjoy it.'

The drinks were delivered. 'Thanks, luv. So I lived for hunting for a while. Then the war came and when I came out I couldn't go back to it.'

'Because?'

'Because I got a job in a trade union and hunting became

35

a guilty secret of my past. You don't get to be a General Secretary by careering around the countryside on the back of an 'orse. You get there by being leftier than the lefties – at least in those days you did.'

He took a thoughtful sip. 'Mind you, I wouldn't want you to think I was a cynic. I believed a lot of that claptrap till I realized in the late seventies we was doing more 'arm to our members than the bosses were. That's why I moved to the right almost as fast as I'd moved to the left post-war. Cigarette?'

'No, thanks.'

'Mind if I do?'

'Absolutely not.'

Deptford produced tobacco and cigarette papers from his pocket and expertly constructed a roll-up. As he put it in his mouth, he caught Amiss's eye and smiled. 'Old habits die hard. Now where was I? Oh, yes. Moving right. What they called a turncoat. Especially when I took the peerage. Not that I bloody cared. The way I see it is that after nearly a lifetime of judging everything according to how it would go down with our members, I've 'ad fifteen blissful years to think for meself, which is why I moved from the Labour benches to the cross benches and why I now say that life should be about more people 'aving a good time rather than less people enjoying themselves.'

He sat up and an angry tone came into his voice. 'I'm sick and tired of all these bloody lefty intellectuals trying to impose austerity on the working classes, disapproving of their drinking and their gambling and their chip butties and all the rest of the things that put a bit of sparkle into hard lives. Me' – he raised his glass – 'I'm in favour of cakes and ale and bugger the bigots. What was it Rosa Luxemburg said? "If I can't dance, I don't want the revolution." Do you want to know 'oo really pisses me off? That cow Beatrice Parsons.'

'You mean the author of *Principled Socialism*?'

'And other sexy romps,' said Deptford sourly. 'She's just the kind I hate most. Born into the fuckin' upper middle classes, public school and Oxford, top job as a barrister, but spends her time slagging off everything the working class in this country like best, from the monarchy to the cops. Lives in a Georgian house in Islington high on the hog, takes a peerage when they're looking for a few women to buy off the left and spends her time lecturing us 'ere about this class-ridden haunt of privilege from which all but the likes of 'er should be expelled when the bleedin' revolution comes. Christ, she'd be first out, I can tell you, with my toe up her arse.'

'Do I gather, Sid, that your leap right includes defending hereditary peers?'

'Bloody certain it does. I mean, leaving out the ones I don't know, who never turn up 'ere and who mind their own business down at the farm, most of them are OK. Me best mates from here are Bertie, the Marquess of Stowe, Reggie Poulteney . . .' He saw Amiss's expression. 'Oh, fair enough. I know 'e's a bore. But not if you're interested in hunting. I go down to his place from time to time, just to watch. Oh, and of course, I'm great pals with Benny Porter, who used to be a boiler maker and sees eye to eye with me.

'You don't find most of the hereditary earls looking down at the likes of us. They're only interested in people being good blokes. And what's more, just because they're selected at random, they're a lot more bleedin' representative of the general population than your MPs. Most of the life peers we get here don't know how ordinary people think, particularly the bloody intellectuals and those retired 'ouse of Commons types who rant away like what they used to do down there and don't understand how to behave like a gentleman. It's pretty refreshing, I can tell you, to come here and meet some people who know they're not that bright, 'ave a bit of modesty and courtesy.' He stubbed out his cigarette viciously. 'I mean, can you imagine how pleasant it is to speak in a place where you don't get interrupted? In the other place they have to shout all the time to drown out heckling yobs.'

'I know, Sid, but you're not going to convince the reformers that the hereditary system is anything other than unfair.'

'Oh bollocks. I'm sick of the word "fair". Life ain't fair. The bleedin' human condition ain't fair. All you can do is muddle on as best you can and try and make life as good for most people as is possible in this world. I don't think we do too badly at that in Britain. What you don't do is reduce it all to the lowest bloody common denominator, as prescribed by pain-in-the-arse blue stockings like Beatrice fuckin' Parsons.'

'Has she got a line on fox-hunting?'

'What do you think?' Deptford made a valiant, if unsuccessful, attempt to mimic an educated upper-class female: 'It's twisted, degenerate, sadistic, anachronistic, aristocratic – need I go on?'

'Your kind of gal, clearly.'

'Oh, yeah. Real fun-lover. Bloody woman probably has 'alf a glass of dry white wine every eighteenth Tuesday. Mind you, it's a big disadvantage for the antis that she's the government spokesman. That could win us over a lot of waverers.'

'What's the tally?'

'Well, we've got to drag a lot of the backwoodsmen up here to vote, I guess. It's all those townie life peers that are the problem. They don't turn up much at the 'ouse but they will come in for what they consider a moral issue. Won't listen to half the arguments, just vote blindly. It's no skin off their nose.'

'Have you an organized campaign?'

'Well we 'ave and we 'aven't. Tell you what. Bertie can tell you a bit about it. He'll be joining us shortly for a drink and then we can all have lunch.'

'Frankly, old boy, I've been a bit worried from time to time. Won't deny the old nightmare that hunting will just be abolished by default. You see, the truth is that many of those who feel most passionately about it are perhaps rather less than articulate. I mean, look what happened with deer-hunting?'

'What did happen? It was last year, wasn't it? I didn't really follow it.'

'First place in the lottery for private members' bills went to Gavin Chandler. Know who I mean?'

Amiss knitted his brows. 'High-minded Liberal Democrat

who goes on a lot about morality in international relations, isn't he?'

'Correct. Without knowing what he's talking about, naturally. That always makes it easier to pronounce on morality . . .'

'He's a perpendicular-looking Puseyite pig-jobber,' interjected Deptford. 'Ooh, sorry, Robert. When I gets really excited I tends to quote Jorrocks.'

'Who, as no doubt you will find out, Robert, was a dab hand at insults. Now, to continue. Chandler's constituency is in the West Country and he absolutely hates and despises all the Tories. So he took a particular delight in abolishing what he considered an important symbol of their depravity – deer-hunting. And since most MPs don't know one end of a deer from another, it passed through the Commons virtually unchallenged. And no one in Lords put up any kind of decent defence. Just lay down under it. I can tell you, we're lucky parts of the West Country haven't seceded.'

'And now the same thing's 'appening with fox-huntin'. And barring a bleedin' miracle . . .'

'Or a spirited campaign . . .'

'We'll be right in the shit this time. Letting deer-huntin' go is bad enough. But fox-huntin' . . .'

'I tend to agree,' said Stormerod. 'Although I don't hunt myself, I take a dim view of abolishing what Trollope called "our national sport", even if it has a smaller following than it used to have. But we've been pretty well ambushed again. Still reeling from the deer-hunting debacle – can you believe it? – we've once more been caught napping.' He sighed. 'It's all been a pretty sorry business. First thing that happened was an obscure backbencher called Coulter drew first place in the lottery for private members' bills. He hadn't any sort of form on hunting so it wasn't until very late in the day we discovered he'd been nobbled by the antis and had agreed to sponsor their bill. It's called the Wild Mammals (Protection) Bill and it's not just about fox-hunting – it also has sensible provisions making it illegal to torture hedgehogs or squirrels.'

'Stopping oiks usin' hedgehogs as footballs, for instance.'

'Precisely. Sid and I and most of us are happy about that, and about outlawing snares. But we're deadly opposed to banning hunting hares, foxes and mink.'

'Mmm,' said Amiss. 'I'm probably with you on the last two, but you're going to have to do a seriously proselytizing job to get me to agree on hare-coursing.'

'Later. Anyway, the whole attention has been focused on fox-hunting, which is what's stirred everyone's imagination. Before we knew it, a huge campaign had started and every MP was getting a couple of thousand postcards saying, "Stop this cruelty now." Now, we're no good at mobilizing those sort of numbers and on top of that we usually put up people on radio or television with plummy accents who get everyone's backs up.

'So with that big Labour majority in the Commons, insufficient time and our lot on the defensive, we didn't stand a chance. Hunting's a nice, easy issue unless you're in a rural constituency — all the electoral advantage is in doing down the so-called gentry.'

Deptford interrupted. 'Do you know that A. P. Herbert poem?

> 'While the Commons must bray like an ass every day
>   To appease their electoral hordes
> We don't say a thing till we've something to say:
>   There's a lot to be said for the Lords.'

Amiss grinned. 'Nice one.'

'So,' continued Stormerod. 'It passed its second reading by three hundred and eighty to one hundred and ten and the government — seeing a popular source of votes — came onside and said it would provide time for a third reading. In the blink of an eye it was through Committee and up to here and this time — because they're determined to get it through — it's a government bill.'

'Aren't you more organized now?'

Stormerod raised an eyebrow at Deptford. 'Better, but not good.'

'But you've got numbers on your side, surely?'

'Not as many as you'd think. It's not like a century ago when most peers would hunt. Nowadays, even among the hereditary ones, you've got a hell of a cross-section of society – probably as many vegetarians as you've got hunters. And we don't really know how half of them would jump. If you try pulling them in to vote, it might go the wrong way.

'No, we're concentrating on the working peers, maybe three or four hundred, who are probably evenly balanced. But Labour have a three-line whip on, while the Conservatives don't, because they're split too. So it's tight enough and damn difficult to read.'

Deptford broke in. 'That's one of the reasons Bertie was so anxious to get Jack in 'ere fast. He thought – and I agreed – she'd put a bit of energy into standing up for us. We're goin' to need her when they try to reform us in all the wrong ways.'

'So who is there who's effective besides you two and Jack?'

Stormerod sighed again. 'No one much. You see, we're stuck with the enthusiasts, many of whom are frankly counterproductive. I mean, can you imagine the sort of speeches Poulteney makes? Listen to him for long enough and we'd have mass defections.'

At that very moment Poulteney entered the bar accompanied by a tall, weedy old man in pince-nez. 'Ah, Bertie, Sid, and . . . oh, yes, Robert. Mind if we join you?'

Stormerod rose and began pushing extra seats into place. Poulteney's companion rushed to help, caught his right hand between the backs of two chairs, yelped, grabbed another gamely and pushed it so that it hit the table and spilled some of Stormerod's drink. Deptford interrupted his distracted apologies. 'Meet Robert Amiss, Tommy. Robert, this is Tommy Beesley.' Drinks were ordered.

'I ran into Tommy in the library,' said Poulteney, 'and he's worried.'

'Very worried.' His voice was high-pitched, reedy and redolent with angst. 'I was saying to Reggie that I wish I knew what was going on. I feel quite in despair. This terrible thing must be stopped, I tell you. It must be stopped.'

'Calm down, Tommy. We're doing the best we can.'

41

'Your best is clearly not good enough, not good enough, I say. Look at what happened to my deer-hunting. We've got to take firm action, this time. Just not stand for it.'

'That's right,' said Poulteney, 'we've got to get them on the run, chase them into cover and if they go to earth we dig 'em out.'

'When I speak in the debate' – emotion drove Beesley's voice so high it periodically went into a squeak – 'I shall tell them I shan't stand for it. This is our birthright. We shall stand and fight. And this time we will not give way, whatever happens.'

'This is a democracy.' Stormerod sounded weary. 'We have to win the argument and the vote and you don't do that by threats but by persuasion. Now, if you'll excuse us, we have a lunch engagement.'

'See what we're up against,' he groaned to Amiss as the three of them walked down the corridor.

'Are they typical?'

'Yes and no. Most people like Tommy Beesley never come here. And indeed Reggie rarely comes. But we're not overendowed with lucid exponents of the virtues of the chase, I can tell you that. And unfortunately, Reggie and Tommy will insist on speaking.'

They entered an L-shaped dining room decorated with the usual seas of mahogany panelling, this time along with sickly yellowy wallpaper and a patterned carpet dominated by sea-green squares on which sat uncomfortably the red gold-monogrammed upholstery.

'Ah, Agnes. And how are we today?'

The waitress was unresponsive. 'Table for three, my lord?'

'Four. We're hoping a lady will join us.'

Amiss looked at him enquiringly.

'Your friend the baroness.'

'That's no lady; that's Jack Troutbeck,' offered Amiss as a whirlwind arrived, clapped him on the back, pulled a chair out noisily, plonked herself down and stuck her legs out in front of her. The legs of her directoire knickers came into view during mid-stretch. Amiss observed the waitress looking at them sidelong in disapproval. An elderly peer who

42

tottered past at the crucial moment stopped momentarily, shook his head and staggered off towards a faraway table.

'Busy morning?' asked Deptford solicitously.

'Not really. Up and down to Cambridge, council meeting for an hour, mopping up various bits of business, telling everyone what to do, then back here.'

'Drink?'

'I'll have a Scotch while I think what I'll have to eat. Now, how've you lot been getting on?'

'I fear' – Stormerod looked over his shoulder – 'that our young friend can hardly be encouraged by having been exposed to Tommy Beesley as well as another dose of Reggie Poulteney, who seem set fair through their advocacy of fox-hunting in next week's debate to bring about its demise.'

'And you can't stop them speaking?'

'No.'

The baroness took a thoughtful swig of her drink. 'This could go wrong, you know. Hunting could actually be abolished in a fit of national absent-mindedness. How's the strategic planning going, Robert?'

He shot her a withering look. 'I don't even know yet if any lobbying's been done.'

'The Defend our Field Sports crowd have done what they can,' said Stormerod, 'but it's not like lobbying MPs. People here don't worry about votes. Really, all we can do is ensure the best people speak and speak well and then keep fighting to the end.'

'So what's the talent?'

'Sid and me. Next most anxious to speak, God help us, are Tommy and Reggie and – possibly even worse – Admiral Lord Gordon.'

'What's the opposition like?' asked Amiss.

'Apart from the benighted Beatrice, who is in the lead, I don't know yet.'

The baroness scratched her head. 'It's clear Robert and I had better have a recce. There's an anti-hunting public meeting being held in Islington tonight. I know the wretched Parsons will be there, as well as someone called Lord Purseglove? Any idea who he is?'

43

'He inherited the title a couple of years ago, but isn't seen here much. He's some sort of monk.'

'OK. Robert will report back to you tomorrow. Now, let's have some lunch. I'm starving.'

'OK, we seem pretty clear about everything. Got all that, Robert. Robert! Concentrate.'

'Yes, yes. Sorry. I'm a bit tired. I was falling asleep.'

The waitress came over with a face like thunder.

'Did you want something, your ladyship? I thought I heard you call.'

Stormerod grinned. 'Now, Agnes, I know Lady Troutbeck has a rather loud voice, but there's no need to look so disapproving.'

Agnes sniffed. 'I like things to be seemly.'

'Seemly and I don't mix,' said the baroness cheerfully. 'If I were you I'd get used to it.' She stuck out her wine glass in Agnes's direction. 'But now that you're here, you can give me some more wine.'

The waitress looked mutinous.

'Come, come. We girls must stick together.'

With a bad grace, the waitress filled the baroness's glass and withdrew tight-lipped.

Deptford shook his head. 'Watch out, Jack. It's one thing upsettin' the peers. They don't matter. But for cryin' out loud don't upset the staff.'

'They'll get used to me,' she said carelessly. 'Everyone does.' She pulled out her pipe and tobacco.

'Sorry, you can't smoke yet. It's not 'alf past one.'

'What does that mean?'

'Can't smoke in the dining room till then.'

'There are more rules in this place than in Alcatraz. That's the trouble with men. They want to tie up all of life in a straitjacket.'

'I wouldn't like to be the chap who tries to do that to you.' Stormerod laughed. 'Now hold your soul in patience for a while and enjoy your lunch. The pipe will have to wait. You can't flout all our conventions in the first twenty-four hours.'

44

6

Outside the town hall demonstrators were surging, milling around and chanting slogans. Most of them had banners bearing graphic pictures. As Amiss averted his eyes, the baroness suddenly appeared at his side, having ploughed a path through the demonstrators with no apparent difficulty. 'I would prefer it,' remarked Amiss, 'if my duties did not extend to having to look at pictures of eviscerated animals. It doesn't exactly encourage me in this particular crusade.'

'Oh, stop being so feeble, Robert. I could equally well show you pictures of gassed and shot foxes. This is propaganda; it has nothing to do with the truth. Now, come on in and let's get a ringside seat.'

The hall filled up quickly. From the front row, Amiss looked round covertly a few times.

'I doubt there are many on our side,' he whispered.

The baroness, who had been searching her bag for her pipe, turned and stared around openly.

'There certainly seems to be an absence of jodhpurs. Fear not. You've got me.' She clamped down the tobacco and sucked on her pipe. A woman behind tapped her on the shoulder. 'No smoking.'

'I'm not.'

'You're just about to.'

'Who says?'

'You've got a pipe in your mouth.'

'I've shoes on my feet but I'm not walking.' She put her pipe on her lap and took from her pocket an enormous handkerchief into which she blew her nose noisily. The complainant sat well back in her seat, evincing a mixture of shock and disgust.

'Hah! That's better.' The baroness returned the handkerchief to her pocket and put her pipe back in her mouth.

'You're just trying to tease them.'

'Of course I am. It puts them in the wrong, this old unlit pipe trick. Anyway, it's quite soothing – gives me something to grit my teeth on. How else would I get through a speech of Beatrice Parsons's?'

By eight o'clock the hall was completely full. The audience ranged from octogenarians in woolly hats with Home Counties accents through to steely-eyed fanatics brandishing banners threateningly – which seemed odd, Amiss thought, since virtually the entire audience could be assumed to be on their side. Perhaps it had become simply a habit.

At eight o'clock precisely, a chap in an Aran sweater, crumpled tweed trousers and sandals emerged from behind the scenes leading three speakers on to the platform. Screams and shouts of approval broke out at the back of the audience. As his team sat down, he stood at the microphone and called the meeting to order.

'My friends.' Silence fell. 'As president of the Friends of Oppressed Animals, I am delighted to be here this evening. We are all friends in this great undertaking – united here in a great cause. A cause in which people who, in other circumstances might be politically at odds, can join hands in defence of the defenceless. Victory is within our grasp but it is important that our champions be shown how much we respect and admire them and how – as they continue to hunt down cruelty and oppression – we will be riding closely behind them. We will not be wearing scarlet jackets, for we are not fine lords and ladies, but we will triumph in the chase nonetheless.'

This was apparently regarded as wit by a large section of the audience; they guffawed and roared with laughter.

'Now, if I may make so bold, I would like to introduce someone who is indeed a fine lady, but not in the sense of one of those battening on the oppressed, be they human or animal. As plain Beatrice Parsons, she has long been a fighter for the poor and underprivileged, and that fight she will of course continue, but it is as Lady Parsons, the proposer in the House of Lords of the bill to outlaw these foul practices, that she comes to us today. So now, without further ado . . .' He bowed low in Parsons's direction.

Baroness Troutbeck gripped tightly on her pipe and out of the corner of her mouth muttered, 'Sycophantic git.'

'Sssh.' Amiss didn't like the look in the eye of an old lady who had overheard this challenging comment.

'Why should I?'

'We're in a rather vulnerable spot,' he hissed. 'I don't want to be beaten to death by those who want to abolish cruelty.'

The baroness threw her head back in a gesture which was presumably meant to imply distress at Amiss's pusillanimity, but, to his relief, she said nothing more.

Lady Parsons was by now on her feet. She was a contained-looking woman, crisply turned out in the uniform now *de rigueur* among ambitious women of the left, conventional wisdom being that the more radical you were, the more you had to dress like something out of a glossy magazine. Her close-fitted and stylish yellow jacket sported epaulettes and brass buttons; her cream shirt was silk; her hair was simple but had obviously benefited from the attentions of a very upmarket practitioner. Lady Parsons's vowels were clearly enunciated in a Home Counties/public school/Oxbridge accent that, at times, she must have wished to be without while she battled her way up the ladder of North London local politics.

'Chair, friends, along with all of you, I am honoured to serve the cause of outlawing the cruelty that so disfigures our countryside. I am gratified to be able to play a part in bringing to Britain civilized standards of the kind the Establishment has always fought against.

'I don't need to tell you, my friends, the provisions of this bill.' She then proceeded to do exactly that at considerable length and in the style of Counsel for the Prosecution making the final damning summing-up speech to the jury. Lady Parsons was clearly someone whose austerity allowed for no such luxury as emotion. Hers was a forensic mind, Amiss thought with distaste, as he listened to the bloodless analysis.

As she grimly went through the bill clause by clause, Amiss began to feel much more sympathy for Jack Troutbeck's point of view, for Lady Parsons's perspective clearly had no room for light, shade or tolerance. She saw no distinction between people kicking hedgehogs to death or setting fire to squirrels just for the hell of it and a sport that had involved whole communities throughout the countryside for centuries. Indeed, if anything, it was clear that hunting was the real butt of her loathing and disdain. At every opportunity she offered a humourless sneer at 'bastions of privilege' and 'luxuriators in inherited wealth' who sought to flaunt their riches and heartlessness in such an obscene manner. She even produced without apology, and as if it were newly minted, Oscar Wilde's epigram about hunting being 'the unspeakable in pursuit of the uneatable'.

Amiss hated her. She oozed moral superiority from every well-tended pore and her intellect was competent, efficient and clinical – the intellectual equivalent of a Swiss laboratory. Without warmth, humour or any kind of doubt, it was clear that on all moral issues, where many people saw pros and cons, Beatrice Parsons would be on the side of tidiness. Aborting the unfit, providing a national euthanasia service on demand and purifying the genetic mix to eradicate inherited defects of physique or character would be right up her street.

'So now, colleagues, the issues are clear. The government has led the way, the voice of the people of the United Kingdom, ninety-four per cent of whom are against fox-hunting, has been already exercised through their elected representatives. It is my duty to ensure that the people's will triumphs in that redundant anachronism, the House of Lords, over the selfish interests of the landed gentry.'

'What a pill,' observed Jack Troutbeck in a whisper that carried several rows back. Amiss kicked her on the shin, eliciting a bellow of pain that would have been heard in the back row by the hard of hearing. If it disconcerted Amiss, it markedly unsettled the speaker. She shot a castigatory look at the author of the disturbance, who beamed back at her and moved her pipe to the other corner of her mouth. Parsons looked down at her notes, failed to find her place and ended lamely, 'Well, that's it, Chair. I'm grateful for your support. Victory is within our grasp.'

'That rattled her.' Jack Troutbeck beamed. She swung her right leg over her left knee with gay abandon, causing her skirt to ride up.

'You're showing your knickers,' hissed Amiss, under cover of the thunderous applause in which he, unlike the baroness, was cravenly, though perfunctorily, joining. She looked down at the eau-de-nil satin that peeked from under the houndstooth tweed and said, 'Good. That should upset the monk.'

The chairman rose and quelled the applause with a gesture.

'We are very, very grateful to Lady Parsons. It is comforting to know our cause is in such capable hands. We are honoured further to have here a man of God whose life has been pledged, not only to the service of his fellow human beings, but to the service of all his fellow creatures. Brother Francis has, over the years, contributed movingly to the literature of the animal world in many, many magazines. His short stories and poems have brought tears to our eyes as we contemplate the nobility and unselfishness of our animal friends and the suffering we impose on them. Fortunately for our cause, Brother Francis is not only an inspiration, he is in a position to help fight directly this last battle for the little fox and all the other wild animals whom we are all here determined to protect from the beastliness of man. For Brother Francis is also Lord Purseglove and his eloquence must move those members of that institution whose hearts are not irretrievably hardened. Please warmly welcome Brother Francis.'

Brother Francis certainly looked the part. His skinny stooping body, his snowy hair and cadaverous face had the true stamp of aestheticism. His slightly hooded eyes were of a piercing blue which was intensified by the pallor of his complexion.

'Savanarola?' whispered Amiss to the baroness.

'Probably.'

49

But there was nothing fanatical about the delivery or the voice of Brother Francis. His tone was gentle, his slightly Welsh accent with its seesaw intonation had an overall rather bardic effect and the content of his speech would have raised few eyebrows at a meeting of the North Gloucester branch of the RSPCA. It was treacly and glutinous rather than threatening.

'Sisters and brothers. I am not here to preach religion to you. I am here to preach faith – a faith that is love of one's fellow creatures. Whether you believe in God, whether you are Christian or whatever you may be, all of you here with me will have sympathy with Jesus Christ's promise that not a sparrow falls without God knowing it. Sisters and brothers, as a small boy in the country, I was lucky enough to have read to me the story of St Francis of Assisi and how he loved Brother Donkey and Sister Rabbit. It was then that I decided to dedicate my life not just to God but to those little creatures that cannot speak for themselves, yet are as noble a part of the world as the greatest saint or genius. Who is to say that Sister Nightingale trilling her matchlessly beautiful song is inferior to Schubert; that Mother Moorhen, selflessly searching from morning till night for food for her brood, has less love and selflessness than Mother Teresa; or that Brother Silverback defending his tribe of gorillas is less courageous than Hercules?'

Amiss gazed sideways at the baroness and caught a look of outrage crossing her face. She changed posture noisily and positioned herself, knees out, feet squarely on the floor, elbows on knees, head in hands. He heard the phrase 'Pass the sickbag' floating out. Her distress was certainly not shared by most of the audience. Thunderous applause broke out every time the tremulous philosopher paused. He went on to share with them a moving fragment of autobiography concerning the moment when he had just decided to apply to the Franciscan order. 'I went out into the grounds of my father's home, wondering if I was making the right decision about what to do with the rest of my life. Then I saw, hundreds of yards away, emerging from a copse, a fox in full flight. That beautiful innocent creature fled across the lawn

50

and through the hedgerow, followed shortly afterwards by the baying hounds. And not far behind were the horses ridden by men and women so enamoured of blood that they wore clothes of scarlet. In the front row, I knew to my shame, would be my father.

'As I stood there despairing at that horrible sight, a little squirrel who had come to love me – and whom I called Tiny Tim, for he represented to me such innocent goodness – jumped from a branch overhead on to my shoulder and rubbed his tiny head against my cheek. I knew then that what I had seen was a sign that I must dedicate myself for life to protecting my little feathered and furry friends against the cruelty of man. For it is man who was the enemy here, not the innocent hounds. As I wrote of them:

> 'That faithful hound, his master's slave
> Serves the serial killer to his grave.

'I can do little but pray and by my trifling pieces of verse awaken in others that understanding and kindness that you, by your presence here tonight, show is within each and every one of you. Let me end with a poem that I am proud to say has become the anthem of our great crusade. You will, I hope, sing the last lines with me.

> 'The cunning fox to you may seem
> A lowly creature in God's scheme,
> But see that vixen with her cub
> Peering at you through the scrub
> As if the frost had froze her .
> She's Madonna Lachrymosa .
>
> And is the small hare in the gorse
> Who flees the hounds and farmer's curse
> Bobbing his fluffy ears in fright
> (So vigilant all day and night) –
> A villain up to his old tricks
> Or martyr on his crucifix?

51

'And now, brothers and sisters, sing out for our little siblings.'

And to the tune of 'Jerusalem', the audience sang out lustily.

> *'And did those paws in ancient times*
> *Scamper on England's mountains green?*
> *And did the duck and grouse divine*
> *Fly forth upon our clouded hills?*
> *Bring me my scroll of burning gold*
> *Bring me my quill, my Muse, my lyre,*
> *I will not cease from Mental Fight*
> *Nor shall my odes sleep in my brain*
> *Till we have every blood sport banned*
> *In England, not just on my land.'*

7

After that there were almost no dry eyes in the house. The entire audience, with the exception of the baroness and – through loyalty to her – Amiss, leaped to their feet in a standing ovation. He gazed at the floor; she was slumped in her chair in an attitude of despair. On closer inspection she appeared to be fast asleep. Since it was her fault he was enduring this agony, Amiss was damned if he was going to be left to it on his own. Mindful of her previous performance, he patted her gingerly on the shoulder and then on the thigh. She grabbed his hand instantly.

'I didn't know you cared.'

'For Christ's sake, Jack. Will you knock it off.'

Not for the first time in their relationship, he envied Jack's complete indifference to public opinion. He was already uncomfortably aware of glances from people further down the line, not to speak of mumblings behind of the 'disgrace-ful-what-a-dreadful-woman' variety.

The ovation eventually subsided, and the chairman got to his feet again.

'Very touching, very touching. I feel we are all privileged to have had such an extraordinarily moving and emotional experience. Even the hard hearts among the so-called gentry can surely not do other than melt when they have the good fortune to be exposed to the loving words of Brother Francis.'

Amiss could hear continuous snuffling from behind. Brother Francis had clearly slain the little old ladies.

'Now, I would like to call on our young friend from the Rights of Animals League, Jerry Dolamore, who though a comparatively recent arrival on our shores from the

Antipodes has made himself an inspiration for the campaign for animal rights. His brilliance and eloquence have earned him many admirers.

'Please, friends, welcome the man who during the last few months has done so much to mobilize popular support for our great cause.'

Thunderous applause greeted Dolamore. Gazing at his squat figure and the pallid face with an outcrop of facial hair that resembled a pile of clippings from a salon floor, Amiss found his popularity hard to understand. He wore a striped cotton collarless shirt four sizes too big for him and well past its best, unbuttoned far enough down to reveal a grimy white vest.

Expecting a bore and a whinger, Amiss shifted in an effort to find a more comfortable position. But from his opening words, and despite the rather nasal quality of his voice and the unattractive Australian accent, Dolamore's effect was even more electric than Brother Francis's.

He eschewed all niceties. 'This is war,' he began. 'We represent the forces of good against the forces of evil.'

Amiss and the baroness looked at each other and simultaneously said, 'Savanarola.'

'Ssshh,' came from behind.

The baroness directed a withering glance over her shoulder at the perpetrator. Dolamore's voice rose. 'This is not about stopping cruelty; this is about wiping out animaphobia. About abolishing speciesism. It is about recognizing that no one has the right wantonly to kill any animal, for eating, for wearing or, above all, for pleasure. This is about rights and equality and before I have finished we will have enshrined in this country a bill of rights for animals, which spells out their right to safety, to protection, to food and to shelter.

'Some say we are extreme. But they are the very people who some generations ago said women had no souls. Now they say it of animals.

'All reformers are condemned as extreme at first. Afterwards, they are praised. But for people like us, little children would still be sweeping chimneys and going down mines. Women would still be denied the vote. Men would still be hanged for stealing a loaf of bread. And those lords of the manor who now try to defend hunting would still be exercising their right to ravage the daughters of their tenants.'

Dolamore's speech was frequently interrupted by cheers, though his fan club, it seemed to Amiss, was mainly at the back of the hall. He couldn't imagine the woolly hats would be entirely supportive of the notion that species egalitarianism put them on a par with mice. Yet he acknowledged Dolamore's astonishing oratorical gift. His apparent sincerity was so overwhelming it was hard not to ignore the content and simply be carried along by the style.

From the premise of the equality of all species, Dolamore took his audience logically through history from barbarism to enlightenment, bringing in and extending to animals insights from an eclectic range from Thomas Paine to Buddha. Movingly, he described the advance from darkness into light. His voice soared and swooped and sometimes fell to a near murmur, but it was clear, often thrilling and always compelling.

Having taken the audience through landmarks like the abolition of bear-baiting and cock-fighting he produced his charter of demands for the future. The whole audience was caught up in the excitement. Even the baroness was rapt in concentration. The sporadic applause increased in frequency and loudness and now came from all round the room. But such was Dolamore's quality as an orator that he could instantly, with no more than a gesture of a finger, restore absolute silence.

When his peroration about the Brotherhood of the Species ended with the exhortation, 'to take this crusade into every home in Britain so as to make it a shining example to the world,' Dolamore sat down abruptly, sweat glinting on his face and staining his vest. His eyes continued to bore into the audience, which rose as one activist and cheered and clapped like crazed pop fans. Even Amiss was sufficiently carried away to stand up, but emboldened once again by his companion's rugged independence in staying in her seat without clapping, he sat down again.

'He hasn't converted you?'

'I never was cut out for Nuremberg rallies,' she said acidly. 'For a moment there I had my doubts about you.'

After about three minutes, Dolamore rose to his feet and made a silencing gesture to the audience, hands up and palms out as if to push them back into their seats. They obliged instantly.

The chairman stood up, seeming a little dazed.

'Thank you, Jerry. My goodness, what an experience this has been for all of us. What an extraordinary trio of champions we have here. Our fine legal mind . . .' He bowed at Parsons. 'Our humble, loving Brother, so attuned to his animal friends.' He bowed at Brother Francis. 'And now our great inspiration, our champion, advancing before us all with the banner of justice and equality. Truly he is the veritable Lord Wilberforce of our time.'

The slightly baffled look on Dolamore's face gave Amiss the impression that the name of that doughty opponent of slavery had not been big in Australia. The chairman looked at his watch.

'Good Lord. How time flies. It's a quarter to ten and we really must be out of here by ten o'clock.'

As bathetic moments went, thought Amiss, this rather resembled a caretaker explaining to the SS that he'd be locking up in a minute so would they please make ready to march out of the stadium. 'So only a few questions. Yes?'

A woolly hat rose.

'Please,' she squeaked. 'I want to know what we are to do?'

The chairman looked enquiringly at Lady Parsons.

'Write in support of this bill to your MPs and local councillors and tell them you want evidence that they are putting pressure on members of the House of Lords through public speeches and private lobbying. I understand the Animal Rights Federation can provide you with lists of companies with peers as board members. Write to the chairmen threatening to boycott their company's products if the peers on their board don't vote the right way. And write individually to peers making it clear that this issue will not go away.'

'Brother Francis?'

'Prayer, of course. And spreading the word to your friends and neighbours so that they too can help in this holy work.'

'Jerry?'

'Demonstrate outside the Lords and outside the homes of the key perpetrators of these foul practices. We will hand you the list at the door. And remember too, that it is, as Brother Francis says, a holy crusade, so we must make it clear that wrongdoing will be punished. And when you demonstrate, do so with fervour and do so with pride.'

This solicited another outbreak of cheering and clapping. From the back of the hall came a truculent North-country accent.

'We don't want to be namby-pamby about this.'

'A man after your own heart,' whispered Amiss to the baroness.

'If the police try to silence us or deny us our right to protest democratically, it is our duty to resist them as we would any forces of fascism.'

'Excuse me, Chair,' said Lady Parsons. 'It is important that no one should damage this cause by any form of violence.'

'The violence,' said the heavy voice from the back, 'will be from the oppressive agents of the state. Self-defence is our right.'

'Yes, well, I'm sure no one will do anything silly,' said the chairman, with more hope than conviction. 'Now if that's all . . .'

To Amiss's alarm, the baroness leapt to her feet. 'Mr Chairman.'

'Yes?'

'I have a question for each of the speakers.'

'Oh, I don't think there's time . . .'

'There will be time if you don't interrupt.'

He subsided into his chair looking sullen.

'First, Lady Parsons. You stated that it was the duty of the Lords, as of the Commons, to respond to the wish of ninety-four per cent of the population that fox-hunting be abolished.'

'Certainly.' Parsons was calm.

'How do you square that with your well-known opposition

to capital punishment. Over ninety-four per cent of the population are in favour of that.'

'That is an absolutely false comparison.'

'How?'

'Because it is the duty of representatives of the people to be morally in the lead. On capital punishment, in due course the people will follow. In this case, the people have been morally ahead of their legislators.'

'What a load of dishonest bullshit.'

'Really,' squeaked the chairman. 'I must protest.'

Hisses and boos came from the audience. She raised her voice. 'Now, I would like Brother Francis, Lord Purseglove, to explain how if animals are all that is good, sweet and innocent, they spend so much of their time hunting and killing each other.'

'Only some of them,' he bleated. 'Think how many of them are vegetarian: the hippopotamus, the squirrel, the hare. It will be for us to wean those still locked in the primitive pursuit of flesh to a vegetarian path. Why, I have as a companion, at this very time, a pussy cat who is fed on soya and biscuits and if you saw her gambol happily when I bring her her food, you would know that she had no need for the flesh of her fellow creatures.'

Her contemptuous snort trumpeted forth.

'My God, you're even barmier than I thought. Some people are daft enough to try to alter human nature, but you're the first person I've come across who's ambitious enough to take this as far as the animal kingdom. I wish you luck.'

He smiled at her in a saintly manner. 'Thank you, sister.'

'Now, Mr Dolamore,' she shouted over the chorus of disapproval which had broken out behind her. Dolamore quelled the audience with a gesture. His eyes bored into hers.

'You make it clear that it's all baloney about this bill being a one-off. That wasn't just rhetoric. Fishing next, then the shooting and killing of animals for meat or clothing. This is what your organization wants. Is that now official?'

'Certainly,' he said. 'I am not a compromiser.'

'Nice company you find yourself in, Lady Parsons,' she said. She picked up her voluminous bag, jerked her head at

Amiss and began to walk down the aisle towards the back door. The booing started halfway down and from the back row suddenly erupted several dozen angry people shouting abuse, waving banners and fists and blocking her exit. Amiss looked around for police, bouncers or just people anxious to defend the right to express dissent. There were none, merely some anxious-looking people who had no intention of getting themselves mixed up in any trouble.

'Let's just stand here, Jack, until they calm down,' he whispered.

'Rubbish. When I want to leave I leave. Out of my way!' she shouted to the group in front of her.

The hubbub grew louder. An unpleasant-looking individual with a banner saying, 'Animal Liberation is THE Moral Issue', stepped forward and waved a piece of paper in front of her.

'Sign this petition.'

She looked at it. 'Certainly not.'

'Sign it!' he shouted. His cohorts took up the chant.

Amiss could hear bleatings from the platform. He looked back quickly and saw all four on their feet calling for calm. But on this occasion even Dolamore's hypnotic influence had no effect; the mob were caught up in their local objective.

'Sign it!' they shouted. 'Sign it, sign it, sign it, sign it.'

Jack Troutbeck began to push forward. Frightened but resigned, Amiss moved with her. Suddenly he felt a stunningly painful blow on his shoulder and emitted a yelp. An ugly-looking youth leered at him, raised his banner high in the air and aimed it at Amiss's head. Within seconds he had screamed, dropped his banner and was clutching his right arm, on which Jack had just landed an energetic blow with a horsewhip. As she brandished it at the youth in front, he hesitated.

'Tally-ho!' she shouted and cracked the whip on the floor with a noise so threatening that ahead of her the demonstrators parted like the River of Jordan. She turned, bowed at the platform and, followed by a rather sheepish-looking Amiss, marched out with her head held high and a happy and triumphant grin.

8

'So that's the opposition. Your next job is to get to grips with our side.' The baroness scooped another snail out of its shell, inserted it into her mouth and crooned appreciatively.

'You like snails?'

'Especially when they get the garlic just right. I like lots.' She looked in a rather troubled fashion at his plate. 'Are you sure that pâté is all right? It looks a bit finely cut to me.'

'It suits me. But thank you for your concern.'

She shook her head. 'Pâté should be coarse and preferably made of wild boar. Anyway, did you enjoy yourself?'

'Well, I certainly wasn't bored. Now, in view of a) your provocative interventions and b) the fact that you just happened to have a horsewhip in your bag, I infer that you set out to stir them up.'

'Just a shot across their bows.'

'Doesn't it alert them to trouble ahead?'

'When in doubt, I always believe in a foray into enemy territory. You can undermine their morale while picking up some gen. This time, for instance, we've seen how they crumble when you show them who's boss.'

'Jack, I think you may be getting muddled between a parliamentary challenge and animal activists. It's a vote that will determine what happens to fox-hunting, not hand-to-hand combat between you and some hairy oiks.'

'All part and parcel of the same thing,' she said carelessly.

A parody of a French waiter oiled his way over to her side. 'I 'ope zat everyzeeng is to your satisfaction, madame, your ladeeship. It ees a very great 'oneur to 'ave you 'ere tonight.'

'The *escargots* were excellent, thank you, but I am perturbed about my companion's pâté.'

The waiter gazed worriedly at the small piece remaining on Amiss's plate.

'It ees not good?'

'Very nice indeed, thank you,' said Amiss firmly. 'I have no complaints whatsoever. It was absolutely delicious.'

The baroness shook her head. 'He has no taste,' she said sadly to the waiter. 'I can see that the texture is all wrong – too smooth. Tell the chef.'

'But, of course, your ladeeship. Immediately, your ladeeship.' He collected their plates and departed with another bow.

'Jesus, am I not to be permitted a view on the food that I'm eating myself?'

''Course you are, but I'm not going to pay any attention to it if it's clearly misplaced.'

'What's with all this bowing and scraping and "your ladeeshiping" anyway? I wouldn't have thought you'd start throwing your title about like some counter-jumper.'

'My dear Robert.' The baroness took another large mouth-ful of wine, smacked her lips appreciatively and sighed with contentment. 'Mmmmm, I am enjoying myself. Nothing gives me an appetite like a bit of exercise before dinner. Didn't the Queen's message yesterday state that I should feel free to use all the . . . what was it? . . . rights, privileges, pre-eminences and all the rest of the goodies that come with being a baroness? And what do you think titles are for if not to fling around in restaurants? Surely you understand that that's one of the main advantages of the ennobled state, playing on the snobbery of restaurateurs. Look around this place.'

Amiss surveyed the packed room. 'We have the best table.'

'Exactly. Even though I didn't book it until six o'clock this evening. If I'd said Miss Troutbeck we'd have been doing well to get a billet at the kitchen door. What you have to learn, my boy, is that one gets on in life only by using all one's assets to the full. You're not wholehearted enough, that's your trouble.'

The waiter reappeared, placed in front of both of them a plate of boeuf bourguignon, stood back and contemplated Jack Troutbeck apprehensively. She dug around investigatively. 'Ah, good, plenty of shallots. Good big lumps of bacon. Excellent. And the beef looks satisfactorily chewy.'

He beamed with relief.

'But where is our claret?'

He clapped his hands above his head in a tragic gesture and disappeared at top speed.

'I'll hand it to you, Jack. I've never seen a French waiter reduced to such a quivering state before.'

'Only way to deal with them.' She speared a piece of beef and chewed it ecstatically. 'They're happiest this way. Dammit, the whole point about the French is that they respect food, so they like you to make a fuss about it, even if you're being critical. That's what the apologetic English never understand. I shall henceforward be a popular pet in this restaurant for reasons unconnected with my title.' The waiter arrived and poised the bottle over her glass. 'No, just pour it. If it's not right I'll send it back.'

He obediently filled first Amiss's and then her glass, bowed, wished them *'Bon appetit'* and withdrew.

'You're not descended from the Duke of Wellington by any chance, are you? You seem to have as short a way with the French as he did.'

'I wish I were. He's always been my hero. A girl can't have a better role model. He understood like nobody else the importance of robustness.'

'Speaking of which, what more do you know about Brother Francis? Is he really what he seems?'

'All *Who's Who* reveals is he was an only son, was educated at Marlborough and later joined the Franciscans. Not your common-or-garden Roman-Catholic Franciscans, mind you – the Anglo-Catholic lot. Much more upper-crusty. Then he began to produce verse and short stories which, God help us, became popular in women's magazines and were collected under titles like *Our Furry Friends* or *My Brother the Donkey.*'

'It's anthropomorphism gone mad.'

'Yes, but it's a powerful strain in the English character at the wimpish end among the sort of people who think their dogs read their minds, their cats think deep thoughts and dolphins are smarter than nuclear physicists. Speaking of cats, how's Plutarch?'

Amiss groaned. 'On my conscience. I haven't yet retrieved her from the cattery. Haven't worked up the courage.'

'The trouble with you is . . .'

'Is that I'm a wimp. I know.'

'I wasn't going to be so tactless as to say it.'

'Makes a change.'

'First you allow yourself to be blackmailed emotionally into having a cat you don't want.'

'Which was weak of me.'

'Then you fail to make the best of it by enjoying her.'

'How can I enjoy Plutarch? She's demanding, bossy and badly behaved.'

'Like me?'

'At least you don't swing out of people's curtains and bring me rats in your teeth. No, I have a grudging respect for Plutarch, I wish to see her well looked after and I've even had the occasional fleeting twinge of affection, but enjoy her I don't. If you want her I'll sign the adoption papers on the spot.'

'I doubt if I can manage more than short-term fosterage. After the unfortunate episode in the kitchen last time I put her up I would probably meet mass revolt if I announced I was keeping her. But if you like I'll take her until next week. You won't be able to look after her anyway, since you'll be away this weekend.'

'I will?' He looked at her with deep suspicion.

'Didn't he tell you? You've been invited to stay with Reggie Poulteney and go hunting.'

'How can I go hunting? I can't ride a rocking horse.'

'In a car and on foot. You've got to get the smell of the chase in your nostrils.'

He groaned. 'Oh, if I must, I must. Why aren't you coming?'

'I wish I could. I can hear the sound of the horn and the

baying of the hounds and the smell of the morning dew . . .'
She took a meditative sip and looked starrily into the middle
distance.

'That was well up to the standard of Brother Francis.
Answer my question.'

'I have to be hostess for a St Martha's Old Girls' gathering
which, *inter alia*, I hope will raise some more loot.'

'You can't abandon me alone with that unspeakable old
bore.'

'Tommy Beesley will be there.'

'Thanks a lot.'

'Come, come. There's more to Tommy than there seems.
He was a major-general once, you know. And was decorated
for conspicuous gallantry in Korea.'

'Good God!'

'I admit I find it baffling too, but we're obviously judging
too much by appearances.'

Amiss shrugged. 'Will Sid be there? He's more my type.'

'Doubt it. He's in his late seventies now, don't forget. Tends
to avoid the open air unless it's pretty balmy.'

'I know Bertie doesn't hunt, but will he come along to
plot?'

'Tied up, I gather, at a Leader of the Opposition's hush-
hush "where are we going?" hugger-mugger with his
intimates.'

'So it's just me, Reggie and Tommy. Terrific. I hope you
realize this will probably put me off hunting for life. Are you
prepared to take that risk.'

'I like risks.' The baroness finished the last forkful, laid
down her cutlery with a clatter, smacked her lips and clicked
her fingers. '*Garçon*,' she said in an execrable French accent.
The waiter came running. '*Une autre bouteille*.' He bowed and
scurried off. 'Come on, Robert. Eat up. You need to build up
your strength for the weekend ahead at Shapely Bottom
Hall.'

'Is it seriously called that?'

'Very suitable for a country seat, surely.' She cackled.
'Come on. You know English rural names are daft. That's no
madder than "Lower Slaughter" or "Nether Wallop".'

'Where is it, how do I get there, when do they want me, what do I wear?'

'Rutland. Tommy will ring you with the details. You'll be travelling with him.'

'Oh, no. I can't stand it.'

'That's the wrong attitude. You must throw yourself into this. Shapely Bottom Hall is not for the faint-hearted. Besides, I want them to admire and love you.'

'Thanks, Jack.' Amiss finished his wine and held his glass out gratefully to the hovering waiter.

9

How Lord Beesley had ever got to be a leader of men was a question that had been preoccupying Amiss. Even though Deptford had told him a few stories of Beesley's courage and dash on the hunting field, they seemed incompatible with a voice like a neurotic nanny goat and an obsession with trivia. But then, recollecting some senior civil servants for whom he had worked and ministers he had known, Amiss reminded himself that you got Tommy Beesleys in positions of authority in every walk of life. That thought just about carried him through their first conversation.

'Are you quite sure you've got that, young man?'

'Yes, thank you. All absolutely clear.'

'Just repeat the directions once more.'

'It's OK, Tommy. I've written it all down.'

'No, no, you must set my mind at rest. It would never do if you got lost. We can't have that happening.'

'Well, it would hardly be the end of western civilization as we know it,' said Amiss irritably.

'What's that?'

'Oh, nothing. Very well. I'll meet you at the entrance to the platform from which the four-forty-five to Market Harborough departs.'

'Which station, which station?'

'St Pancras.' He didn't say 'you old idiot', but it was a close-run thing. 'I'll have a first-class ticket.'

'And if I'm not there?'

'If you haven't arrived three minutes before the train leaves, I'll board it without you.'

'And I'll do the same. You didn't mention that.'

'That was implicit.'

'No, no. In any operation, one can leave nothing to chance. Detail is all.'

Amiss kept his patience. There was no point in getting on the wrong side of this old fool before the weekend had even started. He continued. 'We will leave the train at Market Harborough and catch the six-twenty-seven to The Bottoms, where we will be met by pony and trap and taken to Shapely Bottom Hall.'

'And the clothes, the clothes. You haven't forgotten about the clothes?'

'Dinner jacket, hacking jacket, wellingtons, Barbour and all the accoutrements.'

'Make sure you don't forget anything. Reggie is very particular.'

'Only a cad comes improperly clad,' chimed in Amiss cooperatively, having heard the phrase perhaps ten times in the preceding twenty-five minutes of telephonic fuss.

'All right.' Beesley sounded reluctant to let go, but even he had run out of minutiae. 'Perhaps we should talk about arrangements for returning.'

'We'll have ample time to do that during our journey.'

'If we both catch the same train.'

'Even if we don't catch the same train, Tommy, we'll still have plenty of time to discuss it during the weekend. Forgive me, I have to rush. If I don't put my dinner jacket into the cleaners now it won't be back in time for Friday.'

That horrifying possibility did the trick. 'Go immediately, you must go immediately.'

'Thanks, Tommy. Goodbye, I look forward to Friday.'

'Goodbye. Oh, just . . .'

Amiss put the phone down firmly and dialled his friend Detective Sergeant Ellis Pooley.

'It's like old times, raiding your wardrobe. So that's a hacking jacket, is it? Hmm, I hadn't realized you still rode.'

Pooley was rummaging in a chest of drawers. 'Ah, here we are. A proper stock. Do you know how to wear it?'

'Don't be ridiculous.'

Pooley fussed at Amiss's neck for a couple of minutes and then pushed him towards the mirror.

'My goodness, I look almost like a gentleman. Fine feathers really do make fine birds.'

'Now boots.' Pooley reached into the back of his wardrobe and produced a pair of magnificent, highly polished brown riding boots. Amiss looked at them longingly. ''Fraid not,' he said. 'It's wellies I need.'

'You can't ride in wellies.'

'I'm not riding. I've only ridden once in my life and that was on a donkey in Yarmouth. I'm following the hunt by car and on foot.'

'Well then, you don't need all this stuff. Duffel coat and jeans would be fine.'

'You don't know the Marquess of Poulteney.'

A happy grin spread over Pooley's rather serious features. 'Poulteney? Oh, but I do.'

'Don't tell me. He's a mate of your old man's.'

'Well, let's say that on the rare occasions that the pater drops by the House of Lords, Poulteney would be one of the first he would seek out to fulminate with.'

'Your father hunts?'

'A bit. He's not an obsessive like Poulteney, but he does his bit of hunting and his bit of shooting and his bit of fishing with reasonable regularity. Keeps him out of mischief.'

'And you?'

Pooley looked sheepish. 'Used to hunt a bit in school holidays. Gave it up on principle when I was at university. But I have to admit that a couple of times recently when I was at home I couldn't resist having a go again.'

'Ah, Ellis, this is another way in which you're becoming encouragingly less priggish as the years go by.'

'You, on the other hand, become ever more patronizing. Now, have we finished? I want to hear about whatever nonsense you're up to over a drink.'

'That's it, I think.' Amiss checked his list. 'Barbour, hacking jacket, stock, riding crop.'

'What do you want a riding crop for if you're not going riding?'

'Hunt saboteurs.'

'Ah, you're in for an exciting weekend.'

'Oh yes. Wellies, please, Ellis.'

'Green OK?'

'Natch.'

Amiss surveyed himself. 'What a dash I would have cut with your riding boots. These are not the same at all.' He shrugged and began to change back into his own clothes. 'Thanks, Ellis. I'll look after these to the best of my ability.'

'If you're going to be tangling with sabs, it's going to be more important to look after yourself to the best of your ability. There are some nasty ones about. Here '– Pooley reached into another drawer and produced a silver hip flask – 'you'd better take this as well. If the weather is cold and rainy and the sabs are making their presence felt, Dutch courage may be required.'

'Crikey, things must be serious if Ellis Pooley is recommending me to drink whisky on a Saturday morning.'

Amiss pulled on his sweater. Pooley by now had put the pristine wellies in a large carrier bag and was placing it with his other possessions in an expensive, if slightly battered, soft leather suitcase.

'You'd better have the case too. I expect you've got something modern. Modern is suspect.' He closed the catches and handed the case to Amiss.

'Right,' he said. 'Now, how about some gin?'

The journey did not begin auspiciously. Although Amiss was at the appointed place ten minutes early, Beesley had already been waiting for twenty-five and was in a state of high anxiety.

'I feared you had gone to the wrong platform for, most confusingly, there is, at the same time, a slow train which also goes to Market Harborough and who knows, you might have forgotten my precise instructions. You've cut it very fine indeed, I must say. Will we get a seat, I ask myself?' He plunged through to the platform and Amiss had to accelerate to catch up with him, surprised at how fit the old fool appeared to be. They rushed down the platform and, rather to Beesley's disappointment, found an empty first-class carriage, where he managed through dither to spin out to five minutes much carry-on about where the luggage would be most safely and conveniently stowed and whether they should sit beside each other or opposite. When they settled, some of the worry disappeared from Beesley's face, only to return as Amiss got up and said firmly, 'I'm going to get us a drink.'

'But they won't serve you yet. The train has not yet started to move.'

'I want to be at the front of the queue. Now what would you like?'

It took no more than four minutes for Beesley to decide that Scotch and ginger was the wisest choice of those most likely to be available. The queue was already long when Amiss joined it. He didn't care. Standing in a packed corridor reading Whyte-Melville's *Market Harborough* was pure joy compared to consorting with the Lord Beesley.

By the time they reached The Bottoms, between the fuss over changing trains and his near-hopeless attempt to elicit useful information, Amiss was almost exhausted. For Beesley was expansive only on such subjects as the likely disaster should there be a hold-up, as there often was on Fridays, and they missed the connecting train. More strategic worries like what would become of the whole hunting fraternity if the battle was lost were interspersed with reminiscences of happy boyhood hunts accompanied by incredible detail about which horse, which hounds, which huntsmen, which hunt and the rest of it.

'How many will there be at Shapely Bottom?' cut in Amiss, when Beesley drew breath.

'Oh, just a small family party, I suspect. Reggie doesn't entertain much since his wife died.'

'I didn't realize he was a widower.'

'Oh yes, very tragic. Splendid woman. Broke her neck taking a hedge. Turned out to have wire in it.'

'Wire? How disgraceful.' Amiss had read enough hunting literature by now to know there was no more ghastly deed imaginable, short of shooting a fox, than lacing your hedge with wire.

'Dreadful, dreadful. I was there and I saw it and shouted, "Ware wire!" But it was too late. Elsie had already taken off.' Then he brightened up. 'Still, it was the way she would have wanted to go.'

'Didn't it put you or Reggie off hunting?'

Tommy looked at Amiss as if he were crazed. 'No more than it put me off breathing. If hunting is in your marrow, nothing puts you off. That's why though I'm not allowed to hunt deer any more I go to Reggie's as often as I can to hunt foxes.'

A reluctant admiration for the old fellow overtook Amiss. Fusspot he might be, but he was a brave fusspot.

'When was Lady Poulteney killed?'

'Five years ago.'

'So Reggie lives alone?'

'Jamesie Bovington-Petty visits, of course, with his family. Perhaps they'll be there. Maybe even Jennifer.'

'Jennifer?'

But he had lost his companion. 'Oh my goodness, look at the time. Only five minutes until we get into the station and we might even be early. Quick, quick, we must get ready. Where are our coats? We must get the suitcases. Which door should we leave by? I hope you've given that some thought.'

Amiss took on the expression of a man bent on a task of deep significance. He whiled away the ensuing minutes by counting the hours until he would be home again.

10

The dark-blue Shapely Bottom trap was a very fine affair, adorned as it was with a coat of arms on each side, buttoned-down light-blue leather seats, gleaming brass fitments and an aged but very smartly kitted-out multi-caped retainer whom Beesley hailed warmly.

'Hawkins, how good to see you. Now this is Mr Amiss. Robert, this is Hawkins.'

Amiss held out his hand but Hawkins pretended not to see and instead touched his cap: feudalism was clearly alive and well in Shapely Bottom. Yet there was nothing subservient about Hawkins. He dealt crisply with Beesley's attempt to elevate into a major problem the placing of two suitcases inside a trap.

'No, my lord. They will go here, my lord, as they always do. It is the best place for them. Now in you go. You first, my lord.'

His passengers followed his instructions obediently. Hawkins took the reins and the pony took off at a stately trot. Beesley, however, being a man to whom worries came in droves, for the entire journey addressed anxious questions to Hawkins's back about the condition of the horse he kept at Poulteney's, the weather prospects, the likelihood that the countryside might prove to be fox-free and whether the new virulent strain of canine gastroenteritis was likely to have hit the kennels. Amiss sat happily, relieved of the need to listen and pretend interest, gazing around him in pleasure at the countryside and enjoying the discovery that an open trap proceeding at exactly the right pace was an unsurpassable way to see the landscape. If it was true, he reflected, that fox-hunting had something to do with the richness of the hedgerows and the ubiquitousness of copses and woodland, then that was another one up to the utilitarian argument in favour of hunting.

Within fifteen minutes or so they turned left through ornate, iron gates, twenty feet high, passed a small lodge of lowering granite and trotted up a long straight drive, flanked on either side by regularly spaced young trees. Curiosity led Amiss to interrupt as Beesley came to the end of his eighth worry and was about to embark on his ninth.

'Why are the trees so recently planted?'

'The great hurricane of 'eighty-seven, of course. Poor old Poulteney lost the whole driveway. A tragedy, it was, wasn't it, Hawkins?'

'Indeed it was, my lord. Those limes were his lordship's pride and joy, next to his hounds and horses, that is. His old grandfather had planted them in eighteen seventy-five. Should have had another good century or so out of them. Now it'll be about twenty-five years before they make any kind of a show at all and I won't be here to see it.'

'Nor will I,' said Beesley, and they both fell into reflective silence.

By then Amiss had been distracted by his first sight of Shapely Bottom Hall, a vast edifice that seemed to be a haphazard mixture of neo-Georgian and Victorian Gothic. As they drew up in the forecourt in front of a door large enough, calculated Amiss, to allow a platoon of spear-carriers to march through without breaking step, it opened to reveal — to Amiss's slight apprehension — what looked like a butler of the old school. Too grand to carry their bags — a footman was shooed out to do that — he greeted Beesley with a slight inclination of the head and a 'Pleased to see you again, my lord.' Amiss received a 'Mr Amiss, sir, I presume,' in a tone polite, if hardly warm. 'I am Hooper. Please follow me.'

Hawkins drove off and the visitors entered a hallway that might have become uncomfortably full had it been peopled by a swing band and three hundred dancing couples. Hooper was setting a steady pace, so as he loped obediently after him, Amiss could take in only a confused impression of animal heads and skulls and weaponry of various kinds, all put into relief by a vast mural of a hunt in full cry which covered a wall fully fifty yards long. You certainly, thought Amiss, knew where you were with the Poulteneys.

'I'll take you by the short cut,' said Hooper, leading them out of the hall by a side door, down several long corridors and up a dark staircase. Beesley and the footman were deposited first. 'Palgrave will be along shortly to unpack for you, sir.'

'No, thank you.' Amiss was unusually firm. 'I prefer to do it myself, if you don't mind.'

'As you wish, sir.' Amiss was ready to bet that Hooper knew very well that his reluctance to be ministered to had to do with uncertainties over the tipping etiquette.

'You will have plenty of time to bathe and dress, sir. We gather for sherry in the library at seven-forty-five.' Pausing only to give a series of complicated directions, Hooper abandoned Amiss to a bedroom which was pretty modest by comparison with what he had so far seen. True, the four-poster could comfortably have accommodated three couples, the wardrobe could have hidden half a dozen escaped convicts, and a string quintet could have carried out its duties without difficulty in the fireplace, but otherwise there was room for no more than a full-sized tennis court. The bathroom, on the other hand, was a tight squeeze for one, having been constructed out of what appeared to have been a priest's hole and being almost full with an aged and groaning geyser and a rusty bath which, like the washbasin and high pedestal lavatory, had not been at its best since about 1923.

Both rooms were icy cold, the only form of heating in evidence being a one-bar electric heater beside which stood the dispiriting notice: 'Do not use for more than half an hour or you may blow a fuse'. While the carved wooden bed, the chintzes, watercolours and rugs had once been grand, there was a threadbare, shabby quality about the decor, not improved by damp patches in several places on the ceiling and some rather alarming-looking fungus over the bath. Nor were there any of the signs of the gracious living that glossy magazines would have one believe went with such surroundings. There were no flowers, no whisky decanters, no biscuit barrel to ward off the perils of midnight starvation. The only luxury was a dog-eared copy of Lady Apsley's *Fox-Hunter's Bedside Book*. And in the wardrobe, there were only two wire hangers to take all his borrowed clothing.

A bath proved to be a non-starter, for although the only water available in the washbasin was scalding hot, the bath taps could produce only cold, which Amiss, owing to having missed out on the delights of boarding school, had never in his life had to endure. He washed perfunctorily and fast and then contemplated the challenge of changing in a temperature only a few degrees above zero. A swig from Pooley's hip flask and a crouch in front of the tiny heater gave him the necessary courage and, after stripping off so fast he pulled off one of his shirt buttons, he dressed himself without disaster.

The next daunting task was to make sense of Hooper's authoritative but half-forgotten instructions, which had become a confused jumble of lefts and rights leading to a staircase below the great window, left – or maybe right – at the bottom and on to the fourth door past the suit of armour. For ten minutes Amiss wandered up and down dimly lit corridors with a closed door perhaps every twenty-five feet or so, suggesting that within lay further giants' bedrooms. Ultimately, after a series of false starts, he came to a huge window and a well-lit staircase beside which were hung serried ranks of sporting Poulteneys, this one on horseback, that one with his foot on an expired stag, another with gun cocked, some with hounds. Here and there a regimental uniform demonstrated that their animal-slaughtering duties did not prevent Poulteneys from taking on martial duties also.

At the bottom of the staircase, Amiss turned right, and although he could see no armour, tried the fourth door along the corridor and gamely turned on the light. As he gazed incredulously at a room full of African masks and assagais, a voice hailed him from behind with a long, rather lazy, 'Hi. I expect you're lost.' She was around forty, slim, goodish-looking, well-groomed, with an Alice band in her fair shoulder-length hair and expensively but unostentatiously dressed. She had the voice of one who had always known she would marry someone at least as well-heeled as Daddy. Amiss had seen and heard dozens like her, older and younger, in wine bars and shops in Kensington and Chelsea.

'I think I am. This doesn't look like the library. I'm Robert Amiss.' She shook his proffered hand rather limply.

'I'm Vanessa Bovington-Petty — wife to Jamesie.' She accompanied this piece of information with a rather harsh laugh. 'You a friend of Daddy-in-law's?' she asked, in a tone which seemed to mingle suspicion and incredulity.

'Just an acquaintance. We're working together on this anti-hunting bill.'

Her faced cleared. 'Oh yah. Well, jolly good. I mean, it's just too, too obscene. Ghastly plebs can't keep their hands off anything.'

'Well, it's not so much the plebs we're worried about, Lady Bovington-Petty. More the lords.'

'Oh yah. But the plebs are at the bottom of it. Really frightful people trying to mess everything up for us. Anyway, come on, you must tell me all about it. And do call me Vanessa.' She escorted him back to the hall, down the opposite corridor and past a suit of armour into a room which by Shapely Bottom standards was small, presumably because the Poulteney family had not regarded reading as a high priority. In a couple of moments' scrutiny, Amiss spotted rows of bound volumes of *Country Life*, *The Field* and *Hunting* and shelf after shelf of hunting reminiscences.

True to form, the room was dominated by a vast equestrian painting, this time of a top-hatted woman in hunting jacket and skirt sitting side-saddle on a huge white horse. The background showed the Hall, the drive and a few hounds dotted around the place for effect.

'Who's that?' he asked, as thankfully he joined her in front of a huge fire.

She looked at the picture carelessly.

'Oh, that was Mummy-in-law. Dead now, poor old thing. Sherry?' She jerked her head at the silver tray.

'Is it dry?'

'Sort of. It's Oloroso.'

'Please.'

To Amiss's relief the sherry was superb – nutty and rich but without a hint of sweetness.

'Mmm, delicious.'

'Glad you like it, can't say I do. I've been *at* Daddy-in-law and *at* him to give people what they want.'

Which means you, thought Amiss to himself.

'I mean, actually, I say to him, actually, you know, a lot of people don't like sherry. They prefer champers, or gin, or martinis. But he's such a stick-in-the-mud, one simply can't get through to him.'

Amiss tried to look sympathetic. 'Do you live here?'

'Not yet.' Even Vanessa realized that that sounded a little crude and proceeded hastily, 'That is, we come down as often as possible to keep an eye on Daddy-in-law, but we have our lives in London. Have to earn the money for the school fees. Jamesie slogs away in the wine trade. An absolute slave. I can't *tell* you.'

To Amiss's relief they were interrupted by the arrival of the Lords Poulteney and Beesley, and shortly afterwards by a middle-aged, anxious-looking man, an expressionless adolescent and a much younger boy in a purple velvet page-boy suit with matching bow in which he looked ill at ease. These were introduced respectively as Jamesie, James and Timothy. They seemed to get on their mother's nerves even more than did her father-in-law.

'Actually,' she explained when James's response to being introduced to Amiss was to utter a monosyllabic grunt. 'Actually, that isn't the way to greet strangers. What you're supposed to do, if you've been brought up properly, and gone to a proper and very expensive school, is to say, "Hello, sir, I'm pleased to meet you." To say, "Huh", is actually not on.'

The youth gazed at her with indifference, took a glass of sherry and disappeared to the far corner of the library to study the bookshelves. Timothy performed better. His mother had no occasion to rebuke him until a few minutes later he dropped with a resounding crash a fire-iron with which he'd been fiddling.

'Ghastly child, really ghastly, can't take one's eye off him for a moment. Nothing but trouble. Where *have* I gone wrong? I work my fingers to the bone and this is what I get by way of thanks. Get over there to the corner with your brother, you little nuisance, and don't let me hear another sound out of you.'

As the child skulked away Bovington-Petty essayed an 'Oh really, darling, aren't you being a bit . . .' only to be shot down with a glare so icy that it stopped him in his tracks. Glassy-eyed with embarrassment, Amiss edged into the Poulteney/Beesley conversation, which – though incomprehensible because it concerned some recent hound-breeding disasters – was amicable and devoid of tension.

As Beesley absorbed the frightful news that the most junior breeding hound appeared to have passed on to its entire litter a suspect near hind leg, a gong sounded and the gathering proceeded into a dining hall the size of the chamber of the House of Lords and sat at the end of a table that would comfortably have seated sixty.

Poulteney moved to the head of the table, beckoned Beesley to sit on his right, Amiss on his left and ignored his family. Vanessa immediately made a beeline for the seat beside Amiss and with a jerk of the head directed James to sit by her.

'Sit over there beside Lord Beesley,' she instructed Timothy, 'and remember not to speak unless spoken to.' Having thus put everyone at their ease, she sat down and began interrogating Amiss about possible mutual acquaintances.

Amiss was no novice at the sticky social occasion. As a private secretary to a head of department, for instance, he had often found himself marooned below the salt with people who resented being stuck with someone so junior and unimportant. But he had never, he was to complain later to the baroness, been so simultaneously bored, appalled and nervous, for Vanessa's forceful and voluble discontent with her lot meant that quite frequently it was all too obvious that, during her complaints about Bovington-Petty ('just no get-up-and-go/absolutely won't stand up to those vile people in his firm/doesn't realize how much everything costs'),

James ('sullen little brute/no gratitude') and Timothy ('care-less/messy/cheeky'), the objects of her attack could hardly have avoided hearing every syllable. Poulteney – who had quite clearly offended all the laws of seating etiquette in order to save himself – was far too busy with Beesley to hear anything she said.

On went Vanessa, complaints interspersed with what she regarded as conversation, which was moans about inconveniences, followed by rhetorical questions. Dully, Amiss grunted assent to such inanities as 'I always feel there's nothing worse than underdone fish, don't you?'; 'You simply can't trust anything decent to dry cleaners these days, can you?'; 'Can you believe it, Harvey Nicks was quite out of that matching fabric?'; and 'I mean, you'd have thought, wouldn't you, that simple gratitude would make Filipinos reliable?'

But if Vanessa's non-family-related conversation was boring, it was infinitely preferable to her other line of chat. A description of a simply *disastrous* wedding reception at which the best man had been drunk when he made his speech lulled Amiss into a sense of security, when he was jolted out of it by a hiss from his left directed across the table. The hapless Timothy – caught in the act of trying to rub gravy off his velvet – was summoned to his mother's side, pronounced 'a horrible spastic child' and consigned to the butler for handing on to someone who could limit the damage to an outfit which had cost 'an unimaginable amount of money in the sweetest little children's shop in Knightsbridge, though for all the gratitude I got for buying it . . . you've no idea. "Actually," I said to Timothy. "Actually, 'thank you very much' is what a normal boy would say to his mother." But what can you do?' And then, looking over at the silent James, she added: 'After all, what example does he get?'

Release for Amiss came earlier than expected. As the company finished its cheese and the butler advanced with a decanter of port, Poulteney jerked his head and with a mulish look but without a sound, Vanessa got up and left the room.

'What do you do when asked to leave gentlemen to their port?' Amiss was to ask the baroness later. 'No one's dared to suggest that to me since about nineteen sixty,' she answered comfortably. 'And if they did, I'd pretend to be hard of hearing as I reached for the decanter.'

On this occasion, however, Amiss had no scruples in feeling delighted that this household was so illiberal and anachronistic that such deplorable segregation still prevailed. The simple absence of Vanessa was enough to make Poulteney's revelations about the blocked culverts almost interesting, and if Bovington-Petty — who had moved into Vanessa's place — was a less than sparkling conversationalist, listening to his account of how the wine business had been affected by the fall of the Berlin Wall had moments of interest and one or two of humour. Even James felt moved to intervene on a few occasions in a manner which was positively loquacious. Amiss was hoping they might sit over the port until Vanessa had given up and gone to bed when the butler came in and whispered in Poulteney's ear. His face lit up.

'We must go to the drawing room,' he said. 'Lady Flexingham has arrived for coffee and brandy.'

A sturdy brunette in her early forties, equipped with the English Rose attributes of peaches-and-cream skin, bright-blue eyes and a slightly diffident manner, Miranda Flexingham turned out to be Master of Foxhounds in the hunt next door. That Poulteney was mad about her was obvious from the start. He gazed at her as if she were a favourite hound, huntsman and game old fox all rolled into one. Straightaway, she engaged him, Beesley and Bovington-Petty in a lively discussion about the rival merits of dog foods used by the two respective kennels. James and Timothy disappeared and Amiss found himself alone on a sofa with Vanessa. This time he went on the offensive.

'Tell me about Lady Flexingham. She seems charming.'

'To outsiders, possibly.' Vanessa gave her harsh laugh. 'At least to men. Daddy-in-law's being such an idiot.'

'He's sweet on her?' asked Amiss vulgarly.

'Gooey-eyed. Look at him. Disgusting at his age, isn't it?'

'Is there a Lord Flexingham?'

'She's a widow.'

He piled on the coarseness. 'Wedding bells coming up, eh?'

'I can't imagine Daddy-in-law would do such a cruel thing to Jamesie.' Her voice belied her words. 'I would never speak to him again.'

Amiss thought such an incentive would be sufficient to make him marry Lady Flexingham himself.

The telephone interrupted the merry dog-food chat.

'Yes, yes, yes,' said Poulteney. 'No change of plan. A few horsewhips wouldn't go amiss. Just make sure every available man is in position by six o'clock.' He put the phone down.

'Sabs?' Lady Flexingham looked resigned.

'Yes. The tip-off is they're concentrating on us tomorrow. Might be quite lively.'

'Well, in that case the sooner we all go to bed and recharge our batteries the better. I am looking forward to a good day.' She offered her cheek to Poulteney and Bovington-Petty, smiled at the rest of the gathering, first demurred and then accepted her host's demand that he be allowed to see her to her car.

'I'm off too,' said Beesley.

'Me too,' said Amiss. 'You can guide me to my bedroom.' And with a few insincere expressions of gratitude he left the married couple to their own company.

11

The views were beyond criticism. Amiss, who had grown up looking through his bedroom window at a small suburban garden of relentless neatness, where the flowerbeds had hospital corners and no weed ever survived a day, felt retrospective envy for a background whose privileges included not only being able to watch miles and miles of the English countryside at its best from season to season, but knowing that your father owned it. But then he remembered that Lord Poulteney went along with that package and that as heir one might even be expected to marry someone like Vanessa in order to ensure that the connections were good, the pedigree up to scratch and that she'd know how to behave as a consort: his beloved acerbic, iconoclastic Jewish diplomat would hardly fit their bill. It was the same sort of logic, he reflected, that had got poor old Prince Charles into the marital mess he was in. The feelings of envy disappeared rapidly.

Drawing the predictable blank on the hot bath-water front, he washed as much of himself as he could bear and dressed at maximum speed, although a wrestle with his stock added ten minutes to the proceedings. When he finally surveyed himself in the wardrobe mirror in his finery, he was unable to decide whether he looked like a pretentious prat or was cutting one hell of a dash. The effect was definitely spoiled by the wellingtons, which also posed a serious etiquette problem. Surely one did not breakfast in wellies? But then what *did* one do with them? In the end he put on his town shoes and carried the boots, which – as he entered the breakfast room – the butler discreetly removed with the murmured reassurance that sir would find them adjacent to the front door.

Breakfast was a highly social occasion, for, in addition to Lady Flexingham, who was looking extremely attractive in top hat, black jacket and jodhpurs, half a dozen or so of the local squirarchy were braying happily at each other over porridge laden with brown sugar, cream and whisky, game pies and baked ham. There was a general air of joviality. Even Vanessa, turned out like the rest of her family in full gear, seemed happy. She was having a positively animated reminiscence with a couple of locals about a memorable hour-long chase the previous November.

At 9.50, stopping to tell Amiss that he would have no trouble finding a lift from one of the neighbours, Poulteney led the way to the forecourt where the horses were waiting and within ten minutes the mounted breakfasters had been joined by two or three dozen other riders and a motley collection of cars, among whose drivers and passengers Amiss mingled easily. The entire staff of Shapely Bottom Hall passed amongst the throng offering slices of game pie and a choice of sloe gin or vintage port. Not without misgivings, Amiss chose neat gin, but it tasted unexpectedly good and helped to make bracing the cold that had been intolerable in his bedroom, and the air of expectancy, excitement and good humour was almost palpable.

India had made Amiss much more aware of smells — good and bad — than ever before, so now he took sensual enjoyment in identifying the variety of scents wafting about him, from boot polish to horse dung. He enjoyed too, watching in person so much that he had been reading about but had seen only in the occasional film. The noise of conversation was at a crescendo, when he heard a gnarled chap on a huge brown horse shouting to someone beside him. 'City shits! If I get my hands on them they'll be sorry they're not the fox.' And out of the hubbub, more angry words and phrases emerged, confirming that trouble was afoot. From behind him he heard, 'I'm telling you, I hear they've got gas. Some say some are armed.'

Selecting a weatherbeaten chap in late middle age whose

workmanlike clothes suggested long attendance at events like this, Amiss said, 'Excuse me, I'm new here. Is something up?'

'It's those blasted sabs. The wild people who try to wreck our hunt. Word is they're out in force today.' He took a mighty draught of port.

'Do you usually have trouble?'

'Well, I don't know I'd say usually, but we have had trouble, maybe half a dozen times in the last two years. They've got a lot of hunts to get round, do you see? We're not so important they can afford the time very often to grace us with their presence.'

'Aren't you worried?'

'What's the point? Thing to do is take things as they come,' observed the man phlegmatically.

A dour young man chimed in, 'Well, they're after us now, Dad, in a big way, since his lordship's known to be making a speech next week that's to save us from the radicals.'

'What are they likely to do?' asked Amiss, unenthusiastic about another close encounter with wild-eyed activists.

'They've been foiled so far, so I expect they'll be trying to ambush us,' said Phlegmatic Man.

'Foiled how?'

'Hawkins says some were found before daybreak with a sack of doped meat and were handed over to the police. And then he caught some others trying to lay a false scent and hounded them off the land and put lookouts around. But they'll be back later, certain sure.' He looked at Amiss. 'You should have brought a stick. You might be needing it.'

His own stout piece of ash looked to have the potential to crack a skull. Amiss, who had forgotten to bring Pooley's riding crop, determined to keep as close to him as possible. 'Are you going by car?'

'Yep. Me and Matthew here. Want a lift?'

'Oh, yes, please.'

'Come on then. I think his lordship's ready to go.'

As the three of them clambered inside an aged Land Rover, the sound of a horn cut into the air, and with Lord Poulteney and his huntsman in the lead, following closely after the hounds, the mounted hunters began to move off at speed in the direction of some woodland on the far horizon.

'I thought as much,' said Phlegmatic Man. 'There's been a rumour all week about a fine vixen being seen there.' He put his foot on the accelerator and headed down the drive ahead of the other cars. 'We'll catch them down at Tite Bottom, near Cooper's Cope. Then, if the fox goes where I think she'll go, we'll have to continue on foot.'

They had covered perhaps five miles of a very circular pursuit when they caught sight of the hunt standing around aimlessly near a large wood. 'Like I said,' said Phlegmatic Man. 'Now, listen.'

There was little sound for some time except of the cars drawing up behind them. Then there was suddenly an outbreak of activity on the part of the hounds, who had been running around in circles rather haphazardly. One hound emerged from the bulk of the pack and stood by itself, head up, sniffing.

'That's Rosie,' said Phlegmatic Man. 'You can always rely on her. Haven't had a hound in her class since Rankin died in . . . oh . . .' He pursed his lips and bent his head. 'What do you say, Matthew? Was it 'sixty-eight when Rankin went to his reward?'

'That's about right, Dad. I was only a kid.'

'Rosie,' explained Phlegmatic Man to Amiss, 'must be his great-granddaughter.'

At this moment Rosie emitted a bloodcurdling yowl, instantly picked up by a chorus from her fellows, and they all streaked into the outskirts of the wood at high speed, emerging only seconds later in hot pursuit of a blur of red fur. With a triumphant blast of a horn, something that sounded very like, 'Yoirouseimmelads!' followed by shouts of, 'Yoiks, tally-ho!' Poulteney and his throng set off in pursuit, and the cars all disgorged their passengers. Following closely behind his mentor, Amiss was in the vanguard climbing a stile and stomping across a field whose terrain was sufficiently rough and hilly to make him extremely grateful that it was dry underfoot. The trick, he realized after a while, was to conserve energy by keeping up a steady pace and putting on a turn of speed only when it was necessary to see which way the cavalry were heading. For, as Phlegmatic Man explained, 'That vixen is leading them a merry dance and now she's taking them nor'west they're almost bound to do a circle and be up at Wreckett's Brook no earlier than us.'

And there were, of course, for those in the know, short cuts through dense copses inaccessible to horses. Still, as Amiss saw in the distance the pink coats thundering across the fields and clearing some hedgerows, he felt an onrush of romantic regret that he would never be an equestrian hero. To have negotiated a slippery stile in wellies without falling over did not compare with how it must feel to persuade a horse to jump a five-barred gate successfully. But, as Phlegmatic Man had promised, there was still plenty of action, and as they neared Wreckett's Brook, slightly to his shame, Amiss found himself screaming various sounds of the 'Yoiks!' variety when the fox, hounds and riders suddenly appeared on their right and tore along in front of them. It was then, as they cleared a brook, that they met the promised ambush. As the fox and hounds disappeared across the countryside, the riders were surrounded by a melee of shouting, banner-waving, balaclavaed demonstrators.

'Come on,' said Phlegmatic Man, no longer phlegmatic. 'Let's go after them.'

Obediently, if unenthusiastically, Amiss kept close as father and son ran to the brook, but by then a van had arrived from which leaped two dozen police. Within moments the horsemen were off again and those demonstrators that weren't being strong-armed into the van were on the run. It was Amiss's bad luck that as he gingerly followed across the stepping stones in the deep part of the brook, a youth fleeing from a truncheon-waving policeman came hurtling through a gap in the hedge, swerved to avoid Phlegmatic Man and crashed straight into Amiss, who fell flat on his back into the icy-cold water; neither demonstrator nor policeman seemed to halt in their tracks. As Amiss, bruised and shaken, miserably began to try to stand up, Phlegmatic Man returned and with the help of his stout stick pulled him to his feet.

'Be off home with you, now,' he said, waving aside Amiss's thanks.

'I thought I should go on.'

'Don't be daft. There'll be another hunt along next week. If you catch your death of cold this week, you won't be there to see it.'

'How do I get back to the Hall? I've lost my bearings.'

'Diagonally across those two fields and then left through Cold Bottom Wood and over that hill. You can't miss it.'

As Amiss stammered his gratitude, Phlegmatic Man touched his cap and took off again with surprising speed. Pausing only to empty water from his wellies and to take a long draught of whisky, Amiss set off for the most uncomfortable walk of his life, spurred on his way by shouts from the pursuers and pursued.

When he got to the top of the hill, he paused for another swig and gazed back at the scene behind. To the far west he could see the mounted huntsmen disappearing over the horizon. Grimly marching behind one field away were Amiss's erstwhile companions, and out of the field where the fracas had occurred was driving a procession of three black vans. Teeth chattering, wet through, walking towards the Hall as fast as he could in his clammy footgear, Amiss wondered what he was going to have to do to get a hot bath.

As his hand went out to the antiquated bell pull, he heard the sound of a car racing up the drive. He turned round to see a small red sports car screeching to a halt. Out of it jumped a young woman who hailed him cheerily as she pulled a hold-all out of the back.

'Who is this wet person, Hooper?' she demanded as the butler opened the door. 'And what has been done to him?'

'Now, Lady Jennifer,' said Hooper in an indulgent tone. 'That's not very polite. This gentleman is Mr Robert Amiss who is a guest of his lordship. This is Lady Jennifer Bovington-Petty, sir. Now let me take your bag, my lady.'

She tossed the bag to him, shook hands with Amiss and raised an eyebrow enquiringly.

'Aggro at the brook. I got run into by a sab.'

'Well, we'd better look after you or you'll be staying longer than you expected. Hooper, get someone to run a bath for Mr Amiss, take some hot whisky to his room and . . . have you something to change into?'

He nodded.

'OK. That's it, then. We'll have some lunch in the library, Hooper. Say around one-fifteen.'

'Lady Jennifer, you know you shouldn't . . .'

'Now don't give me that, Hooper. The library's the most comfortable. We only want wine and sandwiches. That OK with you? Or would you prefer beer?'

'Wine would be perfect.' Amiss was overwhelmed with a wave of gratitude for this ministering angel. 'But please, Mr Hooper, could someone show me to my room? I still can't find the way.'

Hooper summoned a hovering footman and gave him orders.

'And Palgrave,' called Jennifer. 'If there's no hot water in his bathroom, put him in mine.'

'Really, Lady Jennifer!'

'Stop being suburban, Hooper. Now, let's see if there's a nice big fire in the library.'

12

Warm, dry and soothed by a powerful hot whisky, Amiss joined Jennifer shortly after one. She was sitting in an armchair by the fire, intently reading a large leatherbound book. .

He wandered over to look. 'What is it?'

She laughed. 'That's almost a first in this house. Mostly they say, "You're not still reading, are you? Get out in the fresh air. Don't you know it's bad for your eyes?" And of course, they may be right. I'm the only one in the family that wears glasses.'

'I infer you're the family intellectual.'

'That's it. I used to think I'd been adopted but then I found I was one in quite a long line of black sheep like this one — hence the various roomfuls of mementoes of exotic foreign countries. Great-great-uncle Horace, for instance, wasn't thick. He wrote this.' She passed him over her book, which the title page revealed to be *Reflections on some Little-Known Tribes of North Borneo by an Observer recently in Her Majesty's Colonial Service.*

He flicked through it. 'Looks positively interesting.'

'I'm not surprised you seem taken aback. Spent a lot of time with Dad and Jamesie?'

Amiss grinned and handed her back the book. 'And with Vanessa.'

'God help you. So what are you doing here?'

'I'll tell you over lunch.' At that moment, Hooper appeared carrying a decanter of wine, followed by Palgrave bearing on a tray a vast plate of sandwiches, a large pie and various accoutrements.

'Mrs Hooper was anxious for you to have some of her game pie, Lady Jennifer.'

'Don't tell me. She thinks I want fattening up. Thank her very much, and thank you both. Just leave the tray. We can do the rest.'

'Let me at least cut the pie for you, Lady Jennifer.'

'No, Hooper. It's kind of you, but I assure you that between us, Mr Amiss and I can manage to do the necessary.'

She gently shooed butler and footman out of the room. 'I hate being hovered around. They think I'm potty, of course. In every regard. They can't wait for me to come to my senses and accept my responsibilities.'

'Husband?'

'Right kind of husband, children, photographs in *Country Life* and, of course, hunting.'

'You don't hunt? A Poulteney that doesn't hunt?'

'Oh I have, but I don't any more. I get my kicks elsewhere.'

'Doing what?'

'I'm an anthropologist. Just like Great-great-uncle Horace. Except I do it for a living. Now, tell me about you.'

It was 3.30 by the time Jennifer had finished giving Amiss what she called her anthropological tour of the house and had taken him to stroll in the gardens.

'I think in your position I'd have turned into an animal activist,' he said. 'How can you grow up amongst deer skulls and fox brushes and elephants' feet and stuffed reindeer heads and not be violently either pro or anti?'

'I took the route of detachment. Besides, even if my parents were on the dull side, they were nice to me and I loved them. So why should I want to abolish the only fun they got out of life?'

'Killing animals?'

'Oh, don't be so banal, Robert. You know it's not as simple as that. All the anti-hunting people I've met know sod-all about animals, while all the pros I grew up with are devoted to them.'

'Yes. I'm beginning to understand something of that. This morning, if not enjoyable, was instructive. And even though

I find the decor of your house pretty grisly, I suppose I see a certain nobility in such a passionately held tradition. I wouldn't quite die to defend the right of your family to kill and be killed in the name of sport . . .' He stopped, closed his eyes in embarrassment, gritted his teeth and said, 'I'm sorry, Jennifer. I forgot.'

'About Mummy? It's OK. Absolutely validates your point. Incidentally, did you meet her putative successor?'

'Lady Flexingham? Yes, just about. She's certainly a dish.'

'Yes, she is, isn't she? I'm all for it.'

'Vanessa isn't.'

'Of course not. What she really wants is for Daddy to retire to the Dower House and let Jamesie take over now. If it wasn't for Miranda he might, and I think that would be a good idea. You must have noticed how much Shapely Bottom Hall needs a chatelaine.'

'Well, it's certainly bloody uncomfortable, if you'll forgive my saying so.'

'You don't often stay with old wealth, do you?'

'No.'

'Well, they don't throw money around much on creature comforts. I mean, my God, to put central heating into a place like this would mean touching capital. Us rich don't do things like that. Still, in Mummy's day the geyser would have worked and you'd have had a fire in your bedroom.'

'But Vanessa's a greedy bitch, isn't she? Wouldn't she help herself to the loot?'

'Good God, no. Vanessa's a Sloane Ranger. Half the reason she's unhappy is that she's not got somewhere like this to look after. That's what she was bred for; that's what she would be good at. She's not good at pretending to be an interior decorator in South Kensington. And Jamesie's much too weak to keep her happy. Put her in a place like this and she'd enjoy doing her duty. That makes Miranda a real nightmare for her. And worse, Miranda might produce children who'd have to get a share of the family financial goodies. That would really upset Vanessa's applecart.'

'Which is?'

'To pass the estate on to James in due course in better

shape than when she and Jamesie took it over, so he can do the same for his children and they can do the same for theirs. And that means having money for upkeep.' She stopped and pointed. 'Look.' Ahead of them in the distance Amiss could see a large area of meadow with several dozen saplings. 'What does that say to you?'

'Somebody's thinking about the future.'

'That's right. Vanessa. Daddy's rather stopped bothering since Mummy was killed. But what you have to understand is that those trees won't really be in their prime until probably the third next Lord Poulteney. That's the main justification for the landed gentry. Because they know their estates will be inherited by their children and their children's children, it gives them a long-term stake in the country and all that sort of thing. Now, let's go in and demand some crumpets to toast and I'll motivate you further to write nice things for Daddy to say in his speech next week.'

'Do you know I've never done this before.'

'You didn't have a nursery at home?'

"'Fraid not. Whoever built number four, Acacia Gardens unaccountably limited it to two bedrooms.'

'But what about at Oxford?' She sounded shocked.

'I fear they stuck me in one of those nasty modern buildings. I gained central heating, a bathroom on my floor but lost the open fireplace. Here.' He removed a crumpet from the end of his toasting fork and passed it to her.

'Perfect.' She nodded approvingly as she lathered it with butter. 'Mmm. I *am* enjoying myself. More, I admit, than I usually do here.'

'So am I.' He spoke with great feeling. 'The pleasure of all this is heightened by my delight in not being out there getting tired and cold. I fear I wasn't bred for the outdoor life. In Acacia Gardens we liked to stay snug.'

He looked at his watch. 'They have been out an awfully long time, haven't they? Surely hunts don't go on for seven hours?'

'I expect they've gone on to someone's place for tea. I thought I heard the hounds coming back an hour or so ago.'

As she spoke the door flew open.

'Jenny, darling.' Bovington-Petty rushed over to her and gave her a hug. 'Gosh, I am pleased to see you. You've missed all the drama. Poor old Daddy took the most terrible toss.'

'Is he all right?' There was a note of terror in her voice.

'He's fine. The casualty juju said just to tuck him up in bed in case of any delayed shock and he'll be as right as rain tomorrow.'

'But his heart!'

'No ill effects. These bally pacemakers are wonderful, aren't they? Oh, I say, can I have one of these?'

'Of course.' Amiss returned to his toasting duties and Jennifer poured some more tea into her cup and handed it to her brother.

She stood up. 'I'll just go up and see Daddy.'

'Give him a few minutes to get settled. And I want a word with you first. There's something I'm worried about.'

There was a silence.

'Come on, Jamesie. Spit it out.'

'Well, it's sort of private, don't you know.'

'Too late for that. Robert knows too many of our secrets already.'

Ever obedient when spoken to firmly by a woman, Bovington-Petty blurted out, 'I don't think this was an accident. Hawkins just told me that the girth gave way and that it seems that someone had been at it with a knife.'

'Who could do that? Who would do that?'

'Don't ask me. Daddy doesn't have enemies, unless you count the frightful sabs, though of course some of those are capable of anything. We'd better call the police.'

'I don't know if Daddy would stand for it. He'd think we were making a fuss about nothing.'

'Attempted murder is hardly nothing,' said Amiss. 'If someone's tried once, they might try again.'

'He's right,' said Bovington-Petty. 'I'll ring the station. You go and square it with Daddy.'

'Get your new tottie to drive you over here for Sunday lunch.'

'Do you have to see everything in terms of sex. She's not my tottie. Just an agreeable new acquaintance. And I can't get her to drive me to Cambridge.'

'Why not?'

'Why should she?'

'She'll enjoy it. Just persuade her. And when you get here, you'd better stay until Thursday. You've got a lot of speeches to write.'

'I can't stay.'

'Why not?'

'I've only got the weekend's clothes.'

'You really are turning into a complete old woman, Robert. If you run out of knickers I'll lend you a pair of mine. This is St Martha's, remember, not some fucking Buckingham Palace garden party. Come on, get cracking. I'll get someone to sling another fatted calf on the fire. Bye.'

'She's rather like a tank,' he explained to Jennifer. 'Every time you produce a little pile of reasons why what she wants done is impossible she just flattens them.'

'Well, I'm delighted she did.' Jennifer put her foot down hard on the accelerator. 'I've always wanted to see what Daddy's old flame looked like.'

'What!'

'Didn't she tell you?'

'Jack doesn't tell. She mostly imparts whatever is necessary to get you to do her bidding. She subscribes to that educational view that you learn best by finding out for yourself.'

'Well, according to Daddy, he fell madly for her when she was about seventeen. Said she had a wonderful seat.'

'Bit broad in the beam these days.'

'He proposed to her but she turned him down and went to Cambridge instead.'

'Surely they're not contemporaries?'

'No. He was in his mid-twenties at the time. She must have been something unusual.'

'She's still something unusual.'

'Well, he did say to me that although he still respected her a great deal, he and Mummy were much better suited.

Seemed to think Baroness Troutbeck would have found country life a bit dull.'

'I expect she'd have livened it up. She certainly livened up the civil service and from all I gather St Martha's has been undergoing a pretty thorough transformation over recent months.'

The dramatic nature of change was evident even at the gates of St Martha's where rusty black had given way to scarlet. The garden – which for years had resembled an untended Victorian cemetery minus the gravestones – had been cheered up by judicious pruning and the addition of flowerbeds and pots full of winter pansies and flowering shrubs. And when the scarlet front door opened there was no longer that subtle aura of mildew and overdone cabbage.

'Mr Amiss. How nice to see you again. We have missed you.'

'Lady Jennifer Bovington-Petty, Miss Stamp.'

Miss Stamp tinkled girlishly. 'Gosh, we are going up in the world, aren't we, what with the Mistress becoming a baroness and lots of titled visitors like you, Lady Jennifer. Now, you won't want to hang around here chatting. Let me take you to the Mistress. She's got a lovely surprise for you, Mr Amiss.'

He didn't like the sound of that at all. 'Where is she?'

'In her study. I'll lead the way.' And she trotted across the hall and tripped happily up the stairs ahead of them.

'It's very nice,' said Jennifer. 'We certainly didn't have vast open fires at St Hilda's.' She sniffed. 'Mmm. Smells like apple logs. And look at those rugs. For a women's college this is a veritable Sybaris.' They stopped abruptly halfway down a corridor. In answer to Miss Stamp's knock, the door was opened swiftly.

'Come on, you two. Quick.' The baroness bundled them into the room and slammed the door behind her. 'Don't want to let the old girl out yet.' And there, pacing moodily up and down the mantelpiece, was a large orange cat.

'This is Plutarch,' the baroness explained to Jennifer, 'who lives with Robert. He should be proud of her, but –

inexplicably – he's not. I take her in from time to time to restore her self-confidence.'

Amiss approached Plutarch gingerly, muttered a greeting and stroked her left ear.

'Go on, go on, pick her up. You haven't seen her for weeks and weeks. You're not worthy of that cat.'

She picked up Plutarch and thrust her into Amiss's unwilling arms. Taking the line of least resistance, he sat down beside the fire and submitted himself to being trampled all over for several minutes until Plutarch decided she had found the most comfortable spot. Within a minute she was asleep.

'You see. She's glad to see you.' The baroness pointed to Jennifer, who was now settled in the other armchair. 'Drink?'

'Yes, please.'

The baroness walked over to the corner of the room, opened a wooden door to a concealed refrigerator and removed a bottle of champagne. 'We're celebrating your reunion with Plutarch, your return to this academic backwater and, of course, Jennifer's first visit, for any daughter of Reggie Poulteney is a daughter of mine.' She reflected for a moment. 'That isn't quite right, but you know what I mean.'

'It's not like you to make pretty speeches, Jack. I suppose it's a by-product of mixing with the nobility.'

There was a resounding explosion as the cork parted company with the champagne. Plutarch took off like a gazelle and, after a brief touchdown in the middle of the mantelpiece, completed several circuits of the room at high speed and landed on the desk, where in short order she knocked over a pile of books, a filing tray of papers, a container of pens and pencils and three glasses.

'Good thing they were empty,' said the baroness cheerfully. 'There, there, Plutarch, steady now. You really must learn to cope with the unexpected.'

She picked her up, dropped her on Amiss's lap, put the scattered articles back in place and poured out the champagne.

'How long has she been here?'

'I picked her up yesterday. As you can see, she hasn't quite got acclimatized yet.'

'Any major disasters so far?'

'Well, she had a slight contretemps with the contents of the mantelpiece, but there were few casualties.' She handed over the glasses. 'Now, enough feline chitchat. What's all this about skulduggery at Shapely Bottom? I take a very dim view of any of those hairy thugs trying to kill Reggie. What do the rozzers have to say?'

'Didn't really have a clue,' said Jennifer. 'The saddle's gone off for examination, but I've no doubt it's been deliberately damaged.'

'Access?'

Jennifer looked puzzled. Amiss, a hardened interpreter of the baroness, interjected, 'Quite easy. A hunting magazine feature on Shapely Bottom Hall last month had a map of the grounds and an illustration of the tack room. Even pinpointed the spot where Reggie's saddle always hung. Couldn't have been more helpful to sabs, really.'

'Any of you with any ambition to rub Reggie out?' asked the baroness.

'I expect my sister-in-law has occasionally, but she wouldn't have the nerve.'

'Hmm,' said the baroness. She looked appraisingly at Jennifer. 'Have some more champagne.'

'Well, I'd better be careful. I've a long drive this afternoon.'

'Rubbish. Now you're here, you'd better stay overnight. Sunday lunch goes on a long time. Besides . . .' She smiled winningly. 'I'd like you to talk to me and some of my colleagues about anthropology. There might be a vacancy coming up here soon.'

13

'Aren't you being rather . . .' Soup spoon halfway to his mouth, Pooley paused to find the right word.

'Weak?'

'Well, if you want to put it like that.'

'I don't, dammit. But it's what you think. The trouble with all you people who want me to do what they think I should do is that you want to operate a monopoly.'

'I'm not sure I followed that.'

Amiss chewed crossly on a piece of asparagus and took an irritable gulp of Chablis. 'You think I am letting Jack push me around.'

'Aren't you?'

'May I remind you, Ellis, that in your time you have pushed me into being not only an unwilling English teacher in a den of corruption but also a waiter in a murderous mausoleum. At least Jack introduces me to a better class of person.'

Pooley looked crestfallen. 'I'm sorry. You're right. I was just worrying that it was bad for your career to be in yet another dead-end job.'

'Yes, yes. I know all that. But it's not for long and it isn't half interesting. I mean, I know all these toffs are what you fled from, but they're a new experience for me and you know I'm a sucker for new experiences. And the more I read about hunting the more I see their point. You can't read Walter Scott and Trollope and all those marvellous Victorians without grasping something of the magic of the whole business. I simply hadn't realized that hunting had a distinguished literature.'

'So has bull fighting.'

'Sure, and that's why though nothing would get me to a bullring, I wouldn't simply abolish bullfighting because it offended my sensibilities. You can't just go blindly against the grain of tradition.'

He saw Pooley's quizzical look. 'All right, I admit it. Of course the real reason I'm committed to this is that it's always exhilarating being in cahoots with Jack. You never know what the day might hold.'

Pooley gave a shiver. 'I think I'd rather be on safer ground.'

'Have you and Jim any interesting murders on your hands at the moment?'

'No. I have to admit things are a bit dull. A few open-and-shut domestics are all I'm dealing with at present.'

'Well, you never know. The way the activists are carrying on, you may yet be landed with a corpse. Their demos are getting nastier. Sometimes I'm quite nervous. I won't be sorry when all this is over.'

'So what's going to happen now? The second reading debate's on Tuesday, isn't it?'

'Yes.'

'How will it go? Will you win?'

'Apparently by convention government bills just don't go to a vote on the second reading. Mind you, at first Jack thought we should bash ahead with a vote regardless. She pointed out that in war it's important to try to win as early as possible so as to minimize your losses. But Stormerod put his foot down. Said we'd lose the waverers if we flew in the face of tradition. Besides, as he rightly said, since some of the provisions are acceptable, it would be hard to vote against. You don't win friends by voting for torturing squirrels.'

'So what's your immediate objective?'

'To win a moral victory and, *inter alia*, give the government notice that this one could be a nuisance. They're full of legislative plans – including Lords reform – so they won't be pleased at the possibility of being tied down on this one. But our side intend to fight it out in hand-to-hand combat in Committee. We won't be able to defeat it, but we intend if we can to emasculate it. And then bung it back to the Commons.'

'Sounds straightforward, but I suppose it isn't.'

'Too right. It'll all involve a lot of work and aggro, especially with these mad clowns demonstrating outside day in and day out. Our worry is that it won't be easy to whip in enough of our chaps to support us in the chamber and turn up regularly to the Committee. However, I'm reasonably optimistic. Jack's managed to form a coherent group that's more or less prepared to follow orders.'

'From whom?'

'Stormerod nominally, though Jack's the driving force and I'm the ventriloquist, writing speeches and doing briefing. It's just like being back in the civil service. Just more fun.'

'And who are your puppets?'

'Beesley and Poulteney mainly. Though I'm doing a fair bit of work with Jack, Sid Deptford and Stormerod to make sure they don't trip over each other in their arguments. We're focusing on the fox-hunting issue, since that's the one everyone's particularly exercised about.'

'You should be all right, shouldn't you? Isn't Stormerod an old master at this sort of thing? Though of course Jack's new to it. It must be a strain for her to have to make her maiden speech on such a high-profile occasion.'

'You speaking of Jack Troutbeck?'

'Sorry. Wasn't thinking.'

'In fact, she and Stormerod have decided to throw discretion to the winds and put her in the vulnerable position towards the end where she'll have to respond to the opponents' arguments. Old Bertie has great faith in her. So do I, really.'

Pooley raised his glass. 'To success. And I promise not to nag you again until it's all over.'

'I've written speeches for some dodos in my time, but nothing to match this. I don't think even the dimmest politician presents a challenge of the magnitude of Tommy and Reggie.'

The baroness laughed. 'Are you seriously suggesting they're stupider than your old minister, Norman Thring?'

'He doesn't even rate. At least when you gave him a speech – admittedly in words of one syllable – he was able to read it out with a bit of expression. But there are moments when I've been seriously wondering if Tommy Beesley can read. However, I've taken both of them through their speeches three times and they might just do.'

'Well, I don't want this to go to your head, Robert, but I have to say that bearing in mind the raw material they gave you and their deficiencies as orators, it sounds as if you've done a notable job of damage limitation.'

'There's always the chance Reggie will lose his speech or Tommy will return to his plan of simply asserting stoutly over and over again that he won't stand for it.'

'Just make sure that doesn't happen. Now, had Reggie heard any more about the damaged saddle?'

'Yes. Forensic tests show definitely it was tampered with, which is borne out by Hawkins, who had polished it within a few days of the hunt. But a lot of people could have had access to it during the day. And at night if they knew where to find the key.'

'Which was kept?'

'On a nail outside the back door. Not very difficult. Anyone could have had access to it. It required no special skill.'

'So is the money on the looney end of the animal activists?'

'Jennifer said the police had given the family a considerable going-over, but that they're now doing routine checks on any violent animal activists they've got on file. But they're not hopeful of finding the culprit.'

'How's Reggie taking it?'

'Very well. Snorted a lot and talked about tosses he had taken in his time and other fox-hunting witterings. What was more disturbing was the letter Tommy showed me.'

'Don't tell me,' she said. 'Threatening vengeance if he didn't support abolition.'

'How do you know?'

'They seem to have gone out to everyone in the Lords, including me. I did a spot check when mine arrived. The only reason Reggie won't have had it is because he wasn't at home.' She went over to her desk, took a piece of paper out of her drawer and tossed it over to Amiss. Printed in red ink on cheap paper, it was headed, 'BEWARE'.

'That's a good opening,' said Amiss. 'They've obviously been reading about the necessity to grab your audience at the very first word.'

He read on.

'Member of the House of Lords – You are trying to defeat a just bill which outlaws evil. Everyone who speaks against any part of the Wild Mammals Bill will be responsible for putting the lives of their families and property at risk. Wrongdoing must be punished.

THE ANIMAL AVENGERS

'I never heard of them, but they sound quite serious. Have you told the police?'

'I rang your pal Pooley and then faxed it to him. Presumably Scotland Yard will be doing something, but it is worrying.'

'You mean you're afraid someone might take a pot shot at you?'

'Don't be ridiculous. What's worrying is the effect it will have on the noble lords without backbone, of whom I fear there may be a few. I'm concerned lest they find themselves on Tuesday with urgent business elsewhere, just when we need a show of strength.

'So with Jock's help I got Reggie to send this out to everyone this afternoon.' She handed him a fax from the House of Lords. The letter read:

Dear

I believe you may have received from a scoundrelly group calling itself THE ANIMAL AVENGERS a threatening communication. Since I have reason to believe that it was they who recently damaged my saddle and caused me to take a toss in the hunting field, I thought I should let you know that I am standing firm. I have no intention of letting terrorists move me from the path of duty to Britain and her way of life. Therefore I still intend to be speaking against the anti-hunting clauses of the Wild Mammals Bill on Tuesday.

I have every confidence that you are as zealous as am I when it comes to upholding free speech and that you will not allow yourself to be persuaded by wicked and un-British threats into abandoning the path of duty.

    I remain,

        Yours sincerely,

           Poulteney

'But I only left him at two o'clock.'

'Yes, but Bertie nobbled him a few minutes later and between his secretary, a word processor and three clerks brought in from a nearby agency, the whole twelve hundred will have been sent out by five o'clock, topped and tailed by Reggie. It's exhausted him more than an all-day hunt. If you work it out, he must have written more than two thousand four hundred words, which is probably as much as he would normally write in the course of a year. Martini?'

'*Martini*?'

'Yes, martini. What's so difficult about that concept?'

'Nothing. It just seems a bit unexpected. I hadn't expected you to indulge in anything as effete as cocktails.'

'There's nothing effete about a good martini, young Robert. Not the way I make them.' She strolled over to the fridge, removed a bottle of gin, poured it into two glasses, added a couple of drops of vermouth and dropped in an already prepared twist of lemon rind. She presented a glass to Amiss, who examined it doubtfully.

'You believe in sixteen parts gin to one of vermouth, I see.'

'I'm not quite as heavy on the vermouth as that.'

He tried it timidly and after a certain amount of choking began to enjoy it. The baroness looked pleased.

'Good. Now you've got some nourishment, I wouldn't mind a chat about my own speech. I'm relying on you to stop me from getting too carried away. I am, after all, a maiden speaker and it behoves me to affect a certain modesty.'

'Aren't you a bit old to change the habits of a lifetime?'

'Stop being smart and take a look at this draft.'

'Have you never felt nervous about anything?'

She raised her head from her newspaper. 'What are you talking about?'

'Tuesday, for instance. Are you at all nervous about making this speech?'

'No, why should I be?' She was clearly baffled.

'In case you make a hash of it.'

'You mean compared to Tommy and Reggie?'

'No, no, no. I'm talking within the bounds of possibility. I mean just do it badly.'

'If I do it badly, I do it badly. Just have to do it better next time.' She shook her head in bewilderment. 'What are you going on about? Is it wrong not to worry?'

'No, no, Jack.' Amiss felt weary. 'It's not wrong. It's just unusual.'

The telephone rang early on Tuesday morning. Bleary from too late a night working on last-minute additions to Stormerod's speech, Amiss climbed miserably out of bed, picked up the receiver and croaked, 'Hello.'

'Are you OK?'

He was baffled at such an enquiry from the baroness. 'Why shouldn't I be?'

'It's just that I've had a letter bomb and I was afraid you might have had one too.'

'Are you all right?' he shouted.

'Of course. I spotted it just in time and chucked it into an armchair. It gave Plutarch a nasty shock when it went off, but she's recovered now. The chair isn't looking too good, but otherwise all is well. Right, you warn Bertie, Sid, Reggie and Tommy and when I've tipped off the fuzz I'll get in touch with anyone else who occurs to me. Tell everyone we proceed regardless. Bye.'

'Jack!'

'What?'

'I . . . I'm glad you're all right.'

'I'm glad you are too,' she said gruffly, and put the phone down.

'I won't put up with it.' Beesley was shaking with rage. 'I tell you I won't put up with it. First threatening letters and now this. You and Sid could have been killed.'

'Well, we weren't. So we go on as normal. We're all here to make sure our speeches complement each other and that we know what we're going to do. I trust no one's got cold feet.'

Beesley, Deptford and Poulteney snorted with indignation at the suggestion. Stormerod merely smiled and Amiss raised his eyes to heaven.

'What I don't understand,' said Poulteney, 'is why you two were the only ones to be sent bombs.'

'I expect because apart from Robert – who doesn't count – we're the only ones likely to have been at home this morning. The senders would appear to have been considerate enough to wish to avoid unnecessarily injuring noncombatants.'

'They weren't so considerate with all those bombs a few weeks ago. Remember one took the hand off an MP's secretary.'

'Maybe they learned from that,' said the baroness. 'Anyway, speculation's a waste of time and we haven't any time to waste. Let's get on with it. Robert, take us through the running order of the arguments again. Then we can have a decent lunch.'

14

There was no doubt that numbers were down. Where Stormerod had originally expected the Conservative benches to be full, there were now several gaps. But although the word was that a few names had been withdrawn from the speakers' list, there were enough for Amiss, sitting in the front row of spectators just to the right of the baroness, to be resigned to a long session.

Lady Parsons kicked off very much in the style of the Islington public meeting. She spent little time on the uncontentious clauses, but when she got to hunting, the detailed facts and figures tumbled out followed by the moral denunciation: there was no place for the anachronistic pursuits of the idle rich in a modern society facing the challenge of the European Union. It was disgraceful that country people should still carry such traditional baggage from the shameful days of Empire.

She sat down to obedient but unenthusiastic 'hear, hears'. Stormerod came next. His unassuming, urbane tone was ideally suited to the Lords. 'I should like to congratulate the noble and learned baroness on her mastery of the evidence for the prosecution. Such is her skill that I wished she might have turned her redoubtable talents to the defence – where I am sure she would have made an even better case. She, whose concern for the underprivileged is so well known, could not have failed to be moving on the subject of the damage that would be done to ordinary people in so many professions if this bill went through.'

He dwelt movingly and in sequence on the plight of the huntsmen and the houndsmen whose lives had been dedicated to the ancient trades in which they took such pride.

'I am not myself a huntsman, so it might surprise you that I am opening for the defence of that sport, but then the noble and learned baroness is not a fox.' This piece of wit elicited polite laughter from all over the house, fortunately drowning out to all but those in the Baroness Troutbeck's immediate vicinity the mutter, 'But she is a bloody vixen.' Gently and in the pragmatic manner that befitted an elder statesman, Stormerod talked of those parts of the bill with which he was entirely happy and then about what made hunting different. Why was it, he asked, that as with capital punishment, every time the House of Commons had given proper consideration to the hunting issue reason had triumphed over prejudice and the visceral popular demand to abolish the one and reinstate the other had been rejected? Now it was for the Lords to make sure that irrationality did not prevail.

Brother Francis, aka the Lord Purseglove, could not compete with this. Where Stormerod fitted in with the ambience of the Lords like a top hat at Ascot, Brother Francis looked as out of place as an anorak. Amiss knew enough of the Lords by now to appreciate that while eccentricity was part and parcel of the place, it had to be within clearly defined parameters. You could be shabby, boring, dotty, absent-minded, repetitive and a bit of a drunk, but anything that smacked of the spiv, the cad, or the crank made you, by definition, an outsider. Brother Francis's dress, from his plastic sandals to his clerical collar, did not put his audience at their ease. Apart from anything else, as Sid had explained to Amiss, there was deep disapproval that he was sitting on the cross benches in clerical gear. To the Lords, clergy were bishops: they sat on the benches of the Lords Spiritual in a properly hierarchical manner, archbishops to the fore on the benches with the arm rests. It was muddling to have a member of the clerical lower orders turning up and suggested that the chap was obviously unsound.

Like Lady Parsons, Brother Francis had made few concessions to a change of audience, though he had the wit to begin with a waffly wringing of hands about how dreadful violence was and how he hated it as much when it was applied to man as to beast. He had also left out his verses and his hymn; clearly he was not such an innocent as to be unaware that the Lords were likely to be a bit conservative about their hymn sheet. But he did produce an apposite verse from Cowper:

> . . . *Detested sport,*
> *That owes its pleasure to another's pain;*
> *That feeds upon the sobs and dying shrieks*
> *of harmless nature . . .*

Yet though his sincerity earned him a sympathetic hearing, he kept annoying their lordships. It was, for instance, clear to Amiss from the shocked expressions within his vision that it did not go down well to address peers as: 'My noble brothers and sisters.' Nor did his syrupy sentimentality appeal either to those of rural background – the majority of the hereditary mob – or to those who had fought their way up the greasy poles of politics, academia, law or business. In choosing him as her seconder, Lady Parsons had shown how little she understood the institution.

Deptford came next and – as an old Lords hand – got the tone completely right. Simply and directly, he told the autobiographical story of how hunting had brought joy, excitement and an understanding of the cycle of nature to a boy from the most underprivileged of backgrounds. And he raised a laugh by telling of his delighted amazement in finding the sport egalitarian. 'As the great hunting journalist, Nimrod, explained: "A butcher's boy upon a pony may throw dirt in the face of the first duke in the kingdom."'

It should not be thought that only the right defended hunting, as the Labour Minister for Agriculture had shown when he opposed the anti-hunting bill of 1949 on the grounds that it was not for townsmen to attack the life of the countryside. Yet here we were now contemplating allowing an 'urban dictatorship' to prevail. The murmurs and 'hear, hears' throughout the speech were frequent and genuine.

The antis had pulled off a coup with the next speaker, for Lord Pangbourne was a convert from field sports, who waxed eloquent about the cruelty he had seen and indeed participated in before he saw the light. He produced gruesome descriptions of foxes being dug out before being thrown to the hounds, and other revolting examples which Amiss recognized as standard in anti-hunting literature – always countered by the pros as exceptions and always cited by the antis as typical. But Pangbourne was lucid and at times shocking and – Amiss calculated – probably cancelled out Deptford.

It was with apprehension that he saw Poulteney rise, though with relief that he saw he was clinging on hard to the typescript Amiss had given him. Without stumbling too much, he talked as instructed about tradition, about how all classes united in this great test of vigour and courage. He talked of how restrictive was the social life of the country with little to do but go to the pub or watch television. What hunting offered was an opportunity for vigorous physical exercise that brought the community together, got people out in the open air, gave them a day's excitement and enjoyment and pride in their own achievement and brought to newcomers from the towns some appreciation of how nature worked.

He went off the point once. It was clearly beyond him to resist telling the story he told over and over again of the foreigner who went to a fox hunt. The people, horses and dogs were in the best of spirits, the sky was blue and the air was brisk but not sharp. Everyone was in rattling good form and a good day's sport seemed certain until disaster struck. The fox, instead of breaking free and leading hounds, horses and men a merry dance, faltered and was caught and killed before he left cover. 'The foreign gentleman,' gurgled Poulteney, as he always did at this point, 'thereupon turned to the Master of Foxhounds and said, "Oh my Lord Duke, I congratulate you on having killed that animal so soon and with so little trouble!"' Amiss ground his teeth. While he had advised strongly against representing hunting as vermin control, he had not wished Poulteney to talk of disappointment at a quick kill. Still, considering Poulteney's normal style and the few speeches of his he had read in Hansard, he marvelled at his own brilliance in managing to produce a performance as good as this one.

The next anti was a gift. As an ex-Minister for Health, he explained, Lord Newman was concerned not with animals but with protecting people – from themselves, if needs be. He launched into a self-congratulatory passage about various reforms he had instituted which had cut back on accidents in school playgrounds, on playing-fields and in the boxing ring. It was his dearest wish that the element of danger be removed as far as possible from British life. Boxing must be banned and helmet and pads made compulsory in all team sports. To pass the anti-hunting bill would be to save a significant number of lives and prevent a large number of injuries. Amiss scribbled a few lines and gave them to an attendant to pass to the baroness, who turned round after reading them and gave him the thumbs up.

The debate wore on for another hour or so, throwing up Admiral Lord Gordon, an apoplectic Master of Foxhounds whom Stormerod had never been able to corral into the group and who spent most of his speech going on about saboteur scum and the need to bring back National Service, flogging, the stocks, capital punishment and a clip across the ear from a policeman to any child who cheeked him in the street. Animals were there for the convenience of man to do with them whatever they liked.

Beesley did rather better than this only because Amiss had done a heroic job in converting his 'We-won't-stand-for-it' thesis into a coolly argued protest against criminalizing a highly respectable section of the population by forbidding people to do what their fathers and forefathers had done. He had also pre-empted Beesley's likely worst excesses by allowing him to dilate on the subject of how hunting brought out in people the qualities of courage, coolness under pressure, presence of mind and concern for one's companion in danger that were of such immeasurable value to members of the armed forces. Amiss winced slightly when Beesley brought in the paragraph he had written himself and was very proud of: 'My noble friends. Often in life we have to say how we judge another man. One may say, "I would go into a slit-trench with him." Another may say, "I would go into the jungle with him." I say, "I would ride to hounds with him and trust him to keep a cool and clear head and act at all times like a sportsman." As a country, as a people, we cannot afford wantonly to throw away this training ground, this breeding ground of our future leaders of men on the battlefield.'

Though Beesley was not a disaster, he was not a great success. However, he was cancelled out by the fifth Baron Neville, a dedicated Marxist, who droned on about the class war and the need to abolish the rich and their degenerate pursuits. By the time the baroness rose, Amiss's notebook was full of the elaborate geometric doodles that always testified to deep tedium. But he sat up when – dressed for the occasion in an arresting scarlet jacket – she began to speak. It was clear from the outset that her homework had paid off, particularly the slogging over Hansard and the confabulations with Stormerod about how to affect the appropriate modesty for a maiden speaker without undergoing a complete personality change. She had taken his advice that when in doubt, one should opt for flattery.

What an old fraud, thought Amiss affectionately, as he listened to her inject into her voice a tremulous note as she begged the indulgence of the noble lords towards a speech which must perforce – because her first in this noble house – be faltering and inadequate. She craved their indulgence for her apparent arrogance in making her maiden speech after such a very short time in the House but begged their forgiveness on two grounds. The first was that when she had been a mere civil servant she had been a frequent member of the audience, for because the standard of debate was here so much higher than in another place, she had taken every opportunity to attend. And second, because this was a subject so important – not just to her but to the nation as a whole and the preservation of its heritage – that she could not have forgiven herself if she had not stood up and been counted. This was more important than ever now, since as the noble lords were aware, a failure to speak or a failure to vote to preserve this aspect of our national life might be taken by the enemies of democracy – spearheaded by the Animal Avengers, the Animal Liberation Army, the Hunt Saboteurs and all the many other extreme groups – as a reward for their evil, threatening tactics. If they were to scent blood, who knew what might follow.

Her main theme was courage, which she used as a prism through which to pick off one by one the speakers for the motion. Lady Parsons was denounced politely as someone who lacked the courage to accept the national character for what it was: brave, individualistic and with a deep sense of history and a commitment to conserving the British way of life that had kept it for many centuries a beacon of sanity and stability in a world of torment and upset.

'The noble baroness would do better to take us as we are,' she announced, as Parsons sat grimly staring into the middle distance, 'with our foibles and peculiarities and our eccentricities. She should not try to legislate us into blandness and homogeneity.'

She skewered Brother Francis on his lack of realism: 'If you push people beyond their level of tolerance, you do more harm than good.' While she applauded deep devotion to animal welfare, he was attempting to bring about not only – as Baroness Parsons had done – a fundamental change in human nature, but also, even more ambitiously, he wished to change, even deny, the nature of animals.

In his mysterious way God had ordained that most animals – and man was an animal – fed on each other. It might seem cruel but it was reality and it was not for us to question in this regard the divine plan. As she came out with this, knowing Jack's happy atheism, Amiss had to suppress a sardonic grin. She did a particularly neat job on Pangbourne, using to tremendous effect to denounce the Nanny State the verse Amiss had passed over to her. Her voice rang round the chamber and earned by Lords standards a tremendous outbreak of approving murmurs with Adam Lindsay Gordon's lines:

No game was ever worth a rap
For a rational man to play.

112

In which no accident, no mishap,
Could possibly find its way.

What had this England that Lord Pangbourne was trying to bring about to do with the England of Alfred the Great and Henry V and Winston Churchill – a world in which Cavaliers rode into battle with daring and derring-do and laughter on their lips?

And, she went on, if she might make so bold, she wished to point out too that courage was not confined to the male sex. Mere women (Amiss feared she was beginning to go slightly over the top here) like Boadicea, Queen Elizabeth I and, more recently, Lady Thatcher, had shown that English-women too have stout hearts. There were those among the noble lords who would remember great exhibitions of courage on the hunting field, which sometimes led to tragedy. But did anyone believe that that great lady, the late wife of the noble Lord Poulteney, would have held back from hunting for a day had she known that her life would end during a chase? Amiss looked rather nervously at Poulteney at this juncture, wondering if she had gone too far and hoping she had cleared it with him first, but he was showing no reaction. He lay back on the bench gazing at the ceiling.

'And courage, my noble friends, is what this debate is about. For not only must we preserve hunting for reasons of conservation of tradition, of the good of the local community and because it is the least cruel method of keeping down foxes, but because it is our duty to resist what can now only be called terrorism. What was once peaceful protest has changed to civil disobedience and has recently degenerated into criminality; it is a veritable threat to the stability of the kingdom itself.

'Those who have sought to intimidate some noble lords into acting against their consciences underestimate their mettle. They have underestimated too the intellect of the Lords whom I have the honour to address for the first time, who cannot fail to realize that to give way on this issue will lead inexorably to terrorist agitation on a host of other issues. If we knuckle under now, we will give great heart to those people who wished to terrorize us into becoming a nation of whey-faced vegans.'

She sat down to more supportive noises than any other speaker had yet attracted, both because the speech had been entertaining and because convention required encouragement for a maiden speaker. Yet a few lords refrained from cheering. Amiss was surprised to see that even within his restricted field of vision two lords on the Conservative benches showed no emotion whatsoever; he assumed them to be vegetarians. He guessed Poulteney's failure to show support meant he thought it bad form to show approval of a speech in which his wife had been praised.

The last three speeches contributed very little that was new and during the last Amiss found himself nodding off. He awoke with a start, feeling slightly guilty, though looking round at the number of recumbent forms he felt his guilt misplaced. It was a relief when Lady Parsons stood up to give the winding-up speech. He found her surprisingly unimpressive, being one of those debaters who merely repeat their earlier points and appear not to understand the questions raised. The hunt employees of whom Stormerod had spoken, she explained, would simply have to retrain in modern skills. She sneered at Beesley's argument about the qualities required by a member of the armed forces by remarking that the days of the cavalry were well and truly over. And to Poulteney's point about the importance of the hunt in the social life of rural communities, she said shortly that when their sport was outlawed, it was for them to find some legal leisure pursuit: principle was all. Brisk, complacent and righteous, she brought the debate to an end at ten-twenty.

'The question is that this bill be read a second time,' called out the Lord Chancellor. 'As many as are of that opinion will say, "Content". The contrary, "Not content".' There was a chorus of 'Content' from Labour and the Bishops' benches and a few more from the Conservative and cross benches. As expected, there were no 'Not contents'.

As Lord Broadsword, the government whip, stood up to

move the adjournment, the baroness bustled out of the enclosure and jerked her head at Amiss, who followed her obediently into the lobby.

15

'Well done. You were very good.'

'Yes, I was, wasn't I?' She smote him playfully in the ribs. His yelp drew a disapproving look from a doorkeeper.

'So what do you think?'

'I think you've broken a bone. Otherwise, I think that undoubtedly our side won the moral and intellectual argument. Did you spot any unexpected defectors from the "Content" group?'

'Two,' she said. 'I kept a sharp eye on old Basil Hawthorne, one of my ex-ministers, whose instincts would be those of cockney-Labour, but I think he was swayed by Sid. He certainly nodded at him enthusiastically. And me. He definitely didn't say "Content". Nor did old Joe Taylor, that vegetarian Tory. Though I think he was asleep.'

'He wasn't alone in that. So was Reggie.'

Beesley emerged at the front of a throng of chattering peers a moment later and engaged in a rapid exchange with one of the doorkeepers. They both returned to the chamber.

'Something's up,' said the baroness, 'we'd better go back in.'

'Gently, Jack, gently,' whispered Amiss. 'Don't crash through them. You're not dealing with demonstrators now.'

She moderated her charge and did her best to insinuate herself through the milling peers rather than run them down. By the time they got through to a view of the chamber, it was almost deserted, save for the alarming combination of a clutch of doorkeepers and Tommy Beesley feeling the pulses of several recumbent bodies. Amiss and the baroness glanced at each other in shared apprehension and – running – joined them.

'What's going on, Tommy?'

He turned and looked at her, ashen-faced.

'They're all dead. Reggie, Robbie, Connie and the others. Dead.'

'My God.' She wheeled on the nearest doorkeeper. 'Get the police.'

'Oh, my lady, do you really think that necessary? Could it not be a frightful coincidence of natural death?'

Her glare looked sufficiently powerful to bring about death by shrivelling. 'Very good, my lady,' he muttered, and left the room at a speed – for once – more urgent than dignified.

The telephone rang at 8.00, startling Amiss out of a nightmare in which he was being strangled by a hairy demonstrator wielding an ermine noose. The culprit turned out to be a sheet that his night-time thrashings had succeeded in winding around his neck. By the time he had disentangled himself and scrambled out of bed, the ringing had stopped. He swore and stumbled back to bed. Within a minute the ringing started again.

'Good morning.'

'It doesn't feel like morning, Ellis. I didn't get to bed till five o'clock.'

'I know it was a rough night, Robert, but what kept you up so late? You sound close to death yourself, if you'll excuse my saying so.'

'I admit it wasn't the best of ideas to go back with Jack to Myles Cavendish's after the hoo-haa had died down, but I always remember too late that whisky exacerbates shock rather than moderating it. Hold on a minute. I'm freezing.' Amiss darted back to his bedroom, pulled on a dressing gown, grabbed a rug from the bed and put it round him before he picked up the phone again. 'OK. What do you want to know?'

'Mostly I wanted to know how you are.'

'Incredulous. Shattered. Horrified. What you'd expect. But thanks for asking.'

'Also, I thought you'd like to know Jim and I are on this case.'

'What? Why? Surely it's got to do with the anti-terrorist lot rather than the Murder Squad?'

'It's all hands on deck. The Anti-terrorist Squad are overwhelmed. Between being run down after the Northern Ireland ceasefire and having a scare blow up on the Islamic Fundamentalist front last week, they're so short-handed they've agreed enthusiastically to having Jim, me and anyone else he can spare come on board.'

'Well, thank God for that.'

'Of course, it will all be done under their auspices and they'll get the credit, but at least we get part of the action. And we can maintain a low profile and stay out of the way of the press, thank heaven.'

'Well, bugger the internal politics of the Met, Ellis. This is terrifying stuff.'

'So I gather. Is it OK if we come round to see you in half an hour or so to get some colour?'

'If you bring breakfast.'

'Done.'

By the time he answered the door to Pooley — well laden with carrier bags — and their friend Detective Chief Superintendent James Milton, Amiss was showered, dressed, halfway through his first cup of coffee and almost clear-headed. Milton put an arm half around his shoulders in the awkward manner of a sympathetic middle-aged man from a macho culture.

'Poor old Robert.'

'Thanks, Jim, but I'm all right.'

'At least it wasn't gory.'

'What a Pollyanna you are.'

'Come on. Let's go into the kitchen and tell us all about it while Ellis plays Mum.'

They sat at the kitchen table while Pooley competently dispensed orange juice, coffee, croissants, butter and jam. Amiss drank all his orange juice in one go and held out his glass for more. 'So what happened to all those poor old sods?'

'Mechanical failure.'

'Don't tell me. Someone jammed their pacemakers.'

Milton put down his coffee and gazed at Amiss in astonishment. 'How did you work that out? I thought you were scientifically illiterate. We've only had that confirmed this morning.'

'Lieutenant-Colonel Myles Cavendish, DSO, MC, ex-SAS and presently some kind of hush-hush consultant on terrorism and intimate friend of the Baroness Troutbeck worked it out double quick. His reasoning was based on the impossibility of eight people dying simultaneously of natural causes, the peaceful nature of their deaths and the fact that nerve gas was a non-starter as the bodies were mostly well separated. When he asked about their health, Jack knew four of them had bad hearts and – in response to his prompting – remembered two definitely had pacemakers. Myles wasn't sure how it had been done but he was sure it was possible. He proffered some theories, but I'd had so much whisky by then that I'm damned if I can remember them. What did the pathologist say?'

'That he'd performed four postmortems and all had stopped pacemakers. And since then we've been told the other four had pacemakers too. It looks pretty open and shut. The anti-terrorist boys are getting down to the how. I'm concentrating on the why and the who.'

'And the which.'

'Sorry, Ellis. I don't quite follow that. I'm feeling a bit dim this morning.' Amiss took another draught of coffee.

'Well, we don't know if the intention was to murder one, some or all of them.'

'Oh, I see what you mean. It's a bit hard to imagine somebody with a grudge particularly directed against people with pacemakers unless, of course, there's a Pacemakers Liberation Front. I guess the most likely scenario is that the Animal Avengers were having a second crack at Reggie Poulteney and the other poor bastards just happened to cop it along with him.'

'Second crack?' Milton was puzzled.

'Of course, that wasn't on your territory. Pour me out

some more coffee, Ellis, and I'll try to give you a coherent story.'

'So what's your hunch? Do you think these Avengers might be behind everything?'

'How would I know?' said Milton. 'My instinct would be that it's too much of a leap from behaving like a lot of yahoos and writing childish letters to committing mass murder. But of course if they were responsible for the letter bombs they might be capable of anything.'

'But you don't know if they are.'

'Too true. Paul Jarrett, my pal on the anti-terrorist side, tells me there are at least a couple of dozen animal activist groups, maybe half of which are in the thick of civil disobedience and around half a dozen of whom he thinks are capable of serious violence. His money was on the Animal Liberation Army. He'd never heard of the Animal Avengers till their threatening letter to the peers.'

'I still think the murderer is more likely to have been after an individual,' said Pooley. 'Just like in Agatha Christie's *ABC Murders*. Maybe Poulteney's daughter-in-law hired a hitman.'

'You can't seriously think that. I'm no defender of Vanessa Bovington-Petty, and I could just about imagine her having the guts to try to murder Daddy-in-law in an indirect way which couldn't be traced back to her, but I'm damned if I could seriously see a disaffected Sloane being behind wholesale murder. It's much too far-fetched. What do you think, Jim?'

'Life isn't like Agatha Christie.' Milton sighed. 'Or not any more, anyway. We live in a world where terrorists have launched devastating attacks on the City of London, the New York Trade Centre, the Tokyo underground and Oklahoma City, just to pick four at random.'

'The IRA, Islamic Fundamentalists, Doomsday cultists and anti-government fanatics,' said Pooley. 'I suppose since foreigners always thought the English were mad about animals it would be appropriate if it is their defenders who make our contribution to terrorism.'

'Dammit, as Jack frequently points out, we're animals too.' Amiss sipped his coffee gloomily. 'I know it's a failure of imagination, but I find it difficult to understand how people who call themselves defenders of the rights of some can be so cavalier with the rights of others.'

'Mad people find causes that enable them to cloak their madness with virtue,' said Milton. 'Now, enough of all this philosophizing. Ellis and I have to get back to the Yard to catch up and plan our course of action. What are you going to do?'

'See what the newspapers have made of it and meet Jack for lunch. You can leave messages there for her and they'll get to me.'

'Robert.' Milton looked serious.

'I know. Be careful.'

'I mean it. If these really are pro-animal terrorists, you're right up there in the line of fire beside your pal Troutbeck.'

'Well, there isn't much chance of persuading her to take care. Myles read her the riot act last night and she kept explaining she'd be fine. Trouble is, she thinks she's invincible.'

'Well, you're not.'

'I'll watch out. I promise. Besides, I should be safe enough today. Jack rang earlier to say that she thought the Lords might be a bit depressing, so she'd told Beesley to take us to the Cavalry Club. I should think the inhabitants of that place would see off any troublemakers in short order.'

16

Amiss's relationship with his Indian newsagent was warm and mutually supportive. He wrote references when Sanjeev Patel applied for citizenship or needed a permit to sell alcohol; in turn, Patel kept Amiss's spare keys and took in his parcels, and they enjoyed chatting over the day's news.

'This dreadful business in the House of Lords is really most extraordinary,' he said, as Amiss leafed through the tabloids, which were in a state of ecstatic hysteria. 'Do you think it's something in the heating or air-conditioning that kills eight people out of several hundred? Picks off the weakest, perhaps. Like legionnaire's disease.'

'Interesting notion, Sanjeev. But according to the papers they all seem to have died at about the same time.'

'What I don't understand . . .' Patel pulled out a paper at random. 'Look here. It says the police think they died at about nine o'clock but nobody noticed them until more than an hour later. How could that be?'

'I suppose they thought they were asleep.'

'There's a difference, Robert, in being asleep and being dead. Mark my words, there's something very sinister going on. If your neighbour looks suspiciously quiet beside you, you investigate.'

Amiss shook his head. 'Sanjeev, I fear you don't understand the British upper classes. If anything untoward happens beside you the etiquette is to pretend not to notice.'

'What? Even if you fear something serious has happened?'

'Let me tell you two stories. Several years ago an enormous lump fell out of the House of Lords ceiling on to a seat in the chamber and just missed one of the lords. Now what would be the reaction if that happened in Delhi in the Lok Sabha?'

'All hell would break loose.' Patel laughed. 'I expect we would have a stampede.'

'Well, in the Lords everyone sat in his place and pretended not to notice. And don't you remember that a couple of years ago some lesbians abseiled down from the gallery in the Lords and everyone ignored them. So you see why I have no difficulty in understanding what could have happened last night. To investigate your neighbour's condition, unless he directly asks you for help, would be seen as impolite and intrusive.'

Patel shook his head. 'Intrusive is not a word we understand much in our culture, and that is bad, for we are much too inquisitive and meddling. But from what you tell me, your aversion to it is worse, for it may be lethal.' And sighing at the irrationality of man, he left Amiss to peruse the papers while he attended to another customer.

'Are you the chap in charge?'

'One of them.'

'I've told them over and over that I'll only talk to the c-in-c.'

Milton assumed his most soothing tone. 'I am a detective chief superintendent on the Murder Squad, Lord Beesley. There is no one more senior here at present who understands as much about last night's atrocity at the Lords.'

'That's not what I want to talk about. Well, only in a way.'

Milton summoned up all his patience and shifted the phone to his other ear. 'I'm here to listen to whatever you have to talk about, sir. Just fire away.'

Beesley sounded dubious. 'It's about Reggie Poulteney. You know someone tried to kill him before.'

'By damaging his saddle. Indeed, yes, sir.'

Beesley was cheered by this evidence of intelligence. 'Oh, good. Now this is very delicate. I don't want it talked about.'

'Why don't you just tell me, sir, and then we can discuss what to do with your information. As I'm sure you'll appreciate, the most important consideration is to bring to justice whoever killed or tried to kill Lord Poulteney.'

'Well, I know. But we don't want any scandal unless it's absolutely necessary.'

'No, sir. And there won't be an unnecessary scandal. Trust me.'

Amazingly, that request worked. 'It's Hawkins, you see. He rang me up and told me what he'd seen the night before Reggie took his toss.'

There was a silence. 'And what was that, sir?'

'He saw Vanessa Bovington-Petty . . . do you know who that is?'

'Lord Poulteney's daughter-in-law. And who is Hawkins?'

'Poor Reggie's head groom. Well, he saw Vanessa coming out of the tack room in the middle of the night. Didn't tell anyone but now he's worried in case she tried to kill Reggie then and had something to do with last night. Asked my advice and I told him I'd have a word with someone and then he must make a clean breast of it.'

'Excellent advice, sir. Now if you tell me what you know, you can then ask Mr Hawkins to ring me as soon as he can do so discreetly. And you can reassure him that I will go to all reasonable lengths to conceal his identity.'

'Lady Poulteney is on her way up.'

'Thanks, Jane. Ask Sergeant Pooley if he'll come in now, please.'

Pooley entered, notebook in hand, looking expectant.

'Ellis, I forgot to ask you if you'd ever met this woman. I mean, you haven't come across her at society weddings or hunt balls or Henley or wherever your sort of person hangs out, have you?' He was pleased to note that Pooley was toughening. A year ago he would have blushed, but now he smiled and said, 'No, sir, not even at Ascot.'

'Good, then you can stay.'

'Before she comes in, sir. Have you heard about her and the Rutland police?'

Milton looked puzzled. 'All I've seen are the not very helpful interview notes faxed to me this morning. Why?'

'Gossip from a friend there is that she was very respectfully treated by Inspector Hill, who's notorious as a pushover for

124

the gentry. Apparently there was a hideously embarrassing moment when, after she left the drawing room after the interview, her fluting voice was heard saying to someone: "What a sweet deferential little man!"'

'Good. With luck she'll still have a false sense of security.' He picked up the phone. 'Send her in, Jane.'

As Vanessa swept into the room, Milton stood up.

'How nice to see you, Superintendent. Oh sorry, have I mucked that up? Aren't you a chief or something?' Her manner reminded Milton irresistibly of the attempts of some of his superiors to be gracious to junior staff at the Christmas party.

'Please sit down, Lady Poulteney. And superintendent will do fine. This is my colleague, Detective Sergeant Pooley.'

'Not one of the Worcestershire . . . ? No, sorry. Of course you wouldn't be.'

She sat down, oblivious to Pooley's look of relief and Milton's twitch of the lower lip. 'Thank you for coming to see me, Lady Poulteney. And may I first offer my condolences on the loss of your father-in-law.'

'Oh, yah. Poor old Daddy-in-law. It's so tragic. We're absolutely devastated. Now, what do you want? I haven't got very long, actually, what with a lunch date and absolutely heaps to do now with the funeral and all that and the move to Shapely Bottom. Can't see how I can help.'

'I want to know your movements on the night before the late Lord Poulteney's hunting accident.'

'Oh, really – not again. I gave all that to some frightful flatfoot simply ages ago. You know, the village bobby, or whoever they sent me.'

Milton's voice was even. 'I have seen the statement you gave to Detective Inspector Hill. However, you appear to have omitted to tell him about your visit to the tack room in the middle of the night.'

'How dare you!' She flushed a violent red. 'It's absolutely not true.'

'You were seen.'

'You're making it up.'

'Lady Poulteney, calling me a liar is not the best way of convincing me that you speak the truth.'

This non sequitur was delivered so crisply and authoritatively that she backed down instantly. 'Oh, sorry. Didn't mean that. I was just upset.'

'I have first-hand evidence that a woman answering to your description came out of the tack room at about four a.m.'

'Oh, so it wasn't anyone who knew me. So they must have been mistaken.'

While Amiss had described Vanessa as 'medium-thick', this piece of stupidity was more than Milton could have hoped for. 'Thank you for as good as admitting you were there. And even if you hadn't, I think you would have found it difficult to convince a jury that two women with straight blonde hair, of medium height and wearing an overcoat identical to yours were likely to have been on the premises of Shapely Bottom Hall that night.'

'But whoever said I was is just a wicked liar trying to blame me for whatever they did themselves.'

'Won't wash, I'm afraid. They couldn't have known about your coat.'

She fiddled with her engagement ring for a minute. 'Well, all right then. I was there. I went to look for a brooch I thought I'd lost earlier that day.'

'You went out in the middle of a January night to look for a brooch?'

'Yes. It might have got trodden on in the morning by the grooms and it's my favourite brooch, and it was only at around half past three in the morning that I remembered I'd had it on when I was in the tack room and hadn't seen it afterwards.'

'Did you find the brooch?'

'No. I mean yes.'

'And did you mention to your husband the following morning your relief at having found it?'

She looked as hunted as a fox in a cul-de-sac with the hounds coming round the corner. 'Er, I don't remember.'

'Please stop insulting my intelligence, Lady Poulteney.

Considering what later emerged about your father-in-law's saddle, it is inconceivable that if you'd been in the tack room innocently you wouldn't remember whether or not your husband knew you'd been there. And it would be very hard to convince a jury that you wouldn't have mentioned your uncomfortable expedition.'

'Jamesie and I weren't speaking that morning.'

Milton sighed. 'It will be very easy to check, ma'am. I can send a police officer round to see your husband now to get his story and hold you here, incommunicado, until he's given it.'

She began to cry. Neither Milton nor Pooley was hard-hearted, but they were completely unmoved. After a few minutes she got tired of snuffling and blew her nose.

'Now, Lady Poulteney, why don't you simply tell me what happened?'

'You'll accuse me of trying to murder Daddy-in-law.'

'The case looks pretty straightforward, I'm afraid.'

'No, it's only those horrid sabs trying to blame me for what they did.'

'Look, Lady Poulteney, it's perfectly simple. Either you tell me what happened – what actually happened – or I charge you now with the attempted murder of your late father-in-law. That will give us plenty of time to discuss at leisure if, having failed on this occasion, you hired a hitman or perhaps even yourself killed Lord Poulteney and in the process murdered seven others.'

This provoked hysterics.

Milton sighed. 'Detective Sergeant Pooley, please open the door so that witnesses can see that we are not actually assaulting Lady Poulteney, apologize to them for the noise and tell them we hope it won't last long.'

It didn't. When she realized that the screaming and wailing were having no effect, she ceased them abruptly, sat up straight and said, 'Very well. I've been making an idiot of myself but I was frightened. But please promise you won't tell my husband if I tell you the truth.'

'I can't make promises, but I won't tell him anything unless it is necessary.'

She gazed intently at her gold-buckled, patent-leather clad feet. 'I went to meet a man.'

'Who?'

'Oh, dear, this is so embarrassing.'

'Less so than being arrested, I imagine.'

'There's no need to be horrid. If you must know, it was one of those awful sabs. We had a date.'

'Just tell us the story.'

She attacked it with a rush. 'I was out riding the afternoon before and I got off near Wreckett's Brook because I thought Betty might have picked up a stone. When I was looking at her hoof this fellow came up and we sort of started to talk. Anyway, he asked me if I'd like to meet him that night and it didn't seem any harm to say yes. I didn't mean to turn up.'

'But you did.'

'Well, I was upset that night. Really furious that Daddy-in-law was getting ready to propose to Lady Flexingham and really fed up with Jamesie, who wouldn't talk about it. He just lay there snoring away – he's an absolutely ghastly snorer – and I love Shapely Bottom so much and I know just what I want to do with it and I was really cross. So I thought it was all too beastly and I thought the hell with them, I'd go and meet this fellow just to spite them.'

'What time was this?'

'About two-thirty. We'd said we'd meet at three. So I got the key from the nail beside the side door and when I went into the tack room he followed me.'

'Who was he?'

'He said his name was Stu and that he was a sab.' She saw Milton's face. 'Yes, yes. I know. You'll think I'm awful and I hate those people, but he was exciting in a sort of sultry way and . . .' She hung her head again. 'You can't imagine how boring Jamesie is. I mean, he's awfully nice, but he's really boring.'

'So then?'

'Well, I don't have to spell it out, do I?'

'I'm afraid you do, ma'am.'

'Oh, well, if you must know we had sex a couple of times and then I went back to the Hall.'

'Leaving him in the tack room?'

'Yes. But he promised to lock up afterwards.'

'After what?'

She wriggled. 'He said he'd paint a few slogans. What could I do? I couldn't tell anyone and I made him promise he wouldn't do any real damage. And I was really relieved when it looked as if he hadn't done anything. But I suppose it must have been him who did that to Daddy-in-law's saddle.'

'But you didn't report that afterwards.'

She spread out her hands in dumb entreaty.

'Lady Poulteney. You may have been leaving a would-be murderer on the loose.'

'Well, I wouldn't have known where to find him anyway.'

'You didn't see him again?'

'Absolutely not. I mean, it's not as if he's the sort of person you have an affair with. He was very common.'

The telephone rang. 'Yes, sir. OK. Now.'

He stood up. 'I've got to go to a meeting now, Lady Poulteney. I would like you to tell Sergeant Pooley everything you remember about this gentleman. He will then type your statement and give it to you to sign and you may then go for the time being. We will have to check out aspects of your account.'

Relief overcame her. 'Oh, gosh, thank you.' And almost humbly, 'Will it take very long?'

'Perhaps half an hour,' said Pooley.

She looked apologetically at Milton. 'Would it be awful to ask you if I can make a phone call to the restaurant to say I'll be a bit late?'

'Not at all, Lady Poulteney. Ellis, when you've finished taking details, show her ladyship to a telephone.'

As he left the room she said to Milton, 'I'm sorry for being such a silly-billy, telling lies and all that, but I was terrified. I mean, what would Jamesie think if he knew what I'd been doing? I'd never hear the last of it.'

'Well, let us hope, Lady Poulteney, that there will be no need for him to know. But I can make no promises. However,

I would like to make one thing clear. The only way you can be proved innocent is if this gentleman can be located and will corroborate your story. If that doesn't happen, you will remain high on the list of suspects for attempted murder at least. So for your own sake I recommend you to be as helpful as possible to Sergeant Pooley. Now, if you'll forgive me . . .' He nodded dismissively and left the room.

By its sheer preposterousness, the Cavalry Club lifted Amiss out of his gloom. As he climbed the staircase to the bar, past the vast canvases of heroes riding boldly into battle with sabres flashing, horses perspiring and officers urging their men forward in dozens of forgotten encounters of imperial days, he felt his troubles to be minor by comparison.

To his regret, the room overlooking Piccadilly to which Beesley took them to lunch bore no resemblance to an officers' mess, for – as a member of the gentler sex – Jack Troutbeck was barred from the main dining room.

'One has to accept casualties in time of war,' announced Beesley. 'I agree that the thing to do is to just get on with it. Just like Reggie would have wanted.'

'And turn our reverse to our advantage,' said the baroness. 'How many of ours have we lost?'

Beesley's forehead puckered as he looked down the list. 'I make it five: Reggie, Connie, Robbie, St John Fostock and Tuffy Dreamer. Joe Taylor was an anti and Campden and Wilson were don't knows.'

'Hmmm. Not good. Still, it could have been much worse. Bertie has a pacemaker.'

'Good God, I didn't know that.' Beesley's jaw went slack. 'How did he escape?'

'He tells me it must have happened when he went out to have what he described as "a quiet word with a bishop".'

'What a blow to the tabloids,' said Amiss. 'A dead duke would have had their cup of joy running over.' He saw Beesley looking at him with incomprehension and continued hastily: 'Funny thing. One of the papers said this morning that six of them were life peers. Isn't that odd?'

'You're not thinking,' said the baroness. 'There's nothing

funny about that. We tend to be older than the hereditary lot. That's why the media are so daft when they go on about new blood. Life peers are usually pretty old blood. Not, of course, that we're necessarily any the worse for that.'

Amiss noticed that she seemed in curiously high spirits, brought on by that combination of adversity and adrenaline on which she always flourished.

'So what next?' asked Beesley. 'What should we do?'

'Propaganda war. Robert will draft a letter of the are-we-men-or-mice? variety.'

'If you were mice, there wouldn't be a problem,' said Amiss sourly. 'They'd be making you a protected species instead of murdering you. Look, before you go on – and I see where you're heading – may I just remind you that these people aren't just murderers. They're crazy. Do you really want to put your heads above the parapet so they can more easily be blown off?'

'Not heads above the parapet. More leading the men over the top.' Tragedy seemed to be a great rejuvenator for Beesley. 'Can't risk a collapse in morale. Got to show fighting spirit, leadership. Just like all the chaps who inspire us in this club. Swords out, break into a gallop, and up and at 'em.'

'What we want to avoid is the Charge of the Light Brigade.'

'Don't like this defeatist talk. Surprised at you, young man. That's what comes of ending military service. Encourages cowardice.'

The baroness responded to Amiss's mutinous glare. 'Lay off, Tommy,' she declared briskly. 'Nothing cowardly about young Robert here. We've seen action together before and I can tell you he played the white man. And he has a point. Even people in the front line should take sensible precautions.'

'Like checking under your car before you get into it,' said Amiss. 'Some nutter tried to blow up a research scientist that way a few years ago.'

But the baroness's attention had wandered. 'Good. So you'll draft a letter to be signed by . . . what do you think, Tommy? Us, Bertie, Sid and a few more of the boys?'

'Well, keeping the numbers down will certainly make it easier for the assassins,' said Amiss.

'All right, all right. We'll make it harder for them and increase the number of targets to a few dozen. You and I can get down to rounding them up, Tommy, starting this afternoon. Now, what about some brandy? And I hope there's no nonsense about barring pipes from the dining room.'

17

Pooley's eyes were shining with triumph. 'Looks as if our hunch was right, sir. There was a "Stewart" and a "Stuart" booked in Rutland for disturbing the peace during Lord Poulteney's Hunt and looks as though the "Stuart"'s our man. He's young, dark and the best of it is he was also booked for possession of an offensive weapon, i.e., a Stanley knife, which, as you'll remember, was given by the lab as the most likely kind of knife to have done the damage.'

'So why in hell didn't they follow that up after they heard about the saddle?'

'They did, but he denied everything and produced a girlfriend in London who said they had been together all night in her camper van.'

Milton thought for a moment. 'Bring the girl in.'

'What about him?'

'Get him when you've already got her.'

Pooley nodded obediently and turned towards the door.

'One more thing, Ellis.'

'Yes, sir?'

'It was your hunch, not ours. Well done.'

'One of the aspects of my job I most dislike is bullying the inadequate,' said Milton, as he and Pooley sat in Amiss's living room late, two evenings after the murders. 'But it worked. The girlfriend was a pathetic washed-out creature who seems to have joined the sabs for a social life, the way girls in the Home Counties join the Young Conservatives. She got so upset when I told her that her pal Stuart had been having it off in the tack room, that he had tried to murder someone and that she would be charged with being an accessory after the fact if she didn't cough up the truth smartly that she burst into tears and blubbed everything out immediately. It was made easier by the fact that he isn't really her boyfriend. He just deigns to screw her occasionally when it's convenient.'

'And Stuart himself?'

'In an effort to keep both ladies out of it I told him that if he confessed immediately to causing criminal damage I would drop the charge of attempted murder. He wanted to know what we'd got on him and I simply said, "Enough", and that if he didn't accept my offer now it would be withdrawn. He shrugged and agreed.'

'But can you be sure you didn't frighten an innocent man into admitting something he didn't do?'

'Give me credit for not being an idiot, Robert. He described the tack room in some detail.'

'Why didn't he split on Vanessa?'

'Who knows? Perhaps he's hoping she might be in the market for a bit of rough trade on a regular basis. Anyway, that's it. She's out of it. So, by the way, is he, since he has a solid alibi for the evening of the murders. So I'm back to the conclusion that it's not credible that anyone would indulge in such an elaborate massacre as a cover for killing one person.'

'But you're not ruling it out,' said Pooley.

'No, no. Don't fret, Ellis. You know nothing is being ruled out. But the fact is that if you want to knock off your granny you can find a hitman for a couple of thousand quid, so it's hard to see why you would decide to mount an operation of such complexity – not to speak of such wickedness.'

'What a nice old-fashioned word, Jim.' Amiss handed him a tumbler of whisky and a jug of water. 'Only the cops, the religious and the very old use it these days.'

'Evil would be better in this case.'

'So how was it done?'

'The assassin, can you believe, was almost certainly located behind the false ceiling of the chamber?'

'What?'

134

'Yes. False ceiling. There's lots of room up there and there was recent disturbance to the dust.'

'Any useful clues?'

Milton shook his head. 'A pro, it would seem. Plastic bags on his feet, protective clothing, all that kind of thing.'

Pooley shook his head sadly. 'Even Freeman Wills Croft wouldn't have had any joy with what he left.'

'Who?'

'Oh Jim, you really should read some old detective stories. You can't imagine what you've missed out on. He had this sleuth, Inspector French, who was always discovering the identity of the murderer by extrapolating from minute clues, like a thread from a sports jacket or the fact that the 5.03 was seventeen minutes late on the evening in question.'

'Thanks, Ellis. I can't wait.' He turned back to Amiss. 'But though he did a pretty thorough job on scattering the dust in the areas he walked on, our lads are pretty convinced from a couple of the better prints that he's of average height and weight.'

'Oh, that's fine then,' said Amiss. 'They'll have him in no time. How did he do it?'

'By use of what the boffins call a "microwave-directed energy weapon".'

Amiss looked blank.

'A kind of souped-up stun-gun.'

'Must be pretty damn souped-up to kill at that range. What are we talking about? A hundred feet from behind the ceiling to the poor old buggers beneath?'

'Something like that.'

'And it just simply jammed the pacemakers.'

'More than that. Most of them could have lasted for hours or days before their hearts gave out. But this weapon induced enough resonance in the pacemakers to give a fatal kick to the heart before complete electrical failure.'

'Where did the power come from?'

'Electrical energy stored in a bank of capacitors. If you really want the technical details, I'll dig them out of my briefcase.'

'Don't bother,' said Amiss hastily. 'I can't even understand how electricity works. Just tell me about size and availability.'

'It probably needed about three feet of capacitors and the same length of tube. As for availability . . . These things can be got easily in America and anything you can get there you can get here for a price.'

'So could he have taken out more than he did? I can't believe the only pacemakers in the House of Lords were on the Tory benches.'

'No, there were about four on the cross benches and about a dozen on the other side.'

'So he was positioned deliberately to get the Tories?'

'Presumably. It was an impressive operation all round. I can't think he'd have slipped up on where to direct his death ray.'

'Yes,' said Pooley. 'Although he could hardly have been certain he would definitely get whoever he wanted to get. So presumably he was relaxed about that.'

'Any clues about the motivation?'

Milton took a piece of paper out of his inside pocket and passed it to Amiss. 'The Avengers sent this to the Press Association this evening.

'We issued a warning that anyone who tortured or defended the torture of animals should expect punishment. We have therefore made an example of Lord Poulteney along with some of his companions in evil.

'In order to bring home to other criminals what will be the consequences of continuing along this path, we had to secure maximum publicity. It was for that reason that the execution of Poulteney was carried out in the manner in which it was. We regret that some innocent people died, but in war innocent people always die. If more deaths are to be prevented, then all those opposing the bill must drop their opposition and agree to have it go through committee unamended. The wages of their sin will be death. The Avengers will show no more mercy than do the hunters.'

'Well, you certainly can't accuse them of ambiguity.' Amiss passed the paper back. 'Although it would be helpful to know on what scale they are proposing to operate.'

Milton shrugged. 'Bombs? Running amok with Kalashnikovs? Nerve gas? Who knows. All we can do is step up security massively, which we've done. But you can imagine what it's like trying to make the Lords secure. For all we know, it's crammed full of murder weapons already.'

'Haven't you searched it?'

'Oh, we've searched it, but it's a bit like sending an army of ants into the QE2. It would take us months of lifting every floorboard and every panel to declare that building safe, and even then we couldn't be sure.'

'Christ.' Amiss ran his fingers through his hair. 'As the Yanks would say, I really can't get my head around this one. There's too much frantic behaviour by too many people on too many fronts.'

'Well, I'm just a simple policeman. Unlike you intellectuals, all I can do is go down the obvious paths along with the rest of my colleagues.'

'And what are they?'

'Our hypothesis is that they really are Avengers and that they mean what they say. These seem to be big-time boys.'

'What do you know about them?'

'Nothing. But we're looking. Our anti-terrorist people — supplemented by resources from the Murder Squad and local police forces — are dredging up all the information they have on animal activists and interviewing those thought to be most dangerous. So we should have a clearer idea of who's who in a day or so. But we are, of course, keeping an open mind and interviewing the family and friends of all the deceased just in case there turns out to be an exceptionally strong motive for murder.'

'I know I have a vested interest here, but what are you doing on the preventative front?'

'Special Branch have been drafted in to guard those seen to be most at risk. But there are an awful lot of them and not enough chaps to guard them. I put you high on the list, but I'm afraid you were turned down as insufficiently important. But we've got a round-the-clock guard on Jack Troutbeck and her pals.'

'I see. You have to be titled to be worth protecting these days.'

'It's more that our people think you have to have a title to be worth murdering. Sorry about that.'

'I fervently hope they're right. On some issues, I have no objection to being discriminated against on grounds of class. Another drink?'

'Please. Now what have *you* been up to?'

'Helping Jack and company regroup their forces. This has so far involved our lunching with Beesley at the Cavalry Club, dining with Stormerod at the Carlton and tomorrow we're lunching with Deptford at the Lords, assuming it's been given security clearance by then. I'm certainly being fed and watered well and regularly on this job.'

'What's the plan?'

'Basically, to conduct what these days is called a charm offensive, but Jack calls it a publicity blitz. Her thesis is that since the media are going to be alive with this story for some time to come, we should capitalize by trying to force people to think rationally about fox-hunting and interfering with the rights of others.'

'Seems sensible if you can find good spokesmen. What else?'

'Hold the group together. Do a good job in committee. Stop any tendency to cave in. We're going to have a meeting to stiffen resolve and cry, "No surrender!"'

'Mind you,' said Pooley, 'I bet there'll be a considerable falling-off in your numbers. I don't want to disabuse your romantic notions, but in my experience not all the aristocracy are heroes. Don't be surprised if there's a lot of backsliding.'

'It's a pretty perilous business backsliding when Jack Troutbeck doesn't want you to. It might require even more heroism than standing firm.'

'Just be careful,' said Milton. 'I had a routine interview with your friend Jack yesterday and I took to her. But while it's one thing for her to risk her own life, I'm not so happy at the cavalier way she's risking yours.'

'Cavalier's the word. That's our Jack. The problem is, you see, that she believes that she is invincible and that therefore by extension so must be anyone under her protection.'

'I see. The way she put it to me was that it was a matter of noblesse oblige.'

'She's certainly getting maximum enjoyment out of her peerage,' said Amiss.

'But she has a great sense of duty as well.' Pooley nodded approvingly.

'Anyway,' said Milton, 'the most useful thing you can do, Robert, is to keep a close eye on what she's up to, let us know if she's being particularly reckless and watch your own back.' He looked at his watch. 'Got to be off. I need to look in at the Yard and then catch up on some sleep.'

'How's Ann?' Amiss asked Milton as he ushered them out.

'Still absent. Possibly permanently.'

'What!'

'She's been offered tenure at that American university, wants me to chuck it all in here, join her and find a new way of making a living.'

'But why?'

'You know she never liked the police. I think she wants to save me.'

'And you?'

'I think I'm unsaveable. It's in my blood. How's Rachel?'

Amiss groaned. 'Latest news is there's no chance of her being back here for at least six months. And now these murders have happened she wants me to go back to Delhi. But I can't. At least, I won't. Not till this is cleared up.'

Pooley looked at them sympathetically. 'I must say, you two are certainly doing your best to bring home to me the advantages of being single. At least then you know where you are.'

As Milton put the phone down, there was a knock on his door. 'Come in.'

'Sir, I've been thinking.'

Milton surveyed Pooley with that familiar mingling of wariness and hope. 'About what?'

139

'About the Animal Avengers. I'm sure they're modelled on the Four Just Men. You know. Edgar Wallace.'

'Sorry, Ellis. You know this stuff is a closed book to me. Elaborate.'

'Well, Wallace wrote about these just men who set themselves up as judge, jury and executioner in cases where the law had failed. They used to get together – with cloaks and black caps and the rest of it, if I remember correctly – survey the case dispassionately and then decide how to carry out the sentence. So, for instance, they once murdered the Home Secretary for passing a bill they thought unjust and another time, and this is more relevant, they killed a man who was about to eradicate the common earthworm.'

'Well, even I would kill someone who was about to eradicate the common earthworm since that act in itself would probably bring about the end of the world.' There was a silence. 'So, Ellis, what particularly makes you suppose that these Avengers, if they exist, are inspired by this low literature?'

'Tone, really. The righteousness seemed very familiar.'

'Almost more in sorrow than in anger, you mean?'

'Yes.'

Milton shrugged. 'You may be right, but so what?'

'Well, nothing much except that it suggests that somebody old is in on it. My guess would be that anybody young wouldn't even have heard of Edgar Wallace, unless they were crime fiction fanatics like me.'

'OK, Ellis. Thank you. I'll bear it in mind. You might bring me a sample of the literature sometime. Just at the moment I could use some tips on how to murder the Home Secretary.'

Pooley rushed out with that eager gait that so endeared him to a boss who often required a respite from the company of his jaded, cynical colleagues.

'You'd have thought the demonstrators would have been a bit embarrassed by what has happened. Instead they seem to have redoubled their efforts.' Amiss sounded slightly breathless, for he and the baroness had just struggled once again through a screaming mob, their path made possible by

140

an honour guard of police which had, from time to time, almost given way under the sheer weight of protestors.

'Don't be silly. We're not dealing with people with finer feelings. If you ask me, we're dealing with a lot of fucking anarchists who choose to march under the banner of animal activism. They're trying to bring down the state, not stop people kicking hedgehogs.'

'I'm sure I saw some woolly hats.'

'Just because you're old doesn't mean you're not an anarchist,' she growled. 'Christ, I need a drink. Come on.' And she sped off in the direction of the bar.

They were sitting at lunch with Deptford at the same table they had occupied the day after Jack's introduction, with the same waitress, the same menu and the same conversations going on around them about the merits of roly-poly over sticky-toffee pudding.

'You know,' said Amiss, 'the place seems completely unaffected by what has happened. It continues to be a sea of tranquillity.'

'The point of great institutions,' said the baroness, 'is that they stand up to disasters without losing their nerve. After all, when you think how the Lords has managed to hold off the waves of modernizers, you can't expect them to be overexcited by a few corpses.'

'Come off it, Jack,' said Deptford. 'And Robert, for that matter. First of all, there's only half the usual number here. And second, I bet quite a few of 'em's covering up blind panic. It's not going to be easy to get 'em to turn out for the Committee, I can tell you.'

'Well, we've just got to stir them up and rally them with the old Agincourt spirit,' said the baroness firmly. 'And we're starting with a meeting of the hard core on Tuesday to take stock and decide who's going to do what.'

She turned to Amiss. 'Book the committee room, then, for eleven o'clock, Tuesday morning. Try and get 4. I like the royal iconography. Order the hard core . . .' She smiled grimly. 'Or at least those that are left, to turn up. Say Bertie said they have to be there. I cleared it with him this morning before he hightailed it to Buttermere. Say there's to be no backsliding. Won't stand for it. Got to show these buggers who's boss.' She became aware of the hovering form. 'Right, Agnes. Yes, please. I'll have the soup. And then the lamb, but make sure it's pink.'

Agnes betrayed no sign of having heard. 'My lord?'

Deptford gestured towards Amiss. 'I'll have the same. But I'd like the lamb well done, if you don't mind?'

'My lord?'

'Soup and sole, please, Agnes. And we'll start with a bottle of Chablis.'

Lips pursed, Agnes made a note.

'Cheer up,' said the baroness. 'The sun's shining.'

'I hardly think cheerfulness is appropriate, my lady.' With a sniff, she stalked away.

'It needs a Scottish accent like hers to extract the maximum venom from a line like that,' observed Amiss. 'You really annoy her, don't you?'

'Can't say she's too keen on anyone,' said Deptford. 'She can't stand Bertie, of all people. And 'ee's usually the waitresses' dreamboat. Tries to avoid serving him. Told Lillian she thought he was patronizing.'

'No point in dwelling on miserable sods.' The baroness laughed. 'Only in a place like this could one be rebuked for inappropriate behaviour a few days after eight of the inhabitants had been mown down by a maniac. You'd think she'd be glad to see someone. The joint's hardly jumping.'

'Are you surprised?' asked Amiss. 'Business has been suspended all week and most of your colleagues seem understandably inclined to sit at home and nurse their wounds rather than instantly plunge into working out next steps on what is, after all, only to do with fox-hunting.'

'It's no good lying down under adversity. At the risk of sounding bathetic, Reggie and the rest of them wouldn't want to have died in vain. It's our job to ensure they haven't. So we'd better get on with it.'

Deptford smiled at her. 'You're an example to us all, luv.'

'Forget the flannel, Sid. To work. Who can we find to share the media burden? Requests are coming in thick and fast

142

and you and I seem to be the only pro-hunting peers left in town. Except for Tommy.'

'No, no. Not Tommy,' said Amiss. 'Not unless you want to throw in the towel with the public immediately. Fox-hunters would become a laughing stock.'

Deptford groaned. 'Robert's right, o'course. I'll back you up by doing the ones you can't do, Jack. But you'd better face it. You're going to have to take the lead for the moment. At least until Bertie gets back on Tuesday.'

'Don't know if I'll be any good at it.'

'Just be yourself. That'll be enough to hold everyone's attention.'

18

'So fill me in then,' requested Milton.

'As I told you before, between mainstream, fringe and splinter groups, there are probably a couple of dozen,' said Paul Jarrett. 'Though I can't say we're really experts on them yet. It's only recently we began to realize that some of them really are terrorists. They fall more or less into four groups. First, what you might call Establishment animal protectors: the Royal Society for the Prevention of Cruelty of Animals, the League Against Cruel Sports and so on. They write letters to MPs, pass resolutions, send out press statements and try to win arguments.'

Milton scribbled a few words. 'OK. Next.'

'Groups like Compassion in World Farming which are ninety per cent full of nice, decent people, concerned about cruelty to animals, whether it be battery farming or transporting animals in inhumane conditions to be slaughtered cruelly abroad. They got strongly involved in the hunting issue in recent months because of the barrage of one-sided propaganda. Groups in this category believe in peaceful protest, but increasingly they've been infiltrated by members of the third group – animal rights people – who to say the least have a pretty loose definition of the word "peaceful". Some of them want straightforward civil disobedience, and others – like the sabs – actively encourage violence.'

Milton nodded. 'With you so far.'

'Now to confuse the issue, what you might call categories B and C have also been infiltrated by Trotskyites – members of the Socialist Workers' Party and others less well known and even more sinister. The Trots don't give a tuppenny fuck for animals; their agenda is simply to foment discord wherever it arises. Poll-tax riots, motorway protests, nationalist street protests in Derry, demonstrations against cuts in the NHS – and now animal issues – it's all the same to them. All they want is to take the peace out of peaceful and try to get us to overreact and injure members of the public. So they shout and scream and throw things and by fanning flames and encouraging a riot here and there hope to undermine our democracy.'

'Are they potential murderers?'

'Doubt it. Not most of them, anyway. Though not everyone would agree with me. But the fourth group certainly are. They're the terrorists who send letter bombs, plant the odd car bomb and are so fanatical I believe them capable of anything. Because they're undercover we don't know much about them. We think Jerry Dolamore is their public face.'

'You mean you think he's in favour of murder?'

'I think so. But I can't prove it.'

'What about the peaceful fruitcakes like Brother Francis. Hasn't he got some organization called something like Bunnies for Jesus?'

Jarrett grinned. 'Not quite. But he calls the manor house he inherited from his father the Sanctuary; it's a kind of retreat for animals and animal activists. Dolamore's been there a lot.'

'Do you think they're in cahoots?'

'Definitely. Though I don't know who is the leader and who the led. At the moment we're dredging up information on Dolamore and we'd be grateful if you'd do the same on Brother Francis. He has to be a suspect since he's such a fanatic. And he could have fired the stun-gun. Contrary to Lords etiquette, he had left the chamber immediately after speaking and at the time of the murders he was allegedly praying in his room. So what we really want to know is what he's capable of, and you're more likely to be able to find that out without attracting attention than we are.'

'Sure. I'll get to it straightaway. Talk to you tomorrow.'

*   *   *

145

'When did he leave his order?'

'Not long after he got the title, I gather, sir. About two years ago. Shall I get the clippings?'

'Please, Ellis.'

The file was thick, but most of the contents were pretty repetitive. Milton glanced through some poems, but when he got to the lines:

> The lion's tender with his cub
> Gently licking and cuffing him in the scrub

he grimaced, and put the rest on one side.

Until very recently material about Brother Francis had been mainly confined to women's magazines, with the occasional saccharine piece in a tabloid. 'Saint Who Puts His Kitten First' was a not untypical article, focusing as it did on how Brother Francis had spent an entire night sitting beside the sick bed of his kitten, Tiddles. 'Millionaire Peer Gives His All To His Animals' came when he announced on his father's death that he would use all his material possessions for the good of animals and would not renounce the Purseglove title, since it would give him a platform from which to defend them. He would not, he explained to a reporter, sell up and give the proceeds to the recognized animal charities, for he felt that they were too much part of the Establishment. He wanted to harness the idealism of the young, so he had decided to set up a little commune of animals and their lovers in his family home.

In a profile in a particularly glutinous women's magazine a few months later there was much about Tiddles and Georgie and Becky and Bobbie, respectively cat, dog, hamster and donkey, and how they and all the other little birdies and animals were in communion at Locksleigh Manor, along with those visitors who came for spiritual refreshment. Brother Francis was happy, but he admitted it had been a great wrench to leave the monastery where he had lived so happily for so many years. But he had had no option, for he knew the legacy to be a sign from God that he had been called to a special vocation. His abbot was quoted as confining his remarks to the press to a terse message on behalf of the community wishing their brother well.

Apart from reports of speeches at public meetings and in the Lords, the only other interesting piece was from a reporter who had recently enquired of inhabitants in his local village what they thought of their saintly lord. Attributed comments included: 'proper gentleman' and 'holy man'; unattributed ranged from 'potty' and 'barmy' to – in an outbreak of rural wit – 'two brain cells short of a halfwit'. A few locals grumbled that the ban he had placed on hunting across his land had caused deep and bad feeling.

Milton sat and thought for a moment, then rang directory enquiries.

'I came alone, I thought it might make it easier to talk.'

'Ah, so you are looking to me, Chief Superintendent, to be indiscreet about my brother in Christ.' The abbot giggled. Although their telephone conversation had led Milton to expect a friendly response, the friar's sheer joviality took him aback. His features were as plump as Brother Francis's were drawn, as rubicund as the other was colourless.

'Well, fire away. What do you want to know?'

Milton put down his tea cup. 'Is he capable of murder?'

'If you're asking me if I think Brother Francis might have been capable of devising such a sophisticated method of dispatching his ideological enemies and of then carrying it out, certainly not. As it was too painfully clear here, he is not what you would call a practical man.

'The jobs he was capable of doing, other than writing his unspeakable poetry . . . You look surprised. Just because I'm a Franciscan doesn't mean I'm daft. It is wretched poetry, which is an insult to human beings as well as to animals. I don't want to be duly anthropomorphic, but if I were a tiger described as "gentle pussy of the jungle", I would be inclined to hire a lawyer and sue for defamation.

'However, as I was saying, Brother Francis was so hopeless with his hands and so entirely without . . .' He paused to search for the *mot juste*. '. . . Without a shred of common sense, that he was frankly an encumbrance.' He tittered. 'I

147

can tell you that it is proof of our Christian charity that we didn't end up murdering him ourselves. I mean, for a start, he couldn't do gardening because he was obsessed about not killing insects. He couldn't look after the hens because he disapproved of eating eggs. He was really a Buddhist, was Francis, masquerading as an Anglo-Catholic friar. So mainly we put him on cleaning duties, but he was so dozy that most of that was beyond him too. If there was anything to break, he'd break it.'

'Nursing?'

'The sick, you mean? Trouble there was that he was frankly irritating. When you're sick you want somebody calm, confident and good with their hands, not somebody who'll fret and drop things. So for most purposes we left him to himself to do the best he could. Treated him essentially as our village idiot – a cross sent to us by God to test us.' The abbot laughed. 'Does that answer your question to your satisfaction?'

'Yes. I can see he doesn't appear cut out to be a criminal mastermind. But might he have helped?'

'You mean is this funny colony of his a mask for taking arms against persecutors of animals?'

'Yes. A violent cult, in other words.'

'I believe that Brother Francis would be more upset at the death of a kitten or indeed a fox than of a human being. I often wondered why, and came to the conclusion that the great attraction of animals was, shall we say, that they were uncritical. But that is not to say that he disliked people. No, by and large, he was a peaceable creature who would not wittingly do anyone any harm. Indeed, I would describe him where people are concerned as tender-hearted.'

'But could he be brainwashed?'

'He's certainly weak-minded enough for that. But I stick to the belief that there is nothing violent in the man. I could see him throwing himself in front of horses and hounds to save the life of a fox and thus cause injury and death, but only unintentionally. And you could, in any case, rely on him to launch himself at the wrong time and generally' – the abbot sighed rather wearily – 'once more demonstrate his capacity for messing everything up.'

He looked appraisingly at Milton. 'You shouldn't depend on my word alone. Why don't you join us for dinner and talk to some of the others. Your driver would be most welcome too, though perhaps lest he inhibit conversation, it might be better for him to eat separately.'

'All in all,' reported Milton to Amiss when he rang him from home the next morning, 'it was rather a jolly break in the proceedings.'

'Are you joining up?'

'I don't think I'll go to quite those lengths, but it's been a revelation to me to find that friars can be fun.'

'And they're all of one mind?'

'Absolutely. No one present ever saw Brother Francis harm his fellow man or beast except by accident. They're glad to be rid of him, but to a man they'd be astounded if he ever committed or helped the commission of a violent act. They would not, however, be astounded if someone succeeded in pulling the wool over his eyes.'

'So what does today hold?'

'Getting the goods on Dolamore. Jarrett's mob have a dossier.'

Jerry Dolamore, it emerged, was forty. Australian sources reported that he had left school in Perth with no qualifications at sixteen, drifting into a beach-based world where he'd proved to be short on athletic talent. He was sacked from a job as a lifeguard, moved to Sydney and for a time dallied with the world of gay liberation, but he seemed to have been neither sufficiently attractive nor committed to be anything other than an also-ran in a world of bronzed and handsome young men.

In his late twenties he had come to England, worked in bars in Earls Court and for a time hung around with gay activists. Yet again he had been sidelined.

'That,' said Jarrett, 'was when he seems to have decided to go in search of a new cause.'

Milton was puzzled. 'What I can't understand, bearing in

149

mind all I've heard about his oratorical talents, is why he got nowhere in the gay movement?'

'Because gays don't want to be led by fanatical demagogues. For the most part they make their case through the use of economic power, the courts and lobbying. Few of them have a penchant for standing in great halls shouting *Sieg Heil*. Besides, at that stage Dolamore had no idea how effective he was as a public speaker. He appears to have drifted into the animal-activist business when he went to a public meeting out of curiosity and made a spontaneous speech which went down a treat. Within six months he was recognized as a great rabble rouser and — like orators often do — having started by saying what would please an audience, he came to believe it himself and so entered a vicious spiral of extremism.

'My guess is that what he actually thinks about animals is as unclear to him as it is to us. No one in Australia ever remembers him passing an opinion on animals, and in that land of huge steaks and barbecues, being a vegetarian — let alone a vegan — would have been a cause for considerable comment. No, I think the truth is that Dolamore was desperate for attention and possibly power and therefore took up the most promising cause.'

'And do you think he would use violence?'

'Only to increase his power. But I have to admit, it's hard to see how these murders could help since he couldn't claim the credit publicly without ending up in the clink.'

'So where does that get us?'

'Fucked if I know. But we're putting the fear of God into some of those around him at the moment. So watch this space.'

19

Media coverage went in three stages. First was extensive coverage of all the victims, with the tabloids printing page after page of photographs of them in robes and coronets, with, where possible, coverage of their more glamorous womenfolk. Vanessa was snapped coming out of her house in a short black suit, with the caption: 'Heartbroken daughter-in-law, the new Lady Poulteney'. The broadsheets were meanwhile conducting exhaustive investigations into the reliability of pacemakers and the argument for a second chamber, reformed or otherwise. Then came the death-ray sensation, which allowed editors to indulge their technically minded readers with acres of descriptions of weaponry. And finally, because of the Animal Avengers, attention was focused on animal activists and the pros and cons of the Wild Mammals (Protection) Bill. To her surprise – but not to Amiss's – the baroness became a celebrity virtually overnight, for the media and public were bored with the traditional adversaries on hunting. Over the preceding few weeks, concerned woolly hats, former huntsmen who'd converted to being anti, former antis who'd converted to being pro, farmers who said hunts conserved the landscape, farmers who complained of wanton damage, toffs who were Masters of Foxhounds, saboteur spokesmen and all the rest of the caravanserie had exhausted the interest of the British people. But the Lords outrage had not only got every pub in the land arguing about the issue, but had found an overnight star. Because of his background, Sid Deptford had a certain curiosity value, but essentially he served up the same old story over and over again. What grabbed everyone was the way the baroness dealt with the opposition – one by one.

For a start, she was the only one who could handle Brother Francis, whose gentleness, sincerity and mawkish verses made him initially a great hit and one whom interviewers found hard to handle. Beating up politicians was one thing, viciously interrogating a self-sacrificing, soft-spoken saint who had given up all worldly delights for what the British public held most dear was another. But once Jack Troutbeck began to temper her tendency to interject 'Balderdash' or 'Rubbish', she became adept at dragging her opponent into the real world, where he cut a poor figure. She would recite lines of Brother Francis's back to him and ask politely what they meant. Most viewers laughed on the occasion when she recited:

> *'Oh for a fluffy bunny king*
> *His paw commanding everything*
> *With a cuddly kitty queen*
> *Whose twitching whiskers rule serene,*
> *Their folk all furry, frisky fun,*
> *Bright-eyed and joyful every one.'*

Was Brother Francis really recommending that we emulate the morals of rabbits? she asked. And surely cats were the greatest hunters on earth? And when he fumbled, she would put the fear of God into the viewers by saying that the logical implications of what he and the animal activists stood for was the outlawing of domestic pets: if animals were our equals we had no right to own them. This notion struck chill into the hearts of the owners of Tibbies throughout the nation.

When they threw Lady Parsons at her, she showed her up for the cold fish she was, eliciting the information that she had never lived with animals, whereas she, Jack Troutbeck, was able to call on sixty years of close companionship with dogs, cats, horses and the rest of it. What had she done when she became Mistress of St Martha's? She had insisted the kitchen use only free-range eggs and meat from properly looked-after animals, she had brought peacocks to live in the front garden and two abused donkeys had been given sanctuary in the grounds. 'I'm extremely fond of animals,' she explained. 'I may eat them, I may chase them occasionally for sport, I'm very clear they have no souls, but I don't want to cause them pain and where possible I like them to have a jolly good time. I think that's a humane position.'

She was even better at dealing with Jerry Dolamore, who, like most demagogues, was unimpressive in conversation and too slow-witted for debate. The febrile quality, the nervous energy and the hint that underneath the surface he was a volcano – which made him so exciting as an orator – came across on television as rather mad. As Amiss remarked to the baroness, if television had only been invented some decades earlier, Hitler would probably have never come to power. Worse again, Dolamore's supporters were incapable of exercising the necessary restraint to keep viewers on their side. Ugly studio-audience scenes of people in their twenties screaming at a feisty grey-haired woman did not go down well with the Great British Public and its notions of fair play. Not that the hecklers bothered the lady herself; she perfected a tolerant look with which she prefaced assaults on Dolamore on the issues of freedom of speech and the use of violence. While she did not accuse him of being one of the Animal Avengers, she pronounced his avowed strategy of intimidation to be incompatible with free speech. Ruthlessly she appealed to xenophobia when she explained to him kindly that as a foreigner he would perhaps have a problem in understanding that the British held free speech dear and that those who understood the very essence of the nation would never give in to threats. It was not for this, she explained, to the cheers of a studio audience, that this little country had stood alone against what – like Winston Churchill – she pronounced the 'Naazi' menace. Fortunately, she explained, she knew that her companions in the Lords would stand firm and not dance to the murderers' tune.

'Why ain't she runnin' the bleedin' country?' asked Deptford of Amiss on the telephone one morning.

'Because it's a democracy, Sid. I fear the populace would

not for long accept being pushed around the way we are. Look at what they did to Mrs Thatcher.'

'Yeah, but Jack's more fun.'

'The British don't like their leaders to be fun. Bet you she's got a media shelf life of only a few weeks.'

'That's OK, me old mate. It's all we need. Now, should we answer that toffee-nosed article in the *Independent on Sunday*?'

'It's Paul, Jim. Charlie's pulled him in.'

'Who?'

'Dolamore. Thinks he might have organized the murders to establish his supremacy over the animal-activist movement.'

'Any evidence?'

'I wouldn't go that far. But after being held for twenty-four hours one of his ex-sidekicks was so anxious to be helpful that he spilled the beans on Dolamore's attempt last year to establish a sort of Grand Council of all the looney groups whom he called together at Locksleigh Manor. Apparently it was mayhem. Most of these groups say they operate by consensus, which means anarchy. Mostly they can never take decisions about anything except making trouble in public. So there was old Dolamore trying to persuade a gaggle of the innocent and well-meaning, as well as of fanatics, fascists, anarchists and in some cases even psychopaths to bend to his will.'

'I'd like to have been there. What happened?'

'It went on for five hours, consisted of about three dozen people because the groups with more than one member sent at least three representatives. They were impossible to control and the whole thing ended in uproar. The only thing which was agreed was that they wanted to take direct action, but couldn't agree what it should be. According to this bloke, that was when Dolamore decided to go his own way, side by side with Brother Francis, hoping, by whipping up public support, to become the great guru of the movement, which to an extent he's done. The bloke suggested he might have teamed up with the most violent end of the movement and tried to establish his supremacy by masterminding the murders in the inner circle.'

'Sounds thin.'

'It is thin. But that won't stop Charlie.'

'I wouldn't like to be Dolamore.'

'I wouldn't like to be Charlie's mother if she got on the wrong side of him. Cheers. I'll keep you posted.'

As Milton put the phone down he wondered once again why he was a policeman.

'Cancel the lot of them.'

'Who? What?' Amiss was only half awake.

'Bertie can't make it.'

'Why not?'

'He's just rung to say he's missed the fast train to London.'

Amiss looked blearily at his alarm clock, which showed 7.30. 'He's still got time to get down, hasn't he?'

'No. He's still surrounded.'

'Jack, will you please tell me what you are talking about?'

She adopted her oh-very-well-if-I've-got-to-spell-this-out tone. 'He rang me, on his mobile phone, from the end of his drive, where he has been trapped for some considerable time by a group of enraged woolly hats and riffraff. The police are on their way – but it is a long way – and he says he has no chance of getting to London until this afternoon.'

'Can't we go ahead without him?'

'Without Bertie? You must be mad. He's the only leader we've got.'

'What about you?'

'I'm disappointed in you, Robert. My leadership as yet has to be exercised by stealth.'

'Hah!' said Amiss. 'What about all that carry-on over the airwaves since Friday?'

'That's different. My peers aren't yet ready for me. Stop arguing and ring round and change them to the same time tomorrow. Can't be helped. Oh, and don't forget to rebook the committee room.'

'It would be easier to serve you, Jack, if you didn't vacillate

wildly between treating me as a mind-reader and a moron.'
But he had already lost her.

'Must fly,' she said absent-mindedly. 'Dragons to slay. See
you.'

Amiss spent half the morning trying to track down peers,
and the other half in the Lords placating those who had
turned up. At the end he felt obliged to have lunch with two
particularly aggrieved old dodderers who had come down on
the night train from Aberdeen and who didn't know what
the country was coming to. That evening, after switching
on the six o'clock news, Amiss was minded to agree.

'Massive explosion at the House of Lords: several feared
dead,' said the announcer expressionlessly. Amiss waited in
a cold panic as she produced a few measured lines on the
latest row between London and Brussels and Europe and
then revealed that a bank clerk had been killed in an armed
robbery in Manchester. After an age she returned to the first
item: 'At four-thirty p.m. a committee room on the first floor
of the House of Lords was racked by a series of minor
explosions.

'Early police estimates are that there have been about ten
fatalities, but owing to difficulties of identification, names
are not likely to be released for some time. The Lord Chancellor has vowed that the upper house will stand firm in
the face of this second outrage and the Prime Minister has
promised that no effort will be spared to bring the perpetrators to justice.'

Switching off the platitudes, Amiss rushed to the telephone. He got straight through to the baroness.

'Thank God. I was terrified it was you.'

'What was me?'

'Blown up. A committee room in the Lords. Haven't you
heard?'

'Well, well,' she said when he had finished. 'Things certainly seem to be hotting up. I'm glad it wasn't us, but I'm
sorry for the poor devils who copped it.'

'Instead of us, presumably?'

'Well, it's certainly as good a working hypothesis as I can
think of. You'd better come down.'

'Why? The action is here.'

'First, because however tasteless it might be, I think we should crack open some champagne once more to celebrate being alive. But also because you're more useful here. You're not going to be able to track down your tame rozzers tonight. Everything that has to be done we can do by phone and I need my Watson by my side.'

'Bloody cheek. I'm a more experienced sleuth than you are.'

'Stop arguing and get cracking.'

By the time Amiss reached St Martha's it was after dinner, but the baroness had laid in supplies of thick slices of cold ham, Stilton and brown bread, which she urged on him as she poured a glass of the claret which, for its richness and robustness, had been chosen as the college's recommended red tipple.

'I had something on the train.'

'Rubbish. You can't get anything on the train except tasteless pap. Eat up, you're going to need all your strength.'

'Why?' He pushed Plutarch away from the ham, took a large swallow of claret and looked at her suspiciously. 'What do I need to be braced for? Whom have we lost?'

'None of our stalwarts. It was a sub-committee to discuss some amendment to a town-planning bill which hadn't much grabbed the interest of the landed gentry, so of the rumoured names only poor old Gussy Barnacle was identifiably one of us. But the other side lost three or four, including . . . have another drink.'

'Who?'

'Beatrice Parsons.'

'Christ! It's not claret I need, it's whisky.'

Ever the perfect hostess, the baroness instantly produced a bottle of Black Bush and poured him a quadruple. He took a large swallow gratefully and subsided into an armchair.

'Why has that rattled you so much?'

'I don't know. I couldn't stand her, but . . .'

'Yes. I feel the same.' She took a meditative pull on her

157

pipe. 'Somehow it seems wrong to have one's enemy slain by another hand.'

'I hope the cops think it's another hand. Have you thought they mightn't?'

'Of course I have. What do you take me for? And so has Bertie, who, I may say, for a man of such usual coolness under fire, is a bit unnerved. He said he hadn't anticipated that a row over fox-hunting was going to turn into the Battle of the Somme.'

'So what do you know?'

'Well, I've checked all our hard core and everyone's safe and well. But it looks as if they and us are only safe and well because of Bertie being taken hostage by the animal activists this morning. The bombs went off in committee room 4, so what's the betting they were intended for us?'

'A hundred to one, I suppose. Though surely whoever was trying to get us would have removed them when we didn't show?'

'Maybe it was too difficult. Who knows? Anyway, the Home Secretary's told Bertie the Bomb Squad's preliminary view is that there was was a bomb under each of the twenty cushions; eleven were set off.'

'But . . .'

'Yes, I know. How could they all have sat down at exactly the same moment? Look, there's no point now in bothering our heads with that sort of speculation. Wait till the boffins come up with the goods. We'll concentrate on what we understand.'

'So if they had been intended for us, they'd have got a clean sweep.'

'Are you sure you don't want that champagne?'

'Not tonight, thanks. I haven't the heart for it.'

The phone rang. As the baroness discussed plans with a still surprisingly calm Tommy Beesley, Amiss closed his eyes and tried to think pleasant thoughts about Rachel. Plutarch, who had just finished the ham, settled in appreciatively to the Stilton. She evinced no interest in the brown bread.

'That's all settled,' said the baroness as she came off the

phone. 'As many of us as can make it will meet at nine a.m. at Bertie's London pad to talk things over.'

'Nine?'

'Only time he could manage.'

'God, we'll have to get up before seven.'

'Six. We'll leave at six-thirty sharp so as to avoid the traffic. Then we can have a decent breakfast in London.'

'What's wrong with the train?'

'I want to drive.'

'How do you drive?'

'How do you think?'

'Could you summon a witness? I think it's time I made a will.' He looked round and saw a large ginger form nestled next to a gnawed piece of Stilton and drifting into sleep. 'And I'm going to leave Plutarch to you.'

'That's no threat.' The baroness rose, walked over to Plutarch and stroked her. 'She's a girl after my own heart – appreciates her vittles. Now stop whingeing and try and get hold of young Ellis Pooley. He might have some useful gen. Then I'll put you to bed.'

'I should have expected you to drive a souped-up nineteen thirties Aston Martin,' said Amiss as, relieved, he got into a comfortable seat in her modern saloon.

'Cars are cars. They should be fast and generously built. Rather like me.' Her chortle almost drowned out the revving of the engine as she sped down the drive.

'That racket should have woken half of St Martha's.'

'Do 'em good. Shouldn't be lazing in bed.'

'If you're awake, everyone should be awake, eh?'

'Naturally.'

Despite urban traffic, it took them less than an hour to cover the fifty-five miles to London, a feat which, because of inevitable hold-ups, involved the baroness taking the car to excessive speeds along several stretches of the motorway.

'Must you drive so fast?' said Amiss – trying to keep the panic out of his voice – the first time he saw the speedometer touch 110 m.p.h.

'I wouldn't call this fast. Stop whining. It's my job to drive

159

and yours to keep an eye out for the rozzers and speed traps and find us the *Today* programme.'

By the time they arrived in London, Amiss's nerves about the baroness's driving had been somewhat eased by his realization that – as in all dealings with her – one might as well lie back and enjoy it. From the radio they had learned little that was new except that the definitive tally was eleven, the names of all the victims and details of the two or three who were eminent enough to attract tributes from the mighty. The Prime Minister had been wheeled on to talk of the work of his beloved colleague, Lady Parsons, whose concern for the underprivileged had been an example to everyone in his party: she had been a dear friend and would be sorely missed by him even more personally than politically.

'Balls!' interjected the baroness. 'Bertie tells me the PM never could stand her and greatly regretted being pushed into giving her a peerage.'

The programme was long on shock and short on facts. All that emerged at the end was that there were now nineteen corpses and nobody was quite clear why – though the finger of suspicion appeared to be pointing firmly at what various commentators kept describing coyly as subversive elements.

'Pretty perfect description of you,' said Amiss, as the baroness took a short cut by driving the wrong way up a one-way street. 'Do you keep *any* rules?'

'Rules are for other people. I like breaking them.' She turned sharp right into a small car park, on the gate of which was a notice saying 'Private – no access except for staff and visitors to M. C. Carter Ltd', drove into a bay marked 'Visitors', switched off the engine, placed on the windscreen a notice saying, 'Attending conference', grabbed her holdall and climbed out of the car.

Amiss climbed out after her. 'You are outrageous.'

'You'll turn my head if you go on paying me such compliments. Now come on, let's step out briskly to the Ritz. We've got a long day ahead of us so we'd better stoke up well.'

20

'I'm knackered.' Amiss collapsed into Pooley's armchair.

'What do you think I am? I only had two hours in bed last night.'

'Yes, but you're spending your time with Jim. I'm spending mine with the Lady Troutbeck, who has just deposited me here after a sixteen-hour day and gone roaring into the night in high good humour, promising to beat her record of forty-five minutes to Cambridge. Her apparently inexhaustible supply of energy wears me out.'

'I take your point. Jim had the grace to admit to being too tired to come here tonight. Do you want a drink?'

'Naturally.'

'Whisky?'

'Yes.'

'Have you eaten?'

'Vast breakfast, huge lunch, don't need any more.'

'Well, forgive me if I get myself something. We were running around so much today we didn't have time for anything.'

Amiss was asleep by the time Pooley returned from the kitchen bearing a tray with two apples, a piece of cheese and a glass of milk. He awoke as a glass of whisky was put beside him.

'What an admirably healthy meal. Doubt if it would go down well with Jack. It's a bit austere, and besides, she thinks milk is for babies and cats.'

'Well, from what I've seen of her –' Pooley placed a piece of cheddar tidily on a brown cracker '– she's the exception that proves every rule. Now, while I'm eating, tell me anything I should know that you've picked up today.'

'Well, most of today has been squiring Jack around television and radio studios as she delivered variations on her we-shall-not-be-moved routine. She had a pretty clear run. Hear any of it?'

'No.'

'It was good stuff. She even managed a graceful tribute to Parsons. Jack prides herself on her ability to outdo the opposition when it comes to hypocrisy, so she came up with much about the sterling work of her fellow baroness and how tragic it was that this life of public service had been cut short by the action of insane supporters of hers in a cause both misplaced and ill-founded.'

'Any opposition to this line?'

'A couple of interviewers suggested the pro-hunting lobby might be behind this, but Jack brushed that aside as an absurd reflection on the stout-hearted people who kept our heritage alive in the British countryside. One of Jerry Dolamore's sidekicks ranted a bit about those who murdered foxes being obvious murderers of people, but he wasn't very convincing. And Brother Francis was too preoccupied with sharing with the listeners his new poem to get into the whodunit controversy.'

Pooley finished his cheese. 'What's the poem like?'

'All I can remember is:

> 'That noble dame, so pure of soul
> With pity for the slave
> Is mourned tonight by every mole
> And fox and vixen brave.

'Deliciously inappropriate for an apparatchik like the said Parsons, don't you think?'

Pooley laughed so much that he almost choked on his apple. 'Thanks, Robert. I enjoyed that. There hasn't been much to laugh at today.'

'What's the state of play with Dolamore?'

'He's being held under anti-terrorist legislation, so in

theory Charlie Friel could hold on to him for another five days, but honestly, from what I've heard, he's going to get nowhere. Dolamore put up a very convincing show of shock/horror over the bombs and seemed genuinely upset about Parsons. Otherwise he's full of self-righteousness and oratorical flourishes, and even Charlie's coming to the conclusion that he couldn't organize his way out of a paperbag, let alone into the Lords to murder its inmates. And the Commissioner's getting twitchy about the protests outside the Yard demanding the release of Saint Jerry. My guess is he'll be out any time now.'

'So you write him off?'

'If you ask me, he's the sort of man who would be dangerous if he had a different calibre of supporter. But the activists don't seem to be throwing up any military talents. They're more like a gaggle of unruly street urchins.'

'So another cul-de-sac?'

'So it seems. How are things with you?'

'Well, I can't say our meeting at Bertie Stormerod's was too cheery. A lot of the poor old boys have lost people they were fond of in one or another of those massacres and a few of them are downright frightened, though rallied by a combination of Jack, Bertie and Tommy Beesley, who now that he actually has a proper enemy in his sights is behaving just like an old cavalry officer.'

'So is there a plan?'

'Just to carry on with business as usual, with all the hard core having the job of rallying the troops and me continuing the back-room stuff and helping them make their case in committee. We've had one boost with today's opinion polls showing that support for the abolition of fox-hunting has slumped from ninety-one per cent to sixty-four per cent. Stormerod gave most of the credit for this to Jack, though she said it should go to the Avengers for offending the English sense of fair play. It's probably a mixture of both.'

He drained his glass and waved it at Pooley. 'So what gives on your side?'

Pooley finished his apple, drank his milk, refilled Amiss's

glass and poured himself a small measure of whisky to which he added an equal measure of water.

'Well, it's all so extraordinary and unprecedented it's very hard to get a grip on. Take the bombs, for instance. The Bomb Squad are pretty certain that what happened was that the members of the Committee trickled in a few minutes before the meeting was due to start, sat down, chatted and were joined by their chairman, Lady Parsons, precisely on time at four-thirty. As soon as she sat down the bomb under her cushion exploded. Naturally everyone leaped up and the bombs under each of their cushions exploded in turn.'

'I don't get you.'

'Two different types of anti-personnel mine. One kind explodes on contact: the other explodes when you release contact.'

Amiss grimaced. 'How very unpleasant.'

'Horribly ingenious and sick at the same time.'

'But what would have happened if the chairman had come in first?'

Pooley shrugged. 'Who knows? Maybe the murderer didn't want to kill everybody. He might have been content with one or a few. That might even be why he didn't use a bigger bomb. Though of course these mines are easier to transport.'

'How big are they?'

'About the size of a compact disk.'

'Difficult to get?'

'Unfortunately not. There were thousands of them sloshing around after the Gulf War and they're even easier to get from crooked arms dealers than the stun-gun.'

'Still, there's specialist knowledge involved, isn't there? Presumably we're looking for someone with a military background?'

'If by military you mean paramilitary, yes, probably. But there's no shortage of such people around these days.'

'So who's the hot favourite for perpetrator?'

'Well, quite apart from the matter of Dolamore, the anti-terrorist boys are still going hell for leather after the animal activists; they're working steadily through the shortlist of particularly dangerous groups. We're still plodding through the list of individuals murdered to see if by any chance all these people were murdered as a cosmetic device to cover up an attempt on the life of one of them.'

'Surely in the light of the second lot of murders, that's outrageously far-fetched?'

'Come on. Don't you remember the guy in America years ago who blew up a whole passenger plane so he could collect the life insurance on his mother? These things happen. Still, I admit it's not likely, and Jim – although because he's thorough he's going through the motions – thinks it's hardly worth entertaining. Having gone through last week's victims, we haven't found a soul whom anyone would have wished to murder except for poor old Poulteney. And since we talked to the ghastly Vanessa, we really don't rate her as a prospect. And of course if any of those killed the first time round were specifically targeted, why were those others murdered yesterday?'

'Well, exactly. If we're to believe in the notion of murdering many to dispose of one, yesterday's bombs would mean that they were aiming, a couple of weeks ago, for someone they missed, so all the ones they got then were irrelevant. So you should really only be investigating those they didn't kill.' He took a meditative sip. 'It's making my head swim.'

'We haven't quite reached that stage. At present we're now focusing on who might have wanted to kill any of the unfortunates blown up yesterday as well as everyone in your group who would have been expected to turn up in committee room 4.'

'So you must be talking about perhaps twenty-five individuals.'

'Yes. But talk about needles in haystacks! We've got a team of CID people investigating everyone but it's an enormous job and God knows what the chances are of turning up motives unless they're absolutely staring one in the face. And what's more, as you can imagine, the security implications are an absolute nightmare. We're going to have to bring in the SAS. We're under ferocious criticism for having let yesterday happen. And since the media are screaming for his resignation, the Home Secretary's hopping mad and is taking it out on the police. Yet how could we have stopped it? You could have fitted twenty of those bombs into a small briefcase and hidden them anywhere. We did as thorough a search as we could but inevitably it just wasn't good enough.'

'Calm down, Ellis. You're sounding very defensive. Now, I'm not attacking you and your stout colleagues, but – if I may be just a touch self-centred for a moment – how likely do you think I am to get knocked off in the service of the humble fox?'

'Less than before, I think. You won't be allowed to meet all together again without security clearance and high-grade protection. Even the mighty Duke of Stormerod got a flea in his ear this morning for having organized that meeting with all of you without telling us first.'

'Where can we meet that's safe?'

'Well, not in the duke's pad for a start. Jim and I have been there to see him and I observed – as no doubt you did – that it's a five-storey house crammed with thousands of *objets* which would probably take us three days to search.'

'I suppose the duke could ask the PM for his bunker.'

Pooley rubbed his eyes. 'Finish up your whisky and go home, Robert. We both badly need sleep. And if you see a dark form behind you when you're waiting for a taxi, don't worry. It'll be one of ours. At least, it should be one of ours.'

'Thanks, Ellis. You make me feel so safe.'

'Why didn't you ring? I was frantic with worry.'

'I did! I left a message last night with Ravi that I was OK and gave a number where I could be reached. And I tried your office phone several times but it just rang and rang.'

'It's out of order,' she said wearily. 'And remind me to kill Ravi.'

'Don't kill him. Just sack him.'

'Killing him would be a lot simpler. The dependants would get his life-insurance policy and you could come out and replace him. That would keep you out of harm's way and also console me in my exile. Now, what the hell's going on?'

Ten minutes later he said, 'That's it. I don't think there are any more salient details.' There was a silence. 'Rachel, are you there?'

'Oh, yes. I'm here.'

'What's the matter?'

'With me? Nothing. With you it seems to me rather a lot.'

'You don't like what I'm doing because it's dangerous?'

'Parachuting is dangerous. Bareback riding cross-country is dangerous. Walking across a motorway is dangerous. What you're doing is suicidal.'

'Don't exaggerate.'

'Exaggerate!' she exploded. 'Exaggerate! Nineteen corpses, half of them in smithereens, and you tell me I'm exaggerating? And now you and that lunatic Jack Troutbeck are proffering yourselves for target practice next time round.'

'Oh, now . . .'

'Don't "Oh, now" me. What are you doing this for? To enable people you don't even like to have the right to continue pursuing foxes around the countryside? Yes, that's clearly a wonderful cause to die for. I'm sure your parents, like me, will see that the sacrifice was not in vain. We can club together to provide a fitting memorial. A stuffed fox, perhaps? Placed tastefully in a glass cabinet with a silver plaque engraved with "Robert Amiss 1964−1995. He died for this".'

'It would be more accurate, wouldn't it,' said Amiss tentatively, 'to make it a stuffed hunter?'

'It depends on how you interpret the word "stuffed".' Her tone was icy. 'Why are you going on with this?'

'On the fox-hunting front, because I hate leaving anything half finished. And on the murder investigatory front, just curiosity, I suppose.'

'Wouldn't your curiosity be satisfied if you let the police sort things out and you were left alive to read about it in the newspapers?'

'It's not the same as being involved. And maybe even helping. Come on, Rachel. We've had this conversation several times before.'

'Normally when we do there are no more than a couple

of bodies on the scene and nobody seems much interested in rubbing you out. This time is different.'

'The curiosity isn't different.'

'You know what you remind me of? Hunters. In fact, everyone involved in this crazy business is a hunter. The pro-hunting ones are the simplest kind. All they want is to career around in pursuit of their foxes. The anti-hunting lot want, metaphorically, to hunt down the hunters. And you now want to hunt down whichever of them is the murderer even if, in the process, you break your neck or have it broken for you.'

Amiss couldn't think of anything to say.

'Do you know what?' she said. 'I admire your tenacity. I admire your intelligence. God help me, I admire your courage. But I would really rather see it employed in making a living and, as your father would put it, bettering yourself, rather than playing Sancho Panza to Jack Troutbeck's Don Quixote.'

'I would prefer Ellis's view that I'm Archie Goodwin to her Nero Wolfe.' He heard an impatient intake of breath and added hastily, 'I'll be careful. Honestly. And cross my heart and hope to die, I'll get a real job when this is over, even if that means going back to the civil service. Is it a deal?'

'There isn't really another one on offer, is there?'

'No.'

'One of the fascinating things about you, Robert, is that you are obliging at times to a point of wimpishness and yet completely stubborn at others. Anyone with a grain of sense would accept the advice to quit now.'

'That's the package, I'm afraid. I can't defend it, but it's how I am.'

'I know. And since I love you as you are I suppose I don't want you to change. But you know that periodically I'll shout at you in the hope that you will.'

'And I wouldn't really want you to stop being a shrew. It would remove some of the spice from the mixture.'

'What a romantic pair we are.' She laughed. 'Right. Now let me read you the letter I've just sent to Personnel. I hope it will prove shrewish enough to shake them up a bit.'

*   *   *

'Have the cops been round?'

'I had a Detective Constable Caudwell waiting for me when I got home last night striving to determine if someone so much wants to murder me that they are prepared to go to all this trouble and expense.'

'What did you tell him? Something inventive, I hope.' The baroness laughed merrily.

'I don't want to add to my troubles by being arrested for wasting police time. So I explained that I had no money except for perhaps ten thousand pounds of capital in the flat, and that neither my parents nor my girlfriend was likely to murder me for such a small sum. I did, however, suggest that you might conceivably murder me in order to gain possession of my cat.'

'Did that interest him?'

'He wrote it down so earnestly that I hastily explained that it was a joke and that if he saw the cat he would understand why. I explained as best I could the nature of the business relationship between you and me and he left, I hope, satisfied. Anyway, since I don't have a pacemaker I'm pretty well ruled out of the reckoning.'

'Ah, good. That should confuse them.'

'What? How?'

There was silence on the line. Clearly her attention had wandered.

'Jack! What were you talking about?'

'Nothing.'

'Have they been to see you?'

'Certainly. Late last night also.'

'What did you say?'

'Oh, nothing important,' she said impatiently. 'Don't fuss. Now, about Plutarch. I'm going to have to return her to you for a while.'

'What's she done?'

'Nothing reprehensible in my book, but what one might call a couple of incidents yesterday in my absence. You remember Greasy Joan?'

'How could I forget? But I thought she'd left you long ago.'

'She came back. We couldn't ref...
thing. Got her cleaned up a bit ar...
form, so she's a bit less greasy the...
to hysteria.'

'What brought it on?'

'Since Plutarch refuses to give her ...
be sure, but the gist is – as I followed it ...
that Plutarch's insistence on wresting from ...
capon which she was bearing to High Table ca...
Grease to proclaim her possessed by satanic forces. So, ...
I don't want a posse of mad incestuous Fen-dwellers arriving
to burn her at the stake, with reluctance I've decided it's at
present unsafe to leave her at St Martha's when I'm away
so much. Myles, I'm sorry to say, has put his foot down and
refuses to give her B & B at his place.'

'What a man! You mean he says no to you?'

'On certain matters, Myles is proof even against the most
feminine of my wiles and one such is any question putting
his rather fine collection of eighteenth-century glass at the
mercy of what I am forced to admit is a tendency to clumsiness on Plutarch's part.'

'Put her back in the cattery.'

'No, no, we can't have that. It would upset her. I'll hand
her over tomorrow after lunch. See you in the Peers' Guest
Room at twelve-thirty. Round up Bertie and Sid.'

'You're not coming up today?'

'Can't. I've a few dragons to slay at the College Council
and Jennifer Poulteney's coming over to lunch. I must cheer
the poor child up. She's very upset about Reggie.'

'You're not . . . ?' He couldn't bring himself to ask the
question.

'No, I'm not. You have a dirty mind, Robert.'

'Which is frequently proved to be right.'

'Not this time. My motives are entirely honourable.
Besides, she's an unregenerate heterosexual.'

'How do you know?'

'I asked her. Life is too short for shilly-shallying round
these topics. You need to know where you stand from the

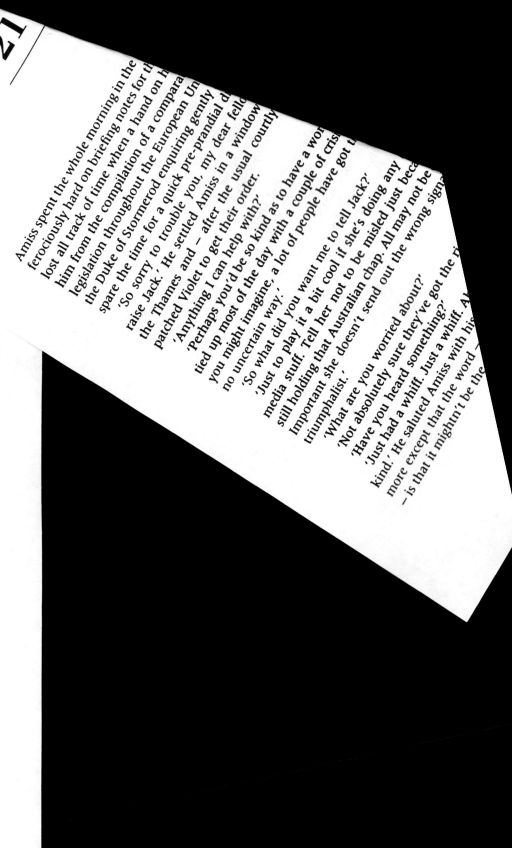

21

Amiss spent the whole morning in the ...
ferociously hard on briefing notes for th...
lost all track of time when a hand on h...
him from the compilation of a compara...
legislation throughout the European Un...
the Duke of Stormerod enquiring gently ...
spare the time for a quick pre-prandial d...

'So sorry to trouble you, my dear fello...
raise Jack.' He settled Amiss in a window...
the Thames and – after the usual courtly ...
patched Violet to get their order.

'Anything I can help with?'

'Perhaps you'd be so kind as to have a wor...
tied up most of the day with a couple of crisi...
you might imagine, a lot of people have got t...
no uncertain way.'

'So what did you want me to tell Jack?'

'Just to play it a bit cool if she's doing any ...
media stuff. Tell her not to be misled just beca...
still holding that Australian chap. All may not be ...
Important she doesn't send out the wrong sign...
triumphalist.'

'What are you worried about?'

'Not absolutely sure they've got the ri...
'Have you heard something?'

'Just had a whiff. Just a whiff. A...
kind.' He saluted Amiss with his ...
more except that the word – ...
– is that it mightn't be the...

done this. Might be something embarrassing for us just round the corner.'

'Really. Like what?'

'Can't tell you that, old chap. Sorry. Top secret, I'm afraid, at the moment. But just rein Jack in a bit. Stop her jumping to conclusions. Tell her I said pious platitudes rather than war cries are what she should be aiming at.' And not another salient word could Amiss get out of the old statesman, who – as Amiss reported bitterly to the baroness – was so discreet he could have doubled for a clam with lockjaw.

'Nonsense. He gave you the necessary. You don't get to be the confidant of all the mighty by being a blabbermouth. Anyway, I've registered what he said. If they call on me I'll rival Brother Francis in sweetness and light and will gently rebuke them if they ask me to make any pre-judgements. Now go off and do something useful. Eavesdrop.' She was gone before he could enquire about Jennifer's state of mind.

He had no more satisfaction from his conversation with Ellis Pooley, who, obviously constrained by the presence of colleagues, did nothing but promise in response to Amiss's urgent entreaty to turn up at his flat for something to eat on his way home, whenever that might be. In the event it was eleven o'clock before he arrived and wolfed down the beef sandwiches that Amiss offered. He even fell gratefully on the claret.

'God, what a day.'

'I hope it was more interesting than mine.'

'What did you do?'

'A lot of the kind of briefing that bored me rigid in the civil service – notes about complicated things rendered simple for idiots, interspersed with fruitless searches for sources of information since the House was mysteriously empty, culminating in drumming my heels all evening in frustration while frantic to know why the Duke of Stormerod should have advised me – insofar as I could understand him – that the murderers may be pro rather than anti-hunting. What the hell is going on?'

'You've got me there. From what Jim said to me before I

left tonight, Charlie Friel's still going hell-for-leather after the activists. Now one more glass of claret, Robert, and I'll be off.'

The baroness looked at her watch. 'Good God, I'd better be off or I'll be late for the interview. Bye, Bertie. Bye, Sid. See you tomorrow. Come on, Robert, we have to have the handover ceremony.'

'Handover of what?'

'My cat, Sid. Jack has kindly been playing host to her.'

'Yes, you should meet her. She's a frolicsome little thing. I'll miss her. Come on, Robert. Come on. There's no time to waste.' She shot out of the bar, down the corridor to the lobby and thence to the cloakroom.

'How's she been, Mr Hudson?'

'Played merry hell for the first fifteen minutes, your ladyship. Caused a lot of comment. Indeed, Lord Purseglove wanted to let her out but I prevented him. He kept saying: "Poor little kitty, poor little kitty". But I told him you had said she can be ferocious when roused and to leave her be.'

'Good thinking.' The baroness sniffed. 'Hmm. I think she needs a pretty drastic change of newspaper. Robert, you'd better take her to the loo.'

'Are you mad? If I get her out of the basket, I'll never get her back in again.'

'Oh, nonsense. You just don't know how to treat her. All she needs is a bit of coaxing, like any woman. Oh, all right then. If you're chicken, I suppose I'll have to do it. The old girl's too fastidious to be left in this condition to journey across London.' She snatched Amiss's newspaper out of his pocket and disappeared off with the basket. Two minutes later she was back with an empty basket.

'Oh no. Please no. You didn't let her get away?'

The baroness looked slightly abashed. 'All would have been fine had it not been for Clarissa Whitney arriving in the loo just as I was on my knees attending to the container. Quite understandably – and she deserves no blame for this – Plutarch thought this was a good moment to take off. When last seen she was streaking up the staircase. I'm afraid you're

174

likely to have a lively time getting her back. Sorry I can't stay and help. Toodlepip.' Grabbing her coat from her peg, she waved merrily and rushed out.

Hudson shook his head admiringly. 'Quite a card, her ladyship.'

Amiss glowered. 'I can think of more appropriate descriptions, but I'll save them for when I see her next.' Picking up the basket, he wandered hopelessly towards and then up the stairs, down a couple of corridors and into the lobby. Two doorkeepers bore down on him instantly. 'Is that your cat that's just invaded the chamber?' asked the smaller giant.

'No, no. It's Lady Troutbeck's. She's asked me to retrieve it.'

'Her ladyship is going to be in trouble with the Lord Chancellor,' observed the larger giant with some satisfaction. 'He didn't look best pleased when the animal launched itself down the table towards him, jumped on the arm of the woolsack and – of all things – straight into the throne itself.'

Amiss grimaced. 'Dear me. I hope this doesn't make her liable for a public hanging on Tower Hill or anything.'

'Judging by the Lord Chancellor's face,' said the smaller giant, 'it'll be disembowelling first.'

'Are we speaking of the baroness or the cat?'

'Both.' He jerked his head. 'Look.'

Amiss peered fearfully into the chamber to see that Plutarch in only a few minutes had succeeded where the abseiling lesbians and a mass murderer had failed. Their lordships were actually admitting to each other that something funny was going on. There was little pretence of listening to old Lord Halliday, who was gamely persevering in addressing them on the subject of the royal parks. Instead, the peers were gazing in fascination at Plutarch's spectacular progress around their sacred surroundings. Leaping on a bench here, clearing a table there, jumping once more on the throne and using the Lord Chancellor's shoulder as a launching pad, she finally, with a leap over the gate that separated the peers from their guests, whizzed into the lobby in a blur of yellow fur. There was no question of catching her. She was out of the lobby and down the corridor to the right before he could draw breath.

'That's some cat,' said the larger giant respectfully.

'The sort of cat you'd expect her ladyship to have,' observed his colleague.

'How very true,' said Amiss. 'Well, I'd better try to find her or her ladyship will be very upset. I could see as she left for her urgent appointment that she was terribly worried.'

Plutarch was not hard to trail. At every corner there was a stunned onlooker who knew she'd gone left, right, up or down and within ten minutes Amiss was being waved by his last informant towards the library. As he opened the door a shrill scream confirmed that Plutarch was indeed among those present.

Amiss peered in cautiously and observed that the dozen or so readers present – like the inhabitants of the chamber – were rapt in fascinated concentration on her progress. The young librarian stood sucking the back of his hand, and not wishing to earn the enmity of someone on whose goodwill he relied, Amiss hastened up to him.

'Has Lady Troutbeck's cat scratched you, Mr Leadbetter? I'm so sorry.'

Leadbetter stuck out his hand. 'Look.' His voice was quavery. 'All I did was try to pick her up.'

It was one of Plutarch's better scratches. Amiss remembered well from the early days of their acquaintance how painful it could be when one incautiously incurred her displeasure. Murmuring apologetic platitudes he began to move towards Plutarch, now crouched on a table in the corner weighing up her options. He was only a foot away – and feeling reasonably optimistic – when the door opened, and aiming for the great outdoors, she sprang off the table, vaulted over a horrified, elderly man and hurtled between the legs of the incoming Lord Harrington, bringing him crashing to the ground. That Harrington had been one of the most odious ministers under whom Amiss had ever worked provided some compensation for what he knew would be further horrors awaiting him. Delivering a weak smile in the general direction of the audience, and leaving others to pick

'Have the cops been round?'

'I had a Detective Constable Caudwell waiting for me when I got home last night striving to determine if someone so much wants to murder me that they are prepared to go to all this trouble and expense.'

'What did you tell him? Something inventive, I hope.' The baroness laughed merrily.

'I don't want to add to my troubles by being arrested for wasting police time. So I explained that I had no money except for perhaps ten thousand pounds of capital in the flat, and that neither my parents nor my girlfriend was likely to murder me for such a small sum. I did, however, suggest that you might conceivably murder me in order to gain possession of my cat.'

'Did that interest him?'

'He wrote it down so earnestly that I hastily explained that it was a joke and that if he saw the cat he would understand why. I explained as best I could the nature of the business relationship between you and me and he left, I hope, satisfied. Anyway, since I don't have a pacemaker I'm pretty well ruled out of the reckoning.'

'Ah, good. That should confuse them.'

'What? How?'

There was silence on the line. Clearly her attention had wandered.

'Jack! What were you talking about?'

'Nothing.'

'Have they been to see you?'

'Certainly. Late last night also.'

'What did you say?'

'Oh, nothing important,' she said impatiently. 'Don't fuss. Now, about Plutarch. I'm going to have to return her to you for a while.'

'What's she done?'

'Nothing reprehensible in my book, but what one might call a couple of incidents yesterday in my absence. You remember Greasy Joan?'

'How could I forget? But I thought she'd left you long ago.'

'She came back. We couldn't refuse her a job, poor old thing. Got her cleaned up a bit and gave her a decent uniform, so she's a bit less greasy these days. But still a bit prone to hysteria.'

'What brought it on?'

'Since Plutarch refuses to give her side of the story, I can't be sure, but the gist is — as I followed it through the sobs — that Plutarch's insistence on wresting from Greasy Joan a capon which she was bearing to High Table caused said Grease to proclaim her possessed by satanic forces. So, since I don't want a posse of mad incestuous Fen-dwellers arriving to burn her at the stake, with reluctance I've decided it's at present unsafe to leave her at St Martha's when I'm away so much. Myles, I'm sorry to say, has put his foot down and refuses to give her B & B at his place.'

'What a man! You mean he says no to you?'

'On certain matters, Myles is proof even against the most feminine of my wiles and one such is any question putting his rather fine collection of eighteenth-century glass at the mercy of what I am forced to admit is a tendency to clumsiness on Plutarch's part.'

'Put her back in the cattery.'

'No, no, we can't have that. It would upset her. I'll hand her over tomorrow after lunch. See you in the Peers' Guest Room at twelve-thirty. Round up Bertie and Sid.'

'You're not coming up today?'

'Can't. I've a few dragons to slay at the College Council and Jennifer Poulteney's coming over to lunch. I must cheer the poor child up. She's very upset about Reggie.'

'You're not . . . ?' He couldn't bring himself to ask the question.

'No, I'm not. You have a dirty mind, Robert.'

'Which is frequently proved to be right.'

'Not this time. My motives are entirely honourable. Besides, she's an unregenerate heterosexual.'

'How do you know?'

'I asked her. Life is too short for shilly-shallying round these topics. You need to know where you stand from the outset. It's amazing how many people give straight answers if you ask straight questions. Bye.'

Amiss sank back on to his pillows wondering how he would summon up the energy to get up. What with Caudwell not leaving till midnight, the row with Rachel at three a.m. and the baroness's breezy wake-up call at seven, he felt exhausted. He fell into a sound and blessedly dreamless sleep and could have cried with frustration when after only a few minutes the telephone rang again.

'Sorry to wake you up so early, son, but I was afraid I might miss you if you had an early interview or anything.'

'That's all right, Dad. Good to hear you. How are things?'

'Fine, fine. In fact, Mum and I were thinking we might come down to London for a day or two to see you. It's been a couple of months now.'

Amiss tried to keep his voice level. 'That would be lovely, Dad. When were you thinking of?'

'How would this weekend be?'

'Terribly sorry.' He summoned his scattered wits. 'Unfortunately I've agreed to visit an old university friend in . . . Devon.'

'What about the weekend after?'

'Not quite sure. Could we make it the one after? I think that'd be safer.'

'Fair enough, son.' Amiss felt the familiar rush of affection for a father who never stooped to emotional blackmail. 'We'll settle on that. Now, how's the job-hunting going?'

21

Amiss spent the whole morning in the Lords Library working ferociously hard on briefing notes for the Committee. He had lost all track of time when a hand on his shoulder extracted him from the compilation of a comparative table of hunting legislation throughout the European Union to the reality of the Duke of Stormerod enquiring gently if he could possibly spare the time for a quick pre-prandial drink.

'So sorry to trouble you, my dear fellow, but I couldn't raise Jack.' He settled Amiss in a window seat overlooking the Thames and – after the usual courtly badinage – dispatched Violet to get their order.

'Anything I can help with?'

'Perhaps you'd be so kind as to have a word with her. I'm tied up most of the day with a couple of crisis meetings. As you might imagine, a lot of people have got the wind up in no uncertain way.'

'So what did you want me to tell Jack?'

'Just to play it a bit cool if she's doing any more of her media stuff. Tell her not to be misled just because they're still holding that Australian chap. All may not be as it seems. Important she doesn't send out the wrong signals by being triumphalist.'

'What are you worried about?'

'Not absolutely sure they've got the right fellow.'

'Have you heard something?'

'Just had a whiff. Just a whiff. Ah, thank you, Violet. How kind.' He saluted Amiss with his glass. ''Fraid I can't say any more except that the word – from a source I can't mention – is that it mightn't be the chaps on the other side that have done this. Might be something embarrassing for us just round the corner.'

'Really. Like what?'

'Can't tell you that, old chap. Sorry. Top secret, I'm afraid, at the moment. But just rein Jack in a bit. Stop her jumping to conclusions. Tell her I said pious platitudes rather than war cries are what she should be aiming at.' And not another salient word could Amiss get out of the old statesman, who – as Amiss reported bitterly to the baroness – was so discreet he could have doubled for a clam with lockjaw.

'Nonsense. He gave you the necessary. You don't get to be the confidant of all the mighty by being a blabbermouth. Anyway, I've registered what he said. If they call on me I'll rival Brother Francis in sweetness and light and will gently rebuke them if they ask me to make any pre-judgements. Now go off and do something useful. Eavesdrop.' She was gone before he could enquire about Jennifer's state of mind.

He had no more satisfaction from his conversation with Ellis Pooley, who, obviously constrained by the presence of colleagues, did nothing but promise in response to Amiss's urgent entreaty to turn up at his flat for something to eat on his way home, whenever that might be. In the event it was eleven o'clock before he arrived and wolfed down the beef sandwiches that Amiss offered. He even fell gratefully on the claret.

'God, what a day.'

'I hope it was more interesting than mine.'

'What did you do?'

'A lot of the kind of briefing that bored me rigid in the civil service – notes about complicated things rendered simple for idiots, interspersed with fruitless searches for sources of information since the House was mysteriously empty, culminating in drumming my heels all evening in frustration while frantic to know why the Duke of Stormerod should have advised me – insofar as I could understand him – that the murderers may be pro rather than anti-hunting. What the hell is going on?'

'You've got me there. From what Jim said to me before I

left tonight, Charlie Friel's still going hell-for-leather after the activists. Now one more glass of claret, Robert, and I'll be off.'

The baroness looked at her watch. 'Good God, I'd better be off or I'll be late for the interview. Bye, Bertie. Bye, Sid. See you tomorrow. Come on, Robert, we have to have the handover ceremony.'

'Handover of what?'

'My cat, Sid. Jack has kindly been playing host to her.'

'Yes, you should meet her. She's a frolicsome little thing. I'll miss her. Come on, Robert. Come on. There's no time to waste.' She shot out of the bar, down the corridor to the lobby and thence to the cloakroom.

'How's she been, Mr Hudson?'

'Played merry hell for the first fifteen minutes, your ladyship. Caused a lot of comment. Indeed, Lord Purseglove wanted to let her out but I prevented him. He kept saying: "Poor little kitty, poor little kitty". But I told him you had said she can be ferocious when roused and to leave her be.'

'Good thinking.' The baroness sniffed. 'Hmm. I think she needs a pretty drastic change of newspaper. Robert, you'd better take her to the loo.'

'Are you mad? If I get her out of the basket, I'll never get her back in again.'

'Oh, nonsense. You just don't know how to treat her. All she needs is a bit of coaxing, like any woman. Oh, all right then. If you're chicken, I suppose I'll have to do it. The old girl's too fastidious to be left in this condition to journey across London.' She snatched Amiss's newspaper out of his pocket and disappeared off with the basket. Two minutes later she was back with an empty basket.

'Oh no. Please no. You didn't let her get away?'

The baroness looked slightly abashed. 'All would have been fine had it not been for Clarissa Whitney arriving in the loo just as I was on my knees attending to the container. Quite understandably – and she deserves no blame for this – Plutarch thought this was a good moment to take off. When last seen she was streaking up the staircase. I'm afraid you're likely to have a lively time getting her back. Sorry I can't stay and help. Toodlepip.' Grabbing her coat from her peg, she waved merrily and rushed out.

Hudson shook his head admiringly. 'Quite a card, her ladyship.'

Amiss glowered. 'I can think of more appropriate descriptions, but I'll save them for when I see her next.' Picking up the basket, he wandered hopelessly towards and then up the stairs, down a couple of corridors and into the lobby. Two doorkeepers bore down on him instantly. 'Is that your cat that's just invaded the chamber?' asked the smaller giant.

'No, no. It's Lady Troutbeck's. She's asked me to retrieve it.'

'Her ladyship is going to be in trouble with the Lord Chancellor,' observed the larger giant with some satisfaction. 'He didn't look best pleased when the animal launched itself down the table towards him, jumped on the arm of the woolsack and — of all things — straight into the throne itself.'

Amiss grimaced. 'Dear me. I hope this doesn't make her liable for a public hanging on Tower Hill or anything.'

'Judging by the Lord Chancellor's face,' said the smaller giant, 'it'll be disembowelling first.'

'Are we speaking of the baroness or the cat?'

'Both.' He jerked his head. 'Look.'

Amiss peered fearfully into the chamber to see that Plutarch in only a few minutes had succeeded where the abseiling lesbians and a mass murderer had failed. Their lordships were actually admitting to each other that something funny was going on. There was little pretence of listening to old Lord Halliday, who was gamely persevering in addressing them on the subject of the royal parks. Instead, the peers were gazing in fascination at Plutarch's spectacular progress around their sacred surroundings. Leaping on a bench here, clearing a table there, jumping once more on the throne and using the Lord Chancellor's shoulder as a launching pad, she finally, with a leap over the gate that separated the peers from their guests, whizzed into the lobby in a blur of yellow fur. There was no question of catching her. She was out of the lobby and down the corridor to the right before he could draw breath.

'That's some cat,' said the larger giant respectfully.

'The sort of cat you'd expect her ladyship to have,' observed his colleague.

'How very true,' said Amiss. 'Well, I'd better try to find her or her ladyship will be very upset. I could see as she left for her urgent appointment that she was terribly worried.'

Plutarch was not hard to trail. At every corner there was a stunned onlooker who knew she'd gone left, right, up or down and within ten minutes Amiss was being waved by his last informant towards the library. As he opened the door a shrill scream confirmed that Plutarch was indeed among those present.

Amiss peered in cautiously and observed that the dozen or so readers present – like the inhabitants of the chamber – were rapt in fascinated concentration on her progress. The young librarian stood sucking the back of his hand, and not wishing to earn the enmity of someone on whose goodwill he relied, Amiss hastened up to him.

'Has Lady Troutbeck's cat scratched you, Mr Leadbetter? I'm so sorry.'

Leadbetter stuck out his hand. 'Look.' His voice was quavery. 'All I did was try to pick her up.'

It was one of Plutarch's better scratches. Amiss remembered well from the early days of their acquaintance how painful it could be when one incautiously incurred her displeasure. Murmuring apologetic platitudes he began to move towards Plutarch, now crouched on a table in the corner weighing up her options. He was only a foot away – and feeling reasonably optimistic – when the door opened, and aiming for the great outdoors, she sprang off the table, vaulted over a horrified, elderly man and hurtled between the legs of the incoming Lord Harrington, bringing him crashing to the ground. That Harrington had been one of the most odious ministers under whom Amiss had ever worked provided some compensation for what he knew would be further horrors awaiting him. Delivering a weak smile in the general direction of the audience, and leaving others to pick

Harrington up and dust him off, Amiss sidled out of the room.

Plutarch, it turned out, was sticking to her favourite haunts; she had retraced her flight path almost exactly. When he next caught sight of her she was circumnavigating the lobby, but although still energetic, she seemed to be slowing down. He was watching in the expectation that after three or four more tours he would be able to ambush her, when a well-meaning attempt by the doorkeepers to corral her started her on a stampede back down the corridor, a detour into the bar and then up a staircase.

As Amiss, cursing, began the climb again, a figure came round the turn of the staircase and Plutarch hit it amidships: cat, man and suitcase rolled to the bottom of the stairs. Amiss grabbed the winded Plutarch, stuffed her in the basket and strapped her in before he turned his attention to the moaning Brother Francis. Apologies, explanations and sympathy followed, until at last the suffering monk was ready to be helped to his feet. Recollecting himself, Brother Francis said, 'I trust Pussy is all right? Why was she in such a hurry? Had she been distressed by someone?'

'Not half as distressed as a lot of people have been by her, I can assure you.'

Brother Francis abruptly lost interest. 'Where's my suitcase?' His battered bag was lying a few feet away. As Amiss picked it up, it opened and out of it fell a large square gilt box. Brother Francis rushed over, picked up the box, grabbed the suitcase, stuffed it inside and took off without another word. Amiss and a protesting Plutarch set off for home.

'I wish I'd been there.'

'Yes, you'd have enjoyed it. In retrospect even I would rather not have missed it. By the way, I said she was your cat. You can expect a wigging from the Lord Chancellor.'

He heard an immense yawn. 'What? A wigging from Perry Ladislaw? Don't be ridiculous. He wouldn't dare.' She sniggered. 'We were on the same delegation once in Amsterdam and he knows that I know what he got up to.

'Now, about Plutarch. I hope you've given her something

decent to eat after all her labours. I worry lest your culinary standards will come as a shock after St Martha's.'

'I treat Plutarch like a cat, Jack, not as some sort of comrade on a pirate ship with whom to share the booty.'

'Brute. I must send her some smoked salmon.'

'What beats me is why he was carrying a tabernacle.'

'Who?'

'Brother Francis.'

'Tool of his trade, isn't it?'

'Yes, but it sits on an altar.'

'Maybe he was taking it to a repair shop. I don't know. You should have asked him.'

'Some of us have a certain delicacy about asking intrusive questions.'

'More fool you if you want to know the answer. Now, I must be off. Myles and I are going to see *Tosca*.'

'That's a busman's holiday, isn't it? All that death and disaster.'

'Yes. But the songs are better than in real life. Give Plutarch my love and tell her I'm proud of her. Her exploits will go down in history. I'm glad I organized things so as to give her the opportunity.'

'You didn't do it on purpose, did you?' howled Amiss. But it was too late. She had gone.

22

Recent events had made Amiss an inveterate news addict, though this evening, like most, had yielded nothing on the Lords investigation that he didn't already know. So when he switched on the ten o'clock news he was expecting nothing but the usual bromide about 'massive police effort', 'no stones unturned', 'every expectation of making an early arrest' that served for information. There was some news on the animal-activist front, however, with a protest outside the Lords for the first time since the latest murders. With the committee stage beginning the following day, they were out in force – woolly hats, cross, bearded people in anoraks. The lot. The camera lingered on the usual revolting banners and focused for a few seconds on 'End This Torture Now', which was held by someone curiously overdressed for such a mild night, the hair being entirely covered by a baseball cap and with a scarf muffling the face from the nose downwards. As Amiss wondered vaguely why anyone should dress his head for Arctic conditions and yet wear no gloves, he noticed something which made him leap up and rush to the telephone. Pooley was still out, but Jim Milton had just got home.

'Can you be sure?'

'How many people have Claddagh rings and a large scratch on the same hand?'

'What's a Claddagh ring?'

'Two hearts entwined.'

'Hmmm. OK. I can't think when I've seen one of those on a man. Fair enough. I guess we'd better have Mr Leadbetter in double quick. I'll have to put Charlie Friel in charge, since the animal activists are his territory. He's going to be furious his people overlooked this fellow. What's Leadbetter like, anyway?'

'No discernible personality. Wouldn't think he's got much guts.'

'Ah well, then he won't enjoy Charlie, poor fellow.'

'You won't finger me as the source?'

'Of course not. I'll say it was an anonymous tip-off. Thanks, Robert.'

'Jim.'

'Yes?'

'What's the news on you and Ann?'

'Stalemate. I've hardly had time to talk to her for two weeks. The time difference makes it almost impossible when I'm so busy, which – as you can imagine – hasn't strengthened my side of the argument.'

Amiss sighed. 'When you do speak to her, give her my love.'

'Of course. And mine to your absent lady. I don't know why we bother with them considering that at the end of the day we end up as celibate as your Brother Francis.'

'Which reminds me . . .'

'Sorry, Robert. My mobile phone's ringing. I'll be in touch.'

'Congratulations.' Pooley's excitement came through even the crackling of the answering-machine tape. 'When they picked up Leadbetter this morning, they raided his house and found all sorts of useful devices from razor blades to detonators for the making of letter bombs, incendiary devices and the rest of it, along with heavily scored volumes of *Who's Who*, list of patrons of field sports groups, editors of hunting magazines, *Country Life* and so on, at least fifty of whom have already had letter bombs in recent months. Bye.'

There was no answer from Pooley's office number, but Milton answered immediately.

'Ellis left a message telling me what was in Leadbetter's house.'

'Encouraging, isn't it?'

'Funny. I wouldn't have thought he was the type.'

'It's just the sort of occupation for a nervous nelly. It's not like hand-to-hand combat, you know, wrapping these things up and sending them off.'

'No, but it requires a certain lack of concern about human life, as well as a certain devil-may-care attitude to something blowing up in your own face.'

'You just don't like to believe people you know are villains.'

'At least you seem to be implying you don't think he did the business in the Lords?'

'But probably made it possible for someone else to do it. I don't know. Charlie's still working him over but apparently he hasn't said anything yet.'

'Let me know when there's anything.'

'Ring me tomorrow lunchtime. Bye.'

Charlie Friel was unusually subdued. 'I can't get any sense out of Leadbetter. He's completely hysterical and just keeps claiming he heard nothing, saw nothing, it was nothing to do with him and he never set foot in the basement.'

'Is he trying to put the blame on anyone else?'

'No, he keeps screaming, "It's impossible! Impossible!" We questioned him all night but got nowhere.'

Knowing Friel's sense of territory, Milton forbore to invite a rebuff by offering his services, but after a few seconds' silence, Friel said, 'I realize how busy you are, Jim, but do you think you could come round and have a word with him? Tell you the truth, I think we might have overfrightened him. I think it's possible he might be more responsive to your technique than ours.'

Milton looked at his watch. 'OK. We'll be round at eleven.'

It took Milton half an hour of making soothing noises to get Leadbetter to emerge from his sobs.

'That's better. Now how about some tea?'

The suggestion went down well. Pooley was dispatched to find a helpful warder and within five minutes – as Leadbetter took a first sip from his mug – Milton felt it safe to start the interview.

'Now, Lucius, I'm not one of the Anti-terrorist Squad. I'm just an ordinary policeman. They think you're guilty of all the murders in the Lords as well as of sending those letter bombs.' He raised his hand. 'No, don't get hysterical again. I've an open mind, so your best chance is to talk frankly to me. Otherwise, reluctantly, I shall have to hand you back to them.' He looked at Leadbetter with what he hoped conveyed a mixture of sympathy and firmness. 'You know they found a lot of very dangerous material, some of which looks as if it has already caused widespread injury. Did you know anything about this?'

Leadbetter blew his nose. 'No, I never went into the basement.'

'So what was the set-up in your house?'

Leadbetter had another gulp of tea, put his mug down, clasped his hands tightly and began with a rush. 'When Mum died, she left me the house. I'd been living in the basement, because Mum always said it was better for us to be separate and it had a private entrance and everything, so I thought I'd move upstairs where I'd have room for my books and music and I'd let the basement to bring me in a bit of income because you don't get much for being a librarian.'

'And when was this?'

'Five years ago last week Mum died. It took me a while to clear up the house and sort everything out and, you know, get over the way I was feeling because Mum and I were very close.'

Milton nodded sympathetically. 'It must have been a terrible wrench.'

'Oh, it was.' He dabbed his welling tears with a tissue. 'But when everything was straight, I let the basement to a nice young couple and that was fine and we had no trouble at all, but then Josephine wanted me to get rid of them.'

'Josephine?'

'A friend.' He blushed. 'I met her on a Concerned Humans Against Animal Exploitation march and we got talking. I asked her home.'

'Yes?'

'And . . .' His eyes flickered round the room as if he were

182

fearful that his dead mother was somewhere around. 'Well, then she, I, we . . .'

'Became more than friends?' Milton wondered how someone like this could function in the 1990s.

'Yes, yes. A lot more. So I wanted to marry her, but Josephine . . . no . . . I mean, she was too good for me. I think she was being kind to me really. She said what it was all about was the cause and we shouldn't put our selfish pleasures above that, so although I could . . . you know . . .' He blushed again and fell into an embarrassed silence.

Milton nodded encouragingly. 'I quite understand, Lucius. Go on.'

'Well, I mean, sometimes it was all right but what I thought was a pity was that she didn't want to go out and do, you know, what people do, like going to restaurants or the cinema or the theatre . . . or even walks. No, she was very dedicated, Josephine. She said all our spare time must be given over to saving animals.'

'So that's how you became more militant?'

'Well, not really. I mean, I got to know them. But I wasn't ever really militant. I'm a pacifist. But Josephine's friends were a bit, and I hung round with them sometimes so I could be with her.'

You poor stooge, thought Milton — a perfect example of all those people dragged into communism, fascism, and all sorts of other unpleasant causes through misplaced trust in a hardhearted loved one.

'I kept asking her to marry me, or at least move in with me, but she wouldn't. She said if we did that we'd end up putting homemaking ahead of principle and duty. But eventually she said she would compromise and live in the basement. We'd be separate, but we'd see more of each other that way.'

'So you gave notice to your tenants?'

'I felt dreadful doing that, though Josephine said I was being soft. She said the convenience of others couldn't be put before the revolution. She put it that way because she said she wasn't just concerned about animals. To get a fair society, individuals had to make sacrifices just like we did.

But there wasn't any unpleasantness because I explained to them about Josephine and me and gave them a lot of compensation and we'd always got on and they were nice about it. I didn't tell Josephine how much compensation I gave them because she would have said I was soft and that the money had to go to the cause. But they found a place quick enough and she moved in three months ago.'

'Did she pay rent?'

He looked shocked. "Course not.'

'So did you spend much time in the basement?'

'I haven't been down there since. Josephine said she had to have her own space, although she'd come up to me. So I left her in peace and if I wanted to talk to her I rang her and if she had time she came up.'

'Did she have visitors?'

'Oh yes. Lots. She's very popular. Some of them she'd bring upstairs so we could spend time together as a group but others, whom she said were colleagues, she'd see on her own, and of course I don't know what she was doing during the day.'

'Josephine is unemployed?'

'That's right. She said she was too principled to take a job because it would come between her and her vocation.'

'Do you know who her visitors were?'

'The ones she introduced me to, yes. Like Bruce, Nigel and Ken. But there were others that came round for meetings. I used to peek out of the window sometimes. I was a bit jealous. I asked her if I could come to some of the meetings but she said not till I'd proved myself.'

'And how were you to do that, Lucius?'

'By showing in demonstrations that I had some bottle.'

'Didn't you realize that you were getting into something violent?'

'I was mad about Josephine and I like animals. I've got some cats. Funnily enough that was one of the reasons Josephine gave for not living with me: she doesn't like cats. But she said that didn't stop her fighting for their rights.'

'How commendably detached of her.' Milton paused. 'Just one thing before you go on. Why are you talking so freely about her? You must realize what you're saying pins the blame firmly on her for what went on in the basement.'

Tears came into Leadbetter's eyes again, but then, in a stronger voice, he said, 'Look, just because I'm gullible, it doesn't mean I'm stupid. I've been thinking it over and I know she's made a fool of me. I think Bruce was probably her fellow all the time and they just used me.'

'But you could have told my colleagues this.'

'I can't talk if people shout at me. I just freeze up and he and the others kept shouting and threatening and they might as well have gagged me.'

'And you're happy to sign this statement naming these people?'

'I'm not happy.' Leadbetter spoke with some dignity. 'Nobody likes to be an informer. But it makes it easier when you've been as badly used as I think I've been, and by your very first girlfriend. Now, what's going to happen to me?'

'You need a good solicitor and you need to stick to your resolve to tell the truth about your former friends. There's a fair chance, if what you say checks out, that no charges will be made against you. But go on cooperating. If the police are on your side, things will go easier. Now, about the Lords murders. Have you any light to cast on that?'

'Only that I know it wasn't Josephine or even Bruce because we were at a meeting the night of the death ray and there'll be lots of witnesses. I'll give you some names. So whatever else she is, whatever sort of Jezebel she's been, she's not a mass murderer and nor is he.'

'Very good. I'll leave you now with Sergeant Pooley to agree your statement. And remember, don't panic, be helpful and if you've been telling the truth, you should be in the clear.'

23

Amiss spent the afternoon of the following day at the opening session of the Committee. It was a subdued affair and low in numbers for a committee of the whole House, since few peers seemed keen to get involved in this issue. The government had appointed a young hereditary peer to Lady Parsons's job, but it was clear from his opening speech that his heart wasn't in this bill.

'If there was ever a foeman unworthy of my steel, it's Littlejohn,' said the baroness. 'What a pathetic, weaselly speech about "people of goodwill", "mutual tolerance at this tragic time" and all that claptrap. While I wasn't looking forward to fighting my way through this bill line by line, eyeball to eyeball with Beatrice, at least it would have been invigorating. This is just plain dull.'

'Poor sod is wet behind the ears. You certainly woke him up, old girl. Your announcement that in view of recent events you felt obliged on principle to oppose every clause of the bill was delivered in a masterly fashion. Littlejohn's face creased in horror.'

'What an idiot! It's no wonder we're in the mess we're in if someone is appointed a minister who doesn't understand the elementary rules of negotiation.'

'Oh, be fair. He knew you used to be a civil servant. He must have thought he was dealing with someone civilized who thought in terms of level playing-fields and fair play.'

She smirked. 'More fool him. It's going to wear him out, persuading our side to make compromises.'

'I still don't see how the government can avoid holding firm on hunting. After all, you simply haven't got enough resources to wage as long a war of attrition as would be needed to wear them down completely.'

'Don't forget our superior cunning. You haven't yet seen Bertie in action making concessions so sadly, so reluctantly and in such a gentlemanly way that the hardest heart will feel honour bound to give a generous quid pro quo. Besides . . .' She attracted Violet's attention and gestured towards their empty glasses. 'That young man is still ambitious and, even if Bertie is on the other side, he's very powerful, influential and nobody is better connected, *and* he is well known to repay favours handsomely by a word in someone's ear at the appropriate time. Thanks, Violet.'

'Tonic, my lady?'

'Certainly not. I never touch the stuff.'

'Sir?'

'Yes, please. Fill it right up. Thanks.' He took a sip. 'I wish you'd stop ordering large measures, Jack. I'm going to end up with cirrhosis of the liver.'

'I like large measures.'

'Where were we?'

'I was complaining about things being dull.'

'What about me? I'm going to be bored senseless. At least you've got some action. What do you think it's like for me just hanging about on the sidelines, briefing your less than scintillating support team?'

'You've certainly got a lonely job. I was more than a little taken aback to discover that I appear to be the only fox-hunting activist who has a research assistant. Not, mind you, that the other side is much better off. They've only got officials. None of the enemy seem prepared to splash out on researchers.'

'Leadbetter told me Brother Francis had someone, but I've never seen him.'

'Judging from the quality of the reverend gentleman's arguments, if he's got an assistant he's no bloody good. Did you hear his contribution today?'

'Something about the wickedness of oppressing other creatures "feathered or furred", wasn't it?'

'Yep. I think he was talking about me. Anyway, enough

of this. Let's run through the order of play for Thursday and then I must be off to meet Myles. Do you want to come?'

'No. I'm expecting Jim Milton and Ellis to look in tonight.'

'I may join you. I want to know what's going on.'

The bell rang. Plutarch, who was curled up on the baroness's lap, opened one eye and grunted. Amiss got up and opened the door to Milton and Pooley.

'You've met Jack?' Milton nodded. 'Good to see you again, Lady Troutbeck.'

'Hello.' Pooley sounded hesitant.

'Good grief, Ellis, just because your gaffer's here doesn't mean you have to get all formal with me. You'd better put him out of his agony, Superintendent, by calling me by my first name.'

'I would be honoured, Jack.' Milton managed a creditable bow. 'And I am Jim.'

'Jack and Jim. There should be a verse about them. Perhaps Brother Francis could oblige.' Amiss ushered his guests to seats and set about getting drinks. 'Something along the lines of "Here come Jack and Jim, with their dear doggy Tim," might fit the bill perhaps.'

He handed them their glasses and sat down again. 'I haven't had a proper update from you for days. Is it still one mad whirl of fanatics of one kind or another with dozens of victims and hundreds of suspects.'

Milton groaned. 'I don't ever want to deal with another murder unless it's the kind Ellis likes reading about with six suspects in a snowbound country house and one – and only one – corpse on the library carpet.' He yawned, shook his head vigorously and took a sip of whisky. 'OK. Now, as you know, we've got the revolutionary Trots who sent the letter bombs, but we're pretty certain they had nothing to do with the murders, so research into animal activists continues. You won't know about the new lot of crazies who believe that to keep a domestic animal is to practise slavery.'

Amiss looked over at Plutarch, who was stretching luxuriously on the baroness's stomach and chest. 'They've got it the wrong way round.'

188

'What exactly do they want?' asked the baroness.

'I have been told they believe that all domestic animals should be freed instantly to go back to their natural state, whatever the consequences.'

'Even though that means that they're being run over in their thousands on the roads and hunted down and eaten by each other,' added Pooley.

'I see,' said the baroness. 'So if I've got a goldfish, a budgie, a cat, a cheetah, a lamb and a fox I open the back door and let them all get on with it?'

'That's about it.'

'Well, that should eradicate domestic pets in no time at all.'

'They say that's not their concern.'

'By the same logic, presumably they are in favour of fox-hunting and are perhaps therefore the murderers of Beatrice Parsons?'

'Ah, no. There's a flaw in that argument. The only people who are not allowed to hunt are us.'

'Us?'

'Man.'

'Because?'

'Because of our record as exploiters.'

'Oh, God.' She rubbed her eyes energetically. 'Come back, Professor Moriarty, Raffles, Fu Man Chu and those happy days when one had master criminals who could read, write and reason, so that at least there was some possibility of getting into their thought processes. These people are an intellectual insult.'

'Mind you,' interjected Pooley, 'we're not taking these weirdos seriously. They seem to be in their infancy as a batty pressure group and are so fixated on the domestic-pet issues I don't think they are up to speed on wildlife.'

'That's reassuring. For now I'll look forward to the moment when they come to release Plutarch into the wild. That should take a few of them out of circulation.' With that she sat up straight, removed the cat from her chest and dropped her on to the sofa beside her. Plutarch emitted a growl of protest but rapidly reassembled herself into a posture suitable for sleep and closed her eyes again.

'I don't know how you dare,' said Pooley respectfully.

'Got to show 'em who's boss.'

'I'll report you to the anti-slavery group,' said Amiss absently. 'Proceed, Jim.'

'Now to move smartly across the spectrum to the loonies on the pro-hunting side.'

'What? Us?' asked the baroness.

'No. Haven't you heard of the Master of the Species Group?'

The baroness groaned, picked up her glass and took a mighty swallow. 'Get me some more, Robert, will you? This whole world is going mad.'

'Well, they're old-fashioned white supremacists, but as well are what would these days be called speciesist. Their basic line appears to be that animals are put on earth to have anything done to them that we wish to, even if it involves torturing them to death for our amusement. They demand the abolition of all legislation protecting animals whether it be against bull-baiting, cock-fighting or experimentation. Their guru is that clown the Admiral Lord Gordon, who made, I understand, a particularly idiotic intervention in the second reading debate.'

'He's a guru?' Amiss's voice rose incredulously.

'The mad right tend not to demand much of their gurus in the way of intellect. He's an admiral, he encourages them in their yobbish opposition to everything that stands between them and their oikish desires to satisfy their nasty appetites and by wittering on about old values, foreign influences and the spirit that was old England, gives them the illusion that they are in some way principled.'

'Are they suspected of blowing up Parsons?'

'Only by Ellis.'

'Well, I know it's far-fetched . . .' Amiss and Milton grinned at each other. 'But it is possible that they murdered the first lot to gain sympathy for the cause and discredit the animal activists and blew up Lady Parsons . . . oh, I don't know, just for the hell of it, or maybe by mistake, or maybe they intended to get your group . . .'

'It doesn't work,' said Milton firmly. 'This crowd are just another lot of thugs who have been enjoying themselves keeping the police bogged down on the streets of London trying to keep the peace. They haven't got the mental equipment to think subtly or undertake a complicated operation.'

'So it's back to Dolamore's lot.'

'He's been released. Charlie's mad with frustration and will keep tabs on him closely, but there's just no evidence.'

'So we can't let go of the possibility of mass murder as cover. Now, of the nineteen murder victims, we can find a discernible motive for murder in only four cases. One was Lord Poulteney, but that doesn't wash any more. One was the Marquess of Havercroft, who had recently dumped his mistress of twelve years when his wife died in order to marry a model. One was Baroness Sedgewick, who has a drug-addict son whom she'd cut off without a penny. And the fourth was Lady Parsons, who had recently brutally and publicly sacked a young barrister from her chambers in a manner that probably ensures that his career is ruined. However, while I think any of these suspects might conceivably have hit their targets over the head with a blunt instrument, I simply can't think they had the skills or the resources either to commit these murders themselves or rent a murderer. Quite apart from anything else, how would they have acquired the necessary knowledge and access to the House of Lords?'

Amiss was following him intently. 'In any case, why should anyone who wanted to murder one of the first eight have murdered the others?'

'Only as a cover-up. But one has to investigate every possibility.'

'I do feel for you.' Amiss went round the gathering with the whisky and the water and sat down again.

'But of course there is the alternative and much more likely scenario, to wit that they were trying to kill more of the pro-hunting crew but the cancellation of that meeting saved you.'

191

The baroness nodded. 'Seems much more likely, except that since the meeting was cancelled because Bertie was enduring a plague of animal activists, it was hardly them.'

Milton shook his head. 'What we have here is a whole lot of different groups, not a tightly disciplined army. I doubt if the crowd in the Lake District have much to do with the London mob, except when they come down for a day to cause a bit of trouble. The odds are it was just coincidence. After all, for several weeks everyone exercised about the wickedness of fox-hunting has been seizing every single opportunity to demonstrate outside the homes of relevant peers. Look at the trouble you had the other day at St Martha's.'

'But if they'd been meaning to do for us, why wouldn't they have taken the bombs away when we failed to show?'

'Lack of opportunity? Needless risk? How would they have known the meeting was cancelled anyway?'

The baroness tickled Plutarch absently. 'What about the further complication of a murderer who might have wanted to knock off any of those of us who were due to be in the committee room that morning?'

'Only four are credible, though it has been suggested that you and Robert were engaged in a tug-of-love battle over Plutarch.'

'Oh God,' said the baroness. 'One should never joke with the constabulary.'

'Not when the constabulary are of the intellectual sophistication of the solid citizen who interviewed you. He said he didn't think it likely, but that stranger things had happened and there was no way of knowing what you were likely to get up to.'

'Including blowing myself up in order to ensure I blew Robert up too.'

'He thought you'd find a way round that. Anyway, it's not entirely your fault. Robert had compounded it by making a similar feeble joke to a not-much-brighter constable from the Met.'

She glowered. 'That's what I hate about the nineteen nineties. You can't say the simplest thing or make the most obvious joke without halfwits or idealogues getting the wrong end of the stick. Bugger the lot of them.'

'So who are the credible ones among our number?' asked Amiss.

'Your pal Beesley's son is very hard up and they don't get on. Lord Pragg's partner in their defunct garden-antique business has had a grievance against him for a long time and is known to have been furious when he inherited the title. Lord Gobbitt won a massive libel action against an historian who accused him of being a KGB spy and he made him bankrupt. And the Earl of Cleveland seems to have contracted AIDS through his frolickings with Filipino bar girls and has passed it on to his wife.

'However, only one of these injured parties seems remotely to be the kind of person one might imagine being able to organize vengeance on this scale, or with so little concern for others, and that's the historian, who is very close to neo-Nazi groups. Oh, and of course there's also the Duke of Stormerod.'

'I tipped you off about that,' said the baroness.

'Indeed you did. Although I don't know yet if it's relevant.'

'I forgot to tell you,' she explained to Amiss, 'that Bertie let drop to me a few weeks ago, apropos of Reggie, that like him he was thinking of getting married again.'

'Before we go on with this,' said Amiss, 'I have a question. Other than Bertie Stormerod, how many, if any, of those of us who were to meet in that committee room had pace-makers?'

Milton looked at him approvingly. 'Very good, Robert. Only Lords Pragg and Goss.'

'Right. So they couldn't have been targets, since Pragg is a cross-bencher and Goss is Labour. So only Bertie comes into the category of a target that could just have been missed through a piece of bad luck on the murderer's part. Now, if his marriage were the reason to kill him, presumably it means a son could supplant the existing heir?'

'Yes. He's an American first cousin once removed.'

'Murderous sort of fellow?'

'Stormerod says he's a perfectly nice chap who lives in a

mid-Western town in America, makes a reasonable living which Stormerod augments pretty generously and has shown little interest in the estate, let alone the title.'

'Hmm,' said the baroness. 'I don't wish to appear cynical, but you'd have to be an awfully high-minded person not to mind about a dukedom, a Scottish castle, the Buttermere estate, the pictures and all the rest of the Stormerod family's ill-gotten gains.'

Milton nodded. 'I agree, but we've had Frederick Sholto thoroughly checked out by the FBI and he hasn't budged from job or home in the last year. His neighbours consider him a model citizen and he's a pillar of the local church.'

'Hmph,' said the baroness. 'That's always bad news in America.'

'No, this is a sensible church. Episcopalian.'

'Did he know Bertie was thinking of getting married again?'

'The duke said he wrote and told him so some time ago and Sholto wished him well.'

'Well, he would, wouldn't he? He'd hardly threaten to murder him.'

'That's why I'm sending Ellis to America to see him.'

24

Westfield, Virginia was a small town like thousands of others in America, right down to the neat white fences. Sholto's pleasant roomy house – clapboarded, painted white and with a verandah – closely resembled those of his neighbours. Like his ducal relative, the man who opened the front door had heavy lids and a very large nose, but there the resemblance ceased. Dressed in blazer, white shirt and grey trousers, of average height with thinning brown hair and with a pleasant face, his ordinariness was a bit of a disappointment to Pooley, whose fertile imagination had been weaving fantasies of murder plotted at long distance.

He shook hands heartily and waved Pooley into the living room. 'You are very welcome. Coffee? Coke?'

'Coffee, please.'

'Excuse me a minute while I get it. My wife's not here, unfortunately. She's at work so she couldn't be here to greet you.'

Pooley sat back and closed his eyes until Sholto reappeared with a tray with coffee and what he averred were the best cookies in Virginia.

'OK,' he said, when the civilities were concluded. 'Now can you explain why you're here? I'm a mite confused as to how those terrible goings-on in London have anything to do with me. Especially since, as I'm relieved to know, Cousin Bertie hasn't been hurt.'

'No. But there is a possibility that he could have been a prime target who escaped twice through good luck.'

'Making me the prime suspect? Yeah, sure. No, don't apologize. That's OK. Of course it must look that way.

Though I'd be real upset if Cousin Bertie saw it like that.'

'Not at all. He spoke most warmly of you and told us we were wasting our time.'

'Knew he would. Bertie's a good guy. Understands that though all that land and money and title would be tempting to most people, it isn't to me. If it comes it comes, as the Lord's will. If it doesn't, it doesn't.'

'You're completely indifferent?'

Sholto scratched his head. 'I just let things take their course. Look at it this way. I'm a patriotic American, I like where I live, I like my neighbours and my wife and I are happily married. I manage the local supermarket and I enjoy the job. She teaches first grade and loves it. Between us we make enough to live decently and Cousin Bertie's generosity has meant that we're a lot luckier than most. My kids had the brains, I'm proud to say, to go to Ivy League universities and Cousin Bertie provided the money. We can afford a new car every few years, a little boat for weekends on the lake and once or twice we've taken a foreign holiday.'

'Recently?'

'You mean did we go over to London to mow down a whole lot of lords in an effort to see off Cousin Bertie? 'Fraid not. We haven't been out of here since two years ago when we went over for the funeral of Cousin Amelia to pay our respects to Cousin Bertie at his time of tragedy.'

'I see, sir. But if you'll forgive my asking – and I don't mean to be offensive. I'm just trying to clear things up.'

Sholto nodded. 'Sure.'

'It's just that most people would find it incredible that you'd settle happily for what you've got when you could have what the duke has.'

'I'll tell you what, Mr Pooley.' He shook his head. 'That sounds much too formal and we're not formal here in Westfield.'

'Call me Ellis.'

'And call me Fred, please. Now look here, Ellis, I may have lived in a small town most of my life, but I'm a keen observer of people and I've seen enough of the harm money can do to see the downside as well as the upside. Now, take my boy. More coffee?'

'Yes, please.'

Sholto emptied the pot into Pooley's cup and sat back. 'My boy Joe worked hard and now he's an engineer and I don't know that he'd have done that if he was sure he was going to be rich. As it was, he wasn't dazzled by being the heir to the heir, if you know what I mean, because I've always pointed out we're a long-lived family and that even if I did succeed it probably wouldn't be until I was seventy and he was nearly fifty, so that kept him sensible. And you see, if I inherit tomorrow it'll probably be the end of what should be a satisfying career, because I could hardly insist Joe make his way as he is now rather than coming with me to England and living the life of an aristocrat. It's just the same with my daughter, Peggy, who's going to be an attorney, all going well. Pretty girl. Nice girl. I'd like someone to marry her because they loved her, not because her old man was loaded.'

'And your wife?'

'She's not crazy about coronets. She's had the odd little fantasy maybe, but mostly she's not interested. She says, "Fred. What do we really want that we haven't got?" And especially since Cousin Bertie made his offer some months back, whatever happens we'll have a very comfortable old age.'

'Sorry. What offer?'

'Oh, didn't he tell you? Here, hang on. I'll find it.'

The Sholto house was so tidy and free of paper that within a minute he had located in the neat bureau a handwritten letter dated the previous April.

'My dear Fred,
This is not an easy letter to write. But I think I know you well enough to believe it will not distress you too much.

I feel it right to tell you that I am contemplating remarriage to someone who is a lot younger than me – in her mid thirties, in fact. So it is possible that we may have children.

It was always a source of great grief to me, and to

197

Amelia, that all her pregnancies ended in miscarriage. I am selfish enough to want to seize a second chance to have what I have always desperately desired – children of my own.

For you this would mean being disinherited, which is why I feel it important to ask if it would be very destructive of your family, or if you could take it in your stride. But since for about ten years you must have assumed you would remain the heir, I will understand if you are appalled by the notion of being supplanted. I love the lady in question, but I give you my word that if it is your wish, then I will draw back. However, if you feel able to give us your blessing, what I propose is that should I marry and should my wife produce an heir, I will settle on you a substantial sum of money to ensure that you have, within reason, all you want materially for you and your family.

My love to Marge,
      Your affectionate cousin,
        Bertie.'

Pooley handed the letter back. 'Nice man, isn't he?'

'A gentleman.' Shotto handed him a photocopy.

'Dear Cousin Bertie,

I appreciated your letter, but don't you worry about a thing. If I end up a duke, I'll try to be a good duke, if I don't, that's OK as well. Like I said to you that time when you asked me if I'd like to move the family to England and learn about the business, you can never know what the future may hold so it's better to plod along unless the Lord calls on you to change. If you get married, you'll have my very good wishes and if you'd like us to be there for the wedding, we'll come. Thanks to you, the kids have had every chance, and we've nothing to grumble about if we don't end up with coronets. I don't know as how I'd know how to wear one properly anyhow.

Marge sends her love and best wishes,
  God bless you.
      Your affectionate cousin,
        Fred.'

'And your wife was happy about this too?'

'Yeah, we think the same about things mostly. When Mom was urging us to up sticks and go and live on Cousin Bertie's estate it was Marge said, "You can't predict what'll happen. After all, Bertie might get divorced or become a widower and who's to say what might happen then."'

'Very sensible woman, your wife.'

'Yep. Never had a day's regret about marrying her.' He pointed proudly at the photographs on the sideboard.

Pooley studied them curiously. 'Are these your children?'

'Yes.'

'Very nice-looking.'

'Yeah, as you can see, they take after Marge, fortunately not after my family. I'm no oil painting. No more than Bertie is.'

'Who's that?' Pooley pointed at a cross-looking, thin woman.

'That's Mom. And there's Dad. He died a long time ago.'

'And that?'

'Oh, that's Will, my twin brother.'

'He doesn't look at all like you.'

'Nope, one of those funny things. Took after Mom's side, while I took after Pop's. It was the same temperamentally.'

Being so far away from home made Pooley forget his usual professional anonymity. 'It's peculiar being a twin when there's inheritance involved, isn't it? I'm the younger by ten minutes and my brother's going to inherit a lot.'

'Yep. The Lord sure moves in mysterious ways. Will would have liked to be a duke much more than me, but life ain't fair. You've just got to take it as it comes. Now, is there anything else I can help you with?'

'No. You've been most kind. Thank you very much, Mr Sholto.'

'Fred.'

'Sorry. Fred. Now I'll be getting back to Washington airport.'

'Not going to stop and see the sights? Not that there are many here.' He laughed.

'No thanks. As you can imagine, with all this going on,

we're short-staffed back at home. Better get back as fast as I can.'

Sholto walked Pooley out to the waiting taxi. As they shook hands he looked sombre. 'If you see Cousin Bertie, tell him Fred was asking for him and that I'm real glad he's safe. I promise you I'll have our congregation pray to the Lord to help you catch that maniac before any more harm's done.'

'I'd be grateful for that. We can certainly use all the help we can get.'

25

'That's really terrific.' Amiss clutched his left temple. 'Sholto's a saint. There isn't a shred of evidence to link those mad Trots in Leadbetter's basement with the Lords murders. Jim says your anti-terrorist boys are out of ideas and no one has a clue who the Avengers are. So it's eight thousand, four hundred and sixty-seven suspects down and none to go. What are you going to do today? Announce it was mass suicide?'

'Probably go through all the files all over again looking for something we've missed. The only bright spot in all of this is that no one's tried to frame the Trots for what they didn't do just because we'd like them to be guilty – which of course is why the press is baying for our blood.'

'Nasty this morning, is it?'

Pooley winced. 'They talk about us like you shouldn't talk about a dog. Or even an animal activist. I'll be in touch.'

'For a man who's been to and from the States in less than twenty-four hours you're looking pretty good, Ellis. It must be all that healthy living. And thanks for your report. Disappointing but very good.'

Pooley flushed with pleasure.

'Thank you, sir. Have you a minute?'

'Yes. I'm just contemplating how to explain to the Commissioner that I'm completely out of ideas.'

'I was just leafing through the file on Brother Francis, and I remembered what Robert had said about him and Plutarch and I still can't work out why he was carting a tabernacle around the place.'

'A tabernacle? I didn't hear that bit of the story – all I

heard was about Plutarch and the Lord Chancellor. Is there more?'

'She crashed into Brother Francis and he dropped a suitcase which turned out to have a tabernacle in it. And I just can't work out why.'

Milton thought for a few moments and then shrugged. 'Why not? Let's go on a wild tabernacle chase. Get Brother Francis's London address, order a car and we'll leave in fifteen minutes.'

Brother Francis's London headquarters was a modest flat in a small terraced house in Highgate. He looked so distressed when he answered the door that as they sat down in his spartan living room on the hard chairs, Milton, to put him at his ease, said, 'Bit far out for you, this, Brother, isn't it?'

'Ah, yes, Superintendent, but it has the incomparable blessing of being beside Highgate cemetery.'

Milton could remember only one thing about Highgate cemetery. 'Do I gather you are an admirer of Karl Marx?'

Brother Francis looked shocked. 'How could you think I could admire such an enemy of godliness? No, no. The cemetery enables me to be in touch with the eternal verities through musings on the afterlife. For instance, every morning, when I walk there, I pass a tombstone which says:

> 'As you pass by, so once was I,
> As I am now, so you will be,
> Therefore, prepare for eternity.

'It is a beautiful piece of poetry.' He simpered. 'I would have been proud to have written it. And I like to reflect on how true it is. But also the cemetery is where I meet my little friends.'

'Ah, yes. Animals, no doubt.'

'Squirrels particularly. At this time of the year I bring them nuts and talk to them. I call them by their names and they come. You can tell them apart, you know. You look surprised, but I assure you it's true, for they all have their own little winning ways and funny habits and charming personalities. It is a privilege to be among them. And among the little birdies, too.'

Milton could not think of any answer to this, so he went straight to the point. 'I'm sorry to break in on you with no notice, but I wanted to know why you were removing a tabernacle from the House of Lords.'

'It's mine.'

'Oh, I'm not disputing that. It just seems odd, and you'll understand that in the present climate we have to investigate anything odd.'

'I thought I'd take it home with me. I no longer feel I can say Mass in a place where so many terrible things have been done.'

'But surely that sad place needs the blessing of God now more than ever before?' Milton felt proud of himself for producing such an unctuous statement without laughing.

Brother Francis wriggled. 'Ah yes, you may be right and I may have been hasty. But I felt the urge to bring this holy object to my little home where I could commune with God more privately.'

'Where used it to be before? In the Lords, I mean.'

'In my little room.'

'May I see it, sir?'

'Yes, I'll bring it in.'

'No, no. You don't want to carry something as heavy as that around unnecessarily. I'll come and look.'

'I'd rather you didn't.'

But Milton was already on his feet and following Pooley out of the room. 'In here, sir?' He walked into a bedroom containing only a narrow iron bed and a clothes rail on which were hung scarlet parliamentary robes, a brown woollen habit and a long overcoat. Behind him Brother Francis was bleating, 'No, please.'

'In here, sir,' called Pooley. Milton joined Pooley at the door of what proved to be the religious sanctum.

'Please, it's sacred.'

'Don't worry, Brother. Nothing will be harmed.' Milton's glance took in the vestments, the monstrance and tabernacle on the altar and the picture of St Francis on the wall with a sparrow in his hand. 'Would you mind opening the tabernacle, Brother?'

Unhappily, Brother Francis walked over, genuflected before the tabernacle and opened the door to reveal a few wafers.

'Very well, Brother. Thank you. Sorry to have disturbed you.'

'Sir!' Pooley called from the kitchen. 'There's another one here.'

The box was lying on the draining board, front downwards, with a bottle of disinfectant beside it. 'I'm a bit puzzled, Brother. Could you explain to me why you brought the tabernacle home when you already had one here?'

'I was going to take this one back to the Sanctuary.'

'Why are you disinfecting it?'

'Hygiene.'

No amount of coaxing could move him from this explanation.

'I'll have to ask you to let me take it for testing, Brother.'

'You can't do that. It's consecrated.'

'If consecration doesn't stop it being disinfected, I'm sure it won't stop it undergoing laboratory tests. But if you wish, you may deconsecrate it and then reconsecrate it once we have finished. On a murder enquiry, inconvenience is, I'm afraid, inevitable. Now, we'll wait for you in your living room while you do whatever is necessary and I'll write you a receipt.'

'That was,' said Milton, as Pooley put the tabernacle in the boot, 'one of the oddest things I've ever committed to paper. "I acknowledge receipt of one tabernacle, silver and gold." What made you think of the kitchen? Just being thorough?'

'No. But I remembered Robert had said it was metal. The one in his chapel was mainly marble.'

'Back to the Yard, please, Donoghue. Well done, Ellis. I'm glad you're thinking so clearly. I have come to feel very addled, with so many lunatics coming at me from all directions. I don't even know why I confiscated the tabernacle, except that I couldn't think what else to do. So what do you think he might have been transporting in it, if anything? Drugs?'

'Or explosives. I think it's big enough to be able to store twenty anti-personnel mines.'

'Good God, what an interesting thought. We'll get the lab to do a rush job and send a team of explosives people and fingerprint experts around to Brother Francis's flat and to his room at the Lords immediately.'

'Nothing, sir.' Pooley was dejected. 'There are no traces of anything in the tabernacle. But the lab said that since the mines were coated in plastic, they wouldn't leave any traces anyway.'

'Fingerprints?'

'Well, there were quite a few but they were probably bona fide visitors. What I was really hoping for was a breakthrough like Jerry Dolamore's prints on the tabernacle.'

'Unlike Brother Francis, I don't believe in miracles. But it was worth a try. Now send it back to him.'

'Yes, Jim. What?'

'Wake up, Robert. Something's happened and you'd better let Jack know.'

'What?'

'Stormerod's been shot.'

'Is he dead?'

'No. The first report is highly encouraging. He's said to be slightly injured and a bit shocked but otherwise fine.'

'Where was he shot?'

'The doctors haven't said.'

'I mean geographically.'

'He was riding from his Buttermere estate to Carlisle station to catch the six-thirty train, with his chauffeur and horsebox following behind, when he suddenly fell off his horse. By the time the chauffeur had established he was alive, though stunned, and learned that he thought he'd been shot, his priority was to rush to the house and ring for an ambulance. By the time the police came there was no sign of a sniper. Not that one would be easy to find in an estate that size. Whoever it was could have been over the hills and far away.'

'Wasn't he guarded?'

'No. Didn't you know? All the protection teams were withdrawn a few days ago. There just weren't the resources. I'll press for putting at least a few back now to look after Stormerod, Deptford and Jack.'

'So you think it was activists?'

'I don't think anything. It could have been a poacher for all I know. I'll be back to you when I do.'

'Curiouser and curiouser,' said the baroness. 'In fact, this is, if I'm not mistaken, Bertie's third life. He seems as resilient as one of our feline friends, I'm happy to say. Now, I'll just ring his house and see when he's going to turn up here. I think it's time we had a chat.'

'There'll be quite a lot of people in the queue, you know.'

'We'll just jump it,' she said airily.

She was back on the phone within five minutes. 'He's catching the next train. Say's he's feeling fine. It was a bullet all right. Deflected, would you believe, by his passport, which was in his left breast pocket. So instead of going through his heart, the bullet bounced off and his only injuries were slight grazes and a few bruises that he got from falling off the horse. He says he's in the pink, so I've fixed a meeting at my club for six. He should be out of the clutches of the constabulary by then and we can get the lowdown. In the meantime, contemplate the evidence. It's time we put an end to all this.'

'Club? Which one? The University Women's?'

'Certainly not. Too respectable for me. It's the one where you worked – ffeatherstonehaughs.'

'I didn't know you were a member of that.'

'They made me an honorary member recently. Now I must be off. See you at six.'

'Jack!'

'What?'

'Please take care. If they've taken to attacking pro-hunters singly, you're a pretty tempting target.'

'Not to say large.' She laughed. 'Oh yes, yes, yes. I'll keep an eye out.'

26

'I've been thinking.'

'How you can think in the middle of this bizarre building is more than I can imagine,' said Stormerod. 'I've read about it but I've never seen it.' His eyes were fixed on the mosaic floor where nymphs and shepherds intertwined passionately.

'Pull yourself together, my boy. This is no time to be indulging in erotic fantasies. I'll take you round another time, or rather Robert can. He used to be a servant here.'

'You seem to have packed in a great deal for one so young, Robert.'

'He certainly has. Ask him to tell you his life story someday. It's a gas. The boy's had more jobs than you've got titles. Now to our muttons. What I've been thinking is that I just don't believe these people have been knocked off for some vague reasons of principle. When in doubt *cherchez la femme ou cherchez l'argent.*'

Her listeners looked at her in bewilderment. 'Come again, Jack?'

'Really, Bertie. What's happened to your French? Look for the woman or look for the money.'

Stormerod's face cleared. 'Oh, I'm with you. *Cherchez la femme ou cherchez l'argent.* I've haven't heard such awful French pronunciation since Winston Churchill.'

'What was good enough for Winston is good enough for me. Now, the point I'm trying to make is that you coppers' – she looked sternly at Pooley –' have allowed yourselves to be given the old runaround. Everything's become overcomplicated. It's obvious all these murders are a smoke screen.'

'I've heard of mixed metaphors,' said Amiss. 'But

207

describing nineteen bodies as a smoke screen is new in my experience.'

'Shut up and listen. My great virtue is that I have a simple mind. Now, this is England and the English don't go round murdering each other in vast numbers to make a political point. The Irish, yes; the Welsh and Scots are capable of it, I grant you, and all sorts of other loonies like the American far right, or Islamic Fundamentalists. But it is not the English way.'

As Pooley opened his mouth to interrupt, she continued, 'And if you start talking to me about global villages and the pooling of cultures I shall become irascible.'

He subsided.

'I walked all the way round St James's Park twice this afternoon and had a serious think and I'm ready to bet a thousand quid that all this was an attempt to murder Bertie. There were only two reasons why they should have gone for him this morning — anti-hunting or anti-Bertie.'

'Hold on,' said Amiss. 'Who were the suspects you were hinting darkly to me about the other week, Bertie, when you routed me out of the library for a drink.'

Stormerod looked embarrassed. 'Sorry, Robert. That turned out to be a bit of misinformation from a source I'd rather not mention who thought that old fool Gordon had a small militia that might be blowing up our side to discredit the bill. Turned out there was nothing in it. Should have told you.'

'As I was saying,' said the baroness impatiently, 'anti-hunting is now out of the question unless they've totally lost their marbles, since to rub Bertie out at this juncture would set up such a wave of public sympathy that hunting would probably become compulsory. Am I right?'

'Not if they're mad,' said Pooley.

'We know they're mad, but they'd have to be stupid. Keep it simple, young Ellis. Your trouble is that you're a complicator. Focus for the moment on Bertie, and only on Bertie.'

She gazed straight at Stormerod. 'We've established, have we not, Bertie, that there are no wronged women in your life who would wish to secure a terrible vengeance. You've ravished no virgins. You are not noted in either Inverness or Buttermere for a propensity to exercise your right to droit du seigneur. And you haven't cast any mistresses off like soiled gloves.

'And since additionally for a politician you're extraordinarily enemy-free, it must be down to loot – in which you are rolling. So we've got to look again at the likely-to-be-disinherited cousin.' She waved at a passing waiter and commanded more champagne. 'Nonsense,' she said when Stormerod protested. 'We have much to celebrate. We're all alive.'

She hushed him with a gesture. 'Now, I accept that the cousin simply can't have done it. His alibi's solid and he's not the type. But what about his son the engineer? He mightn't be such a moral giant as his father. He might feel pretty bad about missing out on the chance to inherit such an extraordinary basket of goodies.'

'Sorry, Jack.' Pooley was smug. 'I thought of that. I checked out his and even his sister's alibis. They've been going to work every day throughout this carry-on.'

'Hitmen,' said the baroness, causing the approaching waiter to start. 'No, no, I'm not talking about you, Walter. Yes, please. Top us up.'

'No, for two reasons,' said Pooley firmly. 'He would need an enormous amount of money – which he hasn't got – and he would put himself in a position to be blackmailed for the rest of his life.'

'You've left something out.' She sounded equally smug. 'The brother.'

'But Will wouldn't inherit unless he knocked off both his own brother and his nephew in addition to Bertie.'

'But think what he stood to gain indirectly from a generous brother, guilty about being the elder twin. And – if he was doing it in collusion with his nephew the heir – he would do even better.'

'Jolly good, Jack,' said Amiss. 'This is a fine foray into Ellis's usual territory.'

She ignored him. 'What do you know about the brother, Bertie?'

Stormerod was looking uneasy. 'Nothing much, to tell the truth. I've never had any reason to meet him and I didn't want to because he's always been very thick with his mother and I've never been able to stick her.'

'Why not?'

'Bit of a tartar.' He looked embarrassed. 'And greedy. It was after they married that Cousin George started writing for money and it was all too obvious whose was the guiding hand.'

'Do you actually know her?'

'Only met her once – at her wedding to George when I was a kid. We all thought her the worst kind of stereotypical unpleasant Scot – hard, hatchet-faced, acquisitive. So I always avoided any invitations.'

'And they never came to see you?'

'My old father wouldn't have them. Said it was bad enough having to disgorge money but he was damned if he was going to put up with their company as well. When I took over and realized Amelia couldn't have children, George was dead and I felt I should get to know my heir, so I established this relationship with nice Fred. He came over a few times but I never saw the other two.'

'So what does the brother do?'

'No idea.'

'And the son. What do you know of him?'

'Very little. Seemed pleasant enough – ambitious, hard-working. Can't read murder into that, Jack.'

Pooley looked serious. 'I should check them out. But when we discover all these people are sitting safely in America, tending to their families, will you be satisfied?'

'Probably not. I'll think of something else. But this must be checked out. Now.'

'I'll have to have a word with Jim first.'

'Nonsense. It's Bertie I want to check it out. Bertie. Off you go and ring your cousin.'

'How do you suggest I approach it? "Excuse me, Fred, but do you think Will might be trying to murder me?"'

She shook her head testily. 'My God, to think you're supposed to be the most subtle brain in the Conservative Party.

That fall must have addled your wits.' She adopted a tone and pace suitable for a nervous and slow learner. 'Ring up and say you want to be the first to tell him about this new murder attempt but that you think everything's over now and the police have it all in hand. Still, a brush with death leaves one anxious to bond with one's nearest and dearest, which is why you're having a chat with him. And you'd like the phone numbers of his mother and brother whom you feel remorseful for having neglected over the years. Have you got that?'

'I'll feel ridiculous doing that. But, yes, if I must. I'll ring him from home. His number's there.'

'Do it now. Ellis, scamper off and extract the number from directory enquiries.'

'I've got it here in my Filofax.'

'Excellent. Right, Bertie. Go for it. And remember, in the guise of solicitude, to extract the maximum amount of information from your cousin about his brother.'

'Such as,' said Amiss helpfully, 'if he's a well-known serial killer.'

'Exactly. Poor old Bertie,' she said, as Pooley shepherded him away to find a discreet telephone. 'This'll be real agony for him. It goes right against a gentleman's grain to spy on his family. But needs must when the bullets fly and he should take care of himself for the sake of that attractive piece of aristocratic crumpet he's taking off with.'

Pooley came back. 'He's got through. It's a bit of luck it's a holiday in the States, so Fred's at home.'

'It seems impolite to ask,' said Amiss, 'but while he's out of the room, is it true the shot was deflected by his passport? And, if so, why was he carrying it?'

'Quite true about the passport,' said Pooley. 'It's not the first time that's happened.'

'Of course, it was the old passport,' said the baroness. 'That nasty new red plastic thing that we've been dished out since we joined the wretched European Union wouldn't deflect a missile from a pea-shooter – another powerful argument against that frightful institution.'

'I'll say for you Jack,' said Amiss, 'that there is nothing, but nothing, that doesn't fuel your prejudices.'

She beamed.

'But why was he carrying it?'

'I didn't like to ask that,' said Pooley. 'It wasn't our business.'

'I did,' said the baroness.

'Naturally. And?'

'He's going to get married to his beloved Georgiana ... Now, this is a big secret and nobody's to tell because he doesn't want the press to know so I'll personally strangle both of you if it comes out.'

'Yes, yes, get on with it,' said Amiss.

'The day after we finish our fox-hunting business they are going to fly straight to Thailand for a honeymoon. So he was bringing his passport down to London so he could pop into the Thai Embassy, fill in the forms and leave it with them. He certainly has the luck of the Stormerods – they were always known for it. Didn't look like it when Amelia died, but it's obviously picked up again.'

'Unless,' said Pooley, 'it's him who's been behind the murders all the time which was why he was out of harm's way at the right times.'

'That's a brilliant idea, Ellis,' said the baroness. 'Presumably he arranged for his own shooting as well in the full confidence the sniper would hit him exactly on target and the passport wouldn't fail?'

Pooley looked slightly crestfallen. 'Sorry. I didn't quite think that one through.'

Stormerod appeared and walked slowly across the saloon. He sat down wearing the impassive expression so well known to his colleagues at party meetings.

'Well?' asked the baroness impatiently.

He spoke slowly. 'It appears that the object of your suspicions is not at present available for a reconciliatory chat since he and his mother are on a lengthy world tour.'

'How lengthy?'

'He's been gone for five months.'

'And where is he now?'

212

'Somewhere in south-east Asia.'

'Any proof?'

'Just that they rang a couple of weeks ago and said they were in Singapore.'

'With modern communications that means nothing. They could be in Dakota or they could be in London. What else?'

'Fred doesn't have much to do with Will.'

'Because?'

'Because – the term he used was "redneck". He said he was sorry to say his brother was one of those redneck Republicans always bragging about his gun collection. He didn't want him to get close to the children.'

'Another bottle of champagne,' said the baroness.

'Easy on, Jack,' said Stormerod. 'It's much too early to celebrate. Wait until we see if there's any more to your hunch than this coincidence.'

'Of course there is. It's plain as the nose on your face.'

Stormerod grinned. 'Only you would be tactless enough to say that to me.'

Pooley had jumped up and was impatiently moving from foot to foot. 'I've got to go.'

'Hold on, hold on. What are you planning to do?'

'Well, start checking him out. Wire for photographs. Check passport controls. All that sort of thing.'

'OK. Get cracking. Bertie, will you stay and have dinner here with me and Robert? We've got to work out how they got access to the Lords and who helped them. Now before you go, Ellis, have you forgotten Brother Francis's research assistant?'

Pooley made a face. 'I had. And I shouldn't have.' He turned and ran.

27

'He came to Britain. And unless he left illegally he's still here. But she didn't.'

'Odd,' said Milton.

'Maybe she's providing cover by sending postcards from around the world.'

'But his brother told me when I talked to him just now that they didn't send any postcards. His mother said they preferred to talk to their dear ones in person on the phone and that they'd share photographs with them later.' There was silence for a moment as they both thought intently. Then simultaneously Milton said, 'Maiden name,' and Pooley said, 'British citizen.'

'Really?'

'Yes. The duke said she was Scots. Maybe she never changed her citizenship.'

'Wait.' Milton pressed the redial button. 'Chief Superintendent Milton again, I'm afraid. I'm very sorry, Mr Sholto, to have to trouble you once more and I know I must be causing you distress, but I have to clear up all loose ends.'

'You've got your job to do, sir. Just ask and I'll try to help.'

'May I have your mother's maiden name, please?'

'Hartley. Mary Agnes Hartley.'

'And was she a British citizen?'

'She was, sir. That is, she is. She always said she saw no reason to change.'

'Thank you, Mr Sholto. Goodbye. OK, Ellis. Mary Agnes Hartley or Mary Agnes Sholto. British citizen.'

*   *   *

It was midnight. Amiss was sitting in an armchair in his flat trying to read, but hopelessly distracted by a hundred speculations and by the rasping purr of Plutarch who was happily ensconced on the rising and falling stomach of the snoring baroness. Not for the first time he found himself resenting his friend's ability to sleep whenever the opportunity presented itself. The bell rang at last and he rushed to the door.

'I thought you'd never come.'

'It's a miracle we did.'

Both policemen collapsed on the sofa and Amiss kicked the baroness awake. With a final loud snort she jerked into full consciousness.

She sat up bolt upright, dislodging Plutarch, who growled menacingly but then grudgingly resettled herself on the baroness's lap. 'Good evening, gentlemen. I was right, wasn't I?'

'Get me a Scotch for God's sake,' said Milton.

'And me,' said Pooley.

'And me,' said the baroness.

'Plutarch?' asked Amiss politely.

'No,' she said. 'Plutarch will pass. She's had quite enough already.'

While Amiss busied himself about his duties, Milton looked at the baroness. 'Possibly.'

'Oh, sir, I mean Jim. Probably.'

'Well, to tell the truth,' said Milton. 'I'd be astounded if you're not.'

Her joyful beam so transfigured her whole face that the others followed suit. The baroness's moods were contagious.

'OK, spill the beans.'

'The airlines and passport control yielded the information that they left Miami on the fifth of August. She was travelling with a British passport under her maiden name. They landed in London and there's no record of them having left.' Milton observed Pooley wriggling impatiently. 'All right, Ellis. You continue.'

'She got a job in the House of Lords as a waitress.'

'How? She's pretty old, isn't she?'

'Very well-preserved, lied about her age, they're not very well-paid jobs and she had excellent references.'

'Didn't they check them?'

'They checked the most recent, which was from a William Sholto, who described himself as manager of a highly regarded Cotswolds hotel. They wrote to him there and asked for confirmation. He was a guest there at the time, the letter went to him and he duly confirmed the reference.'

'Supposing they'd telephoned?'

'Still might have gone to him or the deception might have been found out, in which case they'd have had to think of some other method of infiltration.'

'They're quite smart, these people,' said the baroness.

'You haven't heard the half of it,' said Milton. 'Next thing we know is that about four or five weeks after Mary Agnes Hartley – or Agnes as she's known at work . . .'

'Agnes!' said Amiss and the baroness simultaneously.

'Of course, you'd know her. I hope you didn't like her.'

'You've nothing to worry about there,' said Amiss.

'So Brother Francis finds himself visited by an American in his late forties called William Heston who claims to be doing research on the British constitution and asks if he can be his research assistant. He doesn't want any money, he's prepared to type and help a bit on clerical jobs, he produces references from some mid-West university of which no one's ever heard saying he's a good egg, a worthy mature student who'll be no trouble. Why not? thinks Brother Francis, especially since the guy declares himself to be a great fan and someone who – though coming from a hunting background – has been converted by Brother Francis's eloquence to the cause of animal rights.'

'And of course there's nothing as attractive as a convert,' said Amiss.

'Precisely,' said Milton. 'So Heston/Sholto gets his pass, but rarely turns up in the Lords. He's studying hard, he explains, and prefers to work from home – a service flat in Kensington. But as well as proving obliging and useful, he also begins to take religious instruction from Brother Francis,

216

which involves attending the Masses he says in his home and occasionally his office.'

'So,' said Pooley, 'of course Brother Francis invites him down to his Sanctuary, where he has a chance to observe Dolamore's great meeting.'

Amiss frowned. 'But wasn't he laying himself open to being too easily identified?'

'Egomaniacs and lunatics rarely notice those around them,' said Milton. 'And besides, he was disguised. But we'll come to that later.'

'I don't think I'd have the patience to be that kind of murderer,' said the baroness reflectively. 'I would have been inclined simply to take a pot shot at Bertie. The more you complicate, the more you're likely to fuck up.'

'Yes, but taking a pot shot at Bertie would have led to an absolute focus on the family. Anyway, this was Sholto's view of things, so what he intended was to muddy the waters to the degree that the Loch Ness Monster could be buried for all time undetected. So, so far he had motive and means, but he was looking for the right opportunity.'

'Why is Agnes still in her job? I don't quite see her role in all of this.'

'Nor do we quite yet, but presumably she was some kind of intelligence gatherer. Probably marked Brother Francis out in the first place as a likely stooge and got Sholto to do what he later did.'

The baroness wrinkled her forehead. 'Come again?'

'Keep listening,' said Pooley. 'So then Sholto did his worst with the stun-gun, but the quarry escaped.'

'Is this fact or hypothesis?' asked Amiss.

'A mixture,' said Milton. 'We know from Fred that he had told his mother about Bertie's pacemaker operation. Otherwise, so far our main source is Brother Francis, who of course never suspected that his spiritually minded helper might have anything to do with this frightful happening until said helper tells him he wishes him to swap tabernacles.'

'Aha,' said the baroness. 'The empty one goes out and the full one comes in.'

' "Why?" asks Brother Francis. "Ask me no questions and

217

I'll tell you no lies," says Sholto. "Just something I want done." Even Brother Francis smelled a rat at this juncture and said he didn't like the sound of it and was having no part of it. "Oh, I think you will," says Sholto, "or I'll tell them about Friday and all the other days."'

'What did the poor old sod do on Fridays that he shouldn't?' asked the baroness sadly. 'Pass the bottle over here, Robert.'

'Leather-clad lady with whip, male slaves running round her house in pinnies doing her housework, licking her kitchen floor with their tongues and being beaten at regular intervals.'

'God, I'm so glad I didn't go to public school,' said Amiss.

'We didn't all end up like that,' said Pooley stiffly.

Milton continued: 'The poor devil said he used to flog himself a bit in the monastery for penitential reasons. When he came out into the world the urge to find someone to do it for him became too great so he phoned up one of those people whose ads are plastered all over telephone kiosks: Madam Dominatrix this one was called. Dom for short.'

'And rather than have this revealed he was prepared to allow murder to happen?'

'You do see things in such a black-and-white way, Jack,' said Amiss. 'We're talking about a holy fool, for God's sake. I bet he just chose not to know what was happening.'

'Of course,' said Milton. 'He said what really worried him was the possibility of sacrilege, but he convinced himself that if he deconsecrated and reconsecrated the tabernacles all would be well and that maybe what was being transported – as Sholto claimed – was a bit of harmless contraband.'

'Like what?' asked the baroness.

'Brother Francis barely knew what contraband meant. He certainly wasn't thinking about anti-personnel mines.'

'So the notion of Sholto being a murderer never crossed his mind?'

'He says not until the bombs went off and he read about how small they were.'

'Are you telling me he'd never looked at the contents of the tabernacle he brought into the Lords?'

'Sholto had the key.'

'And nobody tried to search it?'

'It's not the sort of thing people search, especially when it's being carried by a priest.'

'Why didn't the bombs show up when it went through the security screen? Oh, sorry.' The baroness snapped her fingers. 'I'd forgotten. The bombs were encased in plastic, so of course they wouldn't show up.'

Amiss interrupted. 'Now let me get this right. When Plutarch and I ran into him, he had realized a) that the contraband had disappeared, b) that so had his research assistant and c) that this holy of holies had been used to transport instruments of death? So what he was doing was taking it home to disinfect it in case it had traces of explosives and then reconsecrate it.'

'It didn't occur to him to report all this to the police?' The baroness sounded impatient.

Milton shook his head. 'No, because before he left, Sholto told him if he told anyone he'd make him such a laughing stock that his movement and his order would be forever discredited and that anyway he was going out of his life and there was nothing more to worry about and no further harm would be done. That was the straw at which the petrified rabbit grasped.'

'And the stun-gun? How did that get into the Lords in the first place?' asked Amiss.

'Security was almost nonexistent on peers before all this started,' said Milton. 'Brother Francis – who is now frantically cooperating – fears he might have inadvertently imported it in a bag of golf clubs which Sholto left at his flat after Mass and then asked him to take in and leave in his room.'

The baroness gave a mighty yawn. 'Very good. Now if that's all, I think I'll be going home to Myles. Call me a cab, Robert.'

'Mind you,' said Milton, 'we haven't caught them, we haven't proved anything and lots of this is speculation.'

'Don't be daft,' she said. 'It's an open-and-shut case. If I were you I'd hurry up and find the Sholtos.'

219

'Thanks, Jack. Now that you've pointed it out, I suppose that's what we should do next.'

'How did they find them so quickly?'

'Easy. Yesterday afternoon some spark of intelligence illuminated what one might loosely call Brother Francis's brain and he volunteered that though it was true that he didn't know where Sholto lived, he remembered he might have his telephone number somewhere in his office. By the time he'd been taken there and found it, and British Telecom produced the address, Jim and his mob were able to get to the Sholto flat just as mother and son were sitting down to dinner. They were a bit upset, apparently, but since Sholto's arsenal was in another room, they had little option but to go quietly.'

Deptford's usual calm was ruffled. ''E murdered all them poor buggers just to get Bertie? Never 'eard anything like it. What a pestilential son of a pontry-maid!'

'Who? What?' asked the baroness.

'Jorrocks,' explained Amiss.

'So who were the Animal Avengers?'

'Our friend Agnes composed those letters to focus suspicion on to the animal activists. Apparently she was inspired by a book of Edgar Wallace's.'

'Blimey. I knew Agnes was a pill, but this! Violet. Another round, please, luv.'

'Mind you,' said Amiss, 'you have to admit she was unusually devoted to her family.'

'Like a Roman empress,' interjected the baroness.

'Or that American who murdered her daughter's main rival for cheerleadership of the high-school football team.'

'It's beyond everything. Poor old Bertie. 'E must really be upset.'

'He was, but it's been a huge relief to him that neither his heir nor the heir's son had anything to do with it.'

'Are the cops sure of that?'

The baroness nodded. 'Will Sholto confirmed that it was a private entrepreneurial venture to instal the high-minded Fred as duke and then wallow in luxury along with him.

Seems looking forward to that was all mother and son had been living for for years. Fred's announcement that Bertie might get married drove them wild.'

Deptford shook his head again. 'Thanks, Violet,' he said absently. 'Has Agnes said what she actually did?'

'Oh, yes. Since they pleaded guilty apparently they're bragging about how clever they were. Her main contribution was to suss out peers she thought might be vulnerable, whom sonny then followed to see if there was any dirt on them. In nominating Brother Francis she showed herself a good judge of character. And then she stayed on in the hope of picking up useful gossip. For instance, she overheard Jack talking about our planned meeting in committee room 4.'

'Oh, dear,' said the baroness. 'Still, if she hadn't got us one way, she'd have got us another, no doubt.'

Deptford scratched his head. 'Am I bein' stupid? Wasn't she taking a big risk that Bertie might recognize her?'

'They hadn't met for over forty years, and anyway, like her son, between coloured contact lenses, wig and God knows what else she was well disguised.'

The baroness banged the table. 'Let's cheer up. There is much to celebrate, including the news I received from Bertie this morning before he took off abroad that he is to become a father.'

'Why, the old goat!' Deptford smiled with male complicity. 'And them not even married yet.'

'They will be next week. But don't be misled, Sid. This was not a result of unbridled lust. Surely by now you know the ways of the aristocracy. This time he wasn't going to get married unless he was sure the girl could whelp.'

'On that delicate note, shall we go in to lunch?' asked Amiss. 'May I remind you that you are due to spend this afternoon with Littlejohn hammering out the final details of the deal you and Bertie did with him yesterday.'

The media had been excited when the four young members of a far-left group had been charged with sending letter bombs to defenders of field sports. The news that relatives of the Duke of Stormerod had pleaded guilty to nineteen murders was sensational. The leak that Sholto's exotic weapons had been acquired with the help of Ulster Protestant paramilitaries added an extra frisson. And the journalists' cup of joy ran over when it emerged that Brother Francis had been charged with being an accessory after the fact. There followed a stampede of press revelations about the highjacking of the animal rights movement by violent elements in society.

It was a propitious time for Baroness Troutbeck and Lord Littlejohn to announce that the Lords had amended the Wild Mammals Bill in a way that was satisfactory to the majority of people on both sides. The clauses banning wanton cruelty remained, as did the prohibition of hare-coursing, but a huge majority of their lordships agreed it should remain legal to hunt those animals – like foxes and mink – that were themselves predators.

It behoved the sensible people of Britain, explained the baroness over the airwaves, to demonstrate their rejection of the disruptive and violent lunatic fringe. The British treated their animals better than anyone else in the world and it was their job to be evangelists abroad for the decency which characterized their society. Rather than worrying about such minor matters as fox-hunting, the job of the general public was to bombard members of the British and European parliaments with letters demanding that British standards prevail in Europe.

Like the great British public, MPs were terrified of anarchy and the blessed English word compromise was on everyone's lips. So when the bill, duly amended, went back to the Commons, it was backed by the government and passed in its emasculated form with scarcely a fight.

EPILOGUE

Amiss was cold, drenched, tired and wishing passionately that he had never dared Jack to demonstrate her prowess on the hunting field. As he trudged with Jennifer Bovington-Petty through the heavy mud he muttered, 'I'm sorry for dragging you into this. It's a lesson to me to keep my mouth shut when I've been celebrating too well. I couldn't get her to cancel the dare the day after.'

'What do you mean? I wouldn't have missed this for the world. Quite apart from anything else, I had an absolutely wonderful time helping her to dress this morning. It was hilarious to see her normal impatience at war with her notions of the importance of elegance on the hunting field. Getting the apron skirt on over the jodhpurs was difficult enough, but we had a fiendish time getting her hair right for the topper.'

'I admit she looked good.' Amiss stomped on for a moment. 'But to tell you the truth, I'm worried. She hasn't hunted for fifteen years and that horse Jamesie provided is an enormous brute.'

'Roddy's reliable enough. No bigger than what she's used to, apparently. And remember, side-saddle is pretty safe. That's why the Queen didn't fall off when someone fired a starting pistol during Trooping the Colour. Anyway, she certainly took off confidently enough.'

'Confidently! The last I saw of her she looked close to overrunning the hounds. Are we nearly there?'

'Poor Robert. You're not really cut out for country pursuits, are you? Cheer up. That's Rayner's Wood over there, and if the hunt doesn't turn up there within say half an hour honour will be satisfied and we can go back home to the library fire.'

'Only five minutes more.' Jennifer cocked her head. 'I hear something. Come on.'

Amiss reluctantly left the tree against which he had been comfortably propped and squelched after her to the outskirts of the wood.

'Here they come.'

Across the field tore a fox with baying hounds in hot pursuit and Jack Troutbeck careering immediately after them, with three hunters about a hundred yards behind. 'Isn't it a breach of etiquette to be ahead of the Master of Foxhounds?'

'I wouldn't worry. Jamesie knows he's no great shakes.'

As the baroness drew nearer they could see that she had lost her topper, she was red with exertion and drenched through from the torrential rain, but her whole countenance radiated exhilaration. Amiss flattened himself against a tree as the fox and then the hounds hurtled past. Moments later the fox reappeared heading for the covert that lay to the left; it crashed into Roddy's legs. As the hounds came after him Amiss shut his eyes and the baroness let out a lusty roar of 'Hold!' Thrown into momentary confusion, the hounds hesitated for just long enough for the fox to reach safety.

'You can look now,' said Jennifer. 'She's saved it.'

Amiss opened his eyes and looked at the baroness. 'Did you do that for me or for the fox?'

The three hunters drew up behind her and over the horizon the rest came into view. She looked defiant. 'Impulse. Anyway, as Trollope said, "No man goes out fox-hunting in order that he may receive pleasure from pain inflicted." And if they do, they shouldn't. We'd had the ride. Didn't need the fox.'

A hubbub of protest broke out behind her. 'Stymied the hounds.' 'Let him get away.'

Jennifer grimaced. 'I'm afraid they're going to be a bit upset that there hasn't been a kill.'

'Bugger them,' said the baroness, and turned to face her critics.